Secrets & their Lies

By Jo Ann Felton Carter

Prospering Soul Publishing

OTHER TITLES BY JOANN

Abandoned No More
Shame In Me

Published by Prospering Soul Publishing
14455 Gannet Street|Corona, CA |92880
www.aprosperingsoul.com

Prospering Soul Publishing is totally committed to publishing works that
edify and exhort enabling the reader to prosper in their soul as III John 2
states.

Published in the United States of America
ISBN: 978-0-9892671-0-6
Christian Fiction

CONTENTS

Prologue

Let me take a few minutes and explain why I write about issues we have that hinder us from maturing. After years of recapping my day every night to see if I had measured up to the Word, one day during my reading I stumbled on III John and realized my focus should be on getting my soul to prosper and not worry about if I had pleased the Lord or not. Understanding how the soul and the spirit entered into Adam during his making and that he died spiritually, then you understand the importance of becoming 'born again of the spirit'. Being born of our sinful nature, we are totally governed by our five senses; what we see, smell, taste, touch and hear. However we are not totally whole until His spirit dwells in us again. Some of us realize we are missing something at an early age, we just don't know what it is so we seek happiness in things thinking once we achieve whatever; we'll be complete and content. What's missing is the image of God being awakened in us and after we are born again, our life of balancing the spirit and the soul begins.

Our soul houses our thinking and personality; who we really are and aligning who we are with who our Father wants us to become is our life's journey and healing is very important. So, I am motivated to write about becoming healed of the issues we have in hopes of helping others.

III John 2 & 3, states **"Beloved, I pray that you may prosper in all things and be in health, just as your soul prospers. For I rejoiced greatly when brethren came and testified of the truth that is in**

you, just as you walk in the truth." The words, as your soul "prospers" imply an ongoing work in us and life itself produces situations that will cause us to work at having a prosperous soul.

Because the root of our understanding stems from our childhood and, our "method of reasoning" is also developed in our youth. I use childhood memories as the focal point of gaining understanding. When we become "born again" the "mind of Christ" must now become the root of our understanding. Applying the Word must become our method of reasoning. So be encouraged to spend time in studying the Word and, in His presence daily if possible so that your relationship with Christ deepens and your understanding becomes enlightened.

Trust the Holy Spirit and give Him permission to counsel you; He knows your heart and intent even when you don't. Read (Isaiah 9:6) and create an atmosphere of worship and wait for Him to guide you into your "session" with Him. Be confident the Holy Spirit <u>will not condemn you.</u> He has a way of showing you yourself and not condemn you. Study the Word daily so when He speaks, you will know it is Him because He will confirm His Word.

Fiction is my choice of writing because it is so much easier to see our own faults in others and not ourselves. In 2 Samuel 12:1–9 Nathan tells David a parable of a rich man taking a poor man's only lamb to serve as a meal for his guest. David was furious and stated the rich man should repay four lambs to the poor man and be put to death. Nathan told David he was the man in the story; only then was David able to see himself.

This topic on 'secrets & their lies' came about as a result of my birth parents and their families having secrets that affected the lives of their children.

I must remind you, all stories are fictitious; they are not actual events that happened to neither me nor anyone I know. Enjoy!

CHAPTER ONE

Summonsed By Aunt Flora
I do have a life you know!

I push the button to turn off my alarm clock and my phone rings. Immediately I think, '7 am, oh no who died, that's the only reason someone would call this early in the morning.' As I bring the receiver to my ear I hear Aunt Flora, "Oh good, I wanted to catch you before you left for work Angie, I need you to come by this evening. I have something very crucial to talk with you about." I respond, "Aunt Flora is everything alright, because I have a Luncheon this afternoon." She was her usual evasive self and replied, "You will get your answers when you arrive, see you promptly at 5:30 pm. bye Angie." Click. I laid there staring at the dial tone coming from my phone for a few seconds, then shook my head as I placed the handset back onto the receiver. I have a luncheon to cater and she's going to have me in a rush; and I hate to be rushed, ugh Aunt Flora!

As I throw back the cover and get out of bed, my mind immediately goes to how Aunt Flora has always been very peculiar and extremely rigid, now I've added demanding to the list. See, Aunt Flora is the youngest living out of the 6 children now that my mother has passed.

My Big Mama, Gertrude Bowen and Big Daddy, Roy Bowen had Uncle Lester and Aunt Shirley then, Big Daddy was drafted into the Army. As soon as he left for boot camp Big Mama found out she was pregnant with Aunt Brenda. Big Daddy lost his left leg up to his mid thigh and was sent back home. That's when Uncle Howard and Aunt Flora were added to the family tree.

Several years later, Big Daddy died and Big Mama found out she was pregnant with my mother; De Anne, and they all called her "the change baby," because Big Mama was in her 40's.

Aunt Flora is a recluse and has been one for as long as I can remember. She has never spent time with the family and we are very close knit. Sunday dinners are our specialty; we all contribute money for our aunts to cook, and while we eat, we talk about the sermon and some kind of way, Aunt Flora's name always end up in conversation. Maybe it's because she's the only sibling not close and somehow we have to include her. Or, maybe that's just the family's way of including her. I don't know why she's so unsociable but Aunt Brenda says she thinks the reason Aunt Flora is cold and distant is because she was the baby for fifteen years and De Anne; my mother; confiscated her position and she couldn't stand to see the attention shift from herself to my mother.

Now Aunt Shirley, our family "drama queen," thinks Aunt Flora is just spoiled and when things don't go the way she wants, she gets frosty and shuts people out. Personally, I think she feels left out and because we are very close, and this is just me; I think she doesn't know how to ask if she can be a part of us. Kinda like a game of 3 man jump rope, you have to know when to jump in without tripping on the rope, but that's just my opinion.

I'm no therapist or anything, I'm just a caterer. I am 26 years old and own "Taste, And See, Catering, Inc." A full menu catering business I started 7 years ago with my mother. For almost 20 years she was head cook at the "Bottoms Up Buffet," the largest buffet restaurant here in downtown Memphis, Tennessee. Mother taught me everything she was taught about cooking. By the time I was 7 years old, she would come into my room on any Saturday morning she didn't work and wake me by tenderly whispering in my ear, "good morning baby, we need to bake a pound cake today ok, you gonna help mama?" I would always open my eyes to her big warm, loving smile, and after washing my face and brushing my teeth; I would run into the kitchen and gather all of the ingredients she would need, placing each item on the kitchen counter for her. Mother would stand by the kitchen sink flashing her smile as she watched me gather each ingredient; I could feel the love she had for me radiating along with pride. So, for as long as I can remember, I have always loved to cook, it's in my blood.

I'm told Big Mama was an excellent cook and taught all of her children to cook, even my uncles. Mother was a great cook however her specialty was baking. She made cakes, pies, cookies and cobblers for all of our family's Sunday dinners and special occasions. If you wanted to taste a prize winning fried pie; just taste Mothers' and I kid you not; no one else can fry them like she did. I've tried to copy hers but they just don't cut it. Everyone in the family raves about my fried pies but to me, Mother had the exclusive rights on them.

Her baking business as we called it really happened by chance. She would bake cakes for my aunts and uncles when they had to take a dessert to work and their co-workers began making requests for her to bake for them and before we knew it, word was out all over town that the lady who works for "The Bottoms," bakes cakes. She took a cake decorating course at night and began baking specialty cakes for weddings, graduations, baby showers and every special occasion there was, thus launching her part time baking business.

Because cooking and baking was a constant in my surroundings, it was effortless for me so, I decided to do it for a living. I thought, 'why not get paid for doing what I love to do,' hey; my mama didn't have no fool!   Just before I graduated from high school I decided to attend Memphis National College of Business and Culinary School and I also took courses in Business Administration Management. Actually it was while attending Culinary School I had this bright idea to provide free hors d'oeuvres for every event Mother baked a cake for, something simple yet tasteful and not too costly. Soon people were requesting the hors d'oeuvres when placing an order and in less than a year after giving away the hors d' oeuvres, calls began coming in wanting to know if Mother offered main courses. By the time I had completed culinary school I had plenty of customers and when I completed my Restaurant and Catering Management and the Restaurant Ownership courses; I formed my corporation and business took off like a jet.

Catering keeps me very busy and I love every moment of it! I concocted special dry blends of seasonings for red meats and the blends differ according to the cut. I also have special blends for pork and lamb and for turkey and sea foods my blend is real simple; you would be surprised what makes seafood flavors pop! Each blend I make truly enhances the natural flavor of the meats and seafood's. Instead of using seasoned salts and black pepper; I use sea salts, white pepper, fresh garlic and herbs, lemons, limes, dill and cilantro. For my baking I use real butter, fresh eggs, buttermilk, sour cream and cream cheese. Every pastry I make is from scratch and melts in your mouth!

Because my mother was diabetic, I make sugar free desserts also. I believe the reason I have so much business is because my foods are the most flavorful in the catering business; but, I may be a tiny bit biased.

I'm ready for my devotion now and I don't have any scripture in particular I want to study, so since today is the 16th I'll go to Proverbs 16, and meditate on the whole chapter.

Verse 9 really stood out to me, **"A man's heart plans his way, But the LORD directs his steps."** I immediately thought about how my day was planned until Aunt Flora phoned to re-route it, then I figured the Lord is the one in control of my steps so I guess I'll be in agreement to the interruption; after all the Lord knows better than I do; I just wonder what it is she wants to talk to me about.

After devotion I fix my breakfast; toast and tea and while sitting at my kitchen table I can't help but think about Aunt Flora. Maybe because I'm sitting here alone as I imagine she is, anyway I can't get over her being so demanding of me; she knows I have a catering business and for her to have me drop everything and chit chat with her is just downright inconsiderate, ugh that woman! What could she possibly want with me anyway; I haven't done anything to make her mad.

When Aunt Flora's name is mentioned at our Sunday dinners; Aunt Shirley and Aunt Brenda talk about her bad and sometimes Uncle Howard joins in and I mean they say some pretty mean stuff like, "One of the reasons she has never had a man is she is so cold blooded no man wants to shovel ten feet of snow just to get her name." Or, "She is too mean to catch a cold, let alone a man." And the one that makes everybody laugh is, "Yeah, a pound of ground beef could freeze in her arms if she so much as grab hold of it, she's just that cold." It takes Uncle Lester to stop them from talking bad about her. Usually when they get on a roll and the laughter fills the whole room, that's when he stops them from the bashing, he raises his voice and says, "Alright now that's enough, **she is** our sister!" Just like that, the laughter volume goes down to a hush and the subject gets changed. I think hearing about her being so cold hearted all of my life has me afraid of Aunt Flora because honestly, she has never acted cold towards me personally. I guess I'm afraid of her because of what I've heard about her all of my life. Whatever the reason, I'm scared of her and the thought of being alone with her for any length of time; makes me nervous!

I decided to call Dora; my cousin, to see if she knew anything about why Aunt Flora wants to see me; but she hadn't heard anything and told me she would call her mother to find out what she knew and call me back later. Dora is Uncle Howard's baby daughter, her name is Dorinda but she's Dora to family. We are only 3 months apart, I was born June 6th and she was born September 7th and because we all live within a 3 mile radius of each other the two of us grew up together. We walked to and from school every day together and I spent my evenings and Saturday afternoons at her house until I turned 15; then I was allowed to stay home by myself if I wanted. Dora and I are more like sisters than cousins, she knows my thoughts and I know hers and sometimes that can be creepy.

She's 5'9" and I'm 5'7" so most people thinks she's older than me but trust me, I get that straight! She is very beautiful with her copper brown skin tone, keen nose, perfect almond shaped brown eyes, and a full, wide smile. She and Aunt Shirley are thinner than most of us Bowen women; they are both a size 10 but just like the rest of us females; she's got the "Bowen women hips." Dora keeps her hair flawless and spends good money on her clothes and the girl loves her some jewelry. She has been saved for as long as I can remember and filled since we were 13 and yet she has a down to earth personality; she's classy and reachable, yes indeed she is. I, on the other hand, have way more hips than she does and fill out every bit of my size 14's and my hair will be in a ponytail until Sunday, then its French roll time.

I have my mother's bronze colored eyes and I took all of my father's facial features and complexion; russet brown or so they tell me because I have never seen the man. I wear jeans and tee shirts all the time except Sunday then I break out in my designer suits and accessories and as soon as I get home from church, I'm back in my jeans and the only makeup that will ever be found in my purse is lipstick. Dora and I are what you might call night and day but we are definitely the definition of sisters, I honestly don't know what I would do without her in my life and really don't want to ever find out!

After I talked to Dora, I went out to the garage and cooked until 10:30am. Then I went back into the kitchen and called to confirm next Friday and Saturday's events.

I made a sandwich and some iced tea and sat at the kitchen table, gazing out of the window. I thought about how Mother bought this house when I was barely 2 years old. It's small but for me, 1,200 square feet with two nice sized bedrooms and one large bath is plenty room. I remembered how Mother and I would eat here and every once in a while she would tell me some of the ways she saved her money for the down payment to purchase this house and even though it was almost

20 years old when she bought it; she jumped on it because it was within walking distance to her brothers and sisters homes and she said it had a very good price tag.

As I reminisce I realize, except for the usual maintenance and paint; I've kept the house pretty much the way she had it. The only major change I've made was converting the one car detached garage into a commercial kitchen and I added a storage room behind the garage to house my tables, chairs, umbrellas, fountains, trellises and other equipment; and I also added a carport for my truck. It was cheaper for me to convert the garage rather than lease or buy commercial property for the business. Also I had my home phone line added in the garage and added a business line in the house; only in the kitchen. This allows me to cook in the garage and talk on my speaker phone so whether it's business or personal I can cook and talk.

After my confirmation calls and lunch, it was back to the garage to finish getting everything together for the luncheon, and when I was done, I phoned Bobby Ray, my transportation supervisor and notified him the foods were ready. He and Jimmy Lee always set up and break down the tables for the events and they transport the food, they even fill in and serve as waiters.

As I showered and dressed for the luncheon I wondered 'what in the world could Aunt Flora want with me. I can't believe her giving me one more thing to remember to do; like I don't already have enough on my plate.'

I followed Bobby Ray and Jimmy Lee to the luncheon and while we were driving, we drove pass the main street that takes you to Aunt Flora's and I found myself wondering 'maybe she wants to start being included in on the family Sunday dinners. She has to miss being a part of the family; but why would she talk to me about it, why wouldn't she talk to Aunt Brenda. Aunt Brenda is easy to talk to about anything; but Aunt Shirley on the other hand, whew! No getting through to her without a drama session.'

I always follow Bobby Ray in my truck to all of the new booking locations for two reasons. One; so I can make sure everything in the contract is carried out as stated. When I first started catering some clients tried to pull a fast one on me by changing the location or not providing the equipment's stated in the contract. Two; it helps that Bobby Ray has lots of muscles, some people think because I'm female they can run over me. My experience has taught me to be on point at the very start of the event, that way if there are any changes to be made; before anything is unloaded, I get the contract amended.

Well everything on this contract checks out; time to hit it!

The luncheon went well; no snags and I had three requests for my business card. When I returned home Dora had left a message, no one knew or heard a thing as to why Aunt Flora would want to see me and for me to call her when I come home from the meeting and give her the 411. By the time I cleaned the kitchen it was 5:10, good; I am not changing out of my uniform, I have just enough time to get over to Aunt Flora's.

CHAPTER TWO

The Truth Being Told
Disclosure emits understanding

As I drive to Aunt Flora's I'm doing a mind sweep; going over the last Sunday dinner and what I might have said about her that could have gotten back to her. I realize I never uttered a word about her so what in the world could she possibly want with me! Ok, I haven't said nor have I done anything so she must want something, no, wait, what did she say to me on the phone this morning? "I have something very crucial to talk with you about." Ok Angie let's not get intimidated.

I park my truck in her driveway and let out a sigh of relief, that's better! As I began walking up the walkway, I find myself getting nervous again. I'm putting on my best posture and I can almost hear myself saying, "And a left, right, left," I am actually marching up the walkway to her front door. Geez Angela, get a grip!

Aunt Flora lives in the family house; the house all 6 of them grew up in and no one visits her unless it's absolutely necessary. I rang the doorbell and thought to myself, 'I sure hope I haven't done anything wrong, hope I'm not in any trouble.' As the door opens, I take one look at her and I gasped! Her face is aglow. I have never seen her face lit up before, and I think, is she smiling, no, she's, she's smiling, a reaction I'm shocked she's capable of displaying. I'm so thrown off, I stand here staring at her with my mouth open, she reaches her arms out and gives me a warm hug and says, "Well don't just stand there baby come on in." I know this is crazy; but while she's hugging me, I immediately think about the pound of ground beef freezing in her arms and I'm wondering, 'what's going to happen to me? Hey now! What's with her, she has NEVER hugged me before.' I stepped up and through the front door and while she closes the door, as if she had read my mind she says, "I know you're wondering why I hugged you and what could I possibly want to talk to you about." She takes in a deep sigh and her tone turns to serious as she says, "Well Angie, I've prepared you dinner, come into the kitchen, I won't keep you in suspense any longer."

As I follow her through the living room, now the dinning room, I am clutching onto my purse looking around the rooms to see if there's a sign somewhere anywhere warning me to run while I have the chance. Everything in the house is just as I remembered it 6 years ago when I came to get pictures of Mother. Aunt Shirley made me come get them because she wanted the "home going" program full of pictures of Mother's short but full life and Aunt Flora, living in the family house; has all of the family memorabilia.

As I entered the kitchen, I hear some worship music playing softly and while I'm trying to figure out where it's coming from Aunt Flora pulls out a chair for me to sit in. As I slowly sit down, my eyes are busy scanning the kitchen looking at the beautiful green speckled granite counters and I spotted a small CD player and began admiring the latest appliances she has displayed. Hum, she really has good taste.

I didn't notice she was standing in front of me with a clean empty plate in her hand, and tears streaming down her face, not until I focused off the kitchen counters and onto her; I was stunned. I placed my purse on the table, stood up, rubbed both her arms to console her and asked what was wrong.

She placed the plate on the table next to my purse and stood there staring at it and slowly said to me, "Angie," she looks up directly into my eyes and continues, "Angela Elise Bowen. I have a shocking family secret to tell you, you had better sit down." Now I'm getting scared again, so I sit as she has commanded but I don't take my eyes off hers. My stomach is taking a giant leap up to my throat and I feel as though I'm going to be sick. She's staring at me with a frightened look on her face and the suspense is killing me! I leap up out of my chair and ask hastily, "Aunt Flora what is it?"

She slightly turns and pulls up a chair to sit down, then she shifts her eyes back to mine and gives me this stare as she reaches out and grabs hold of both my arms and as she sits; I sit. Never taking her eyes off mine; she reaches one hand back and draws her chair up close to me with her knees touching mine. She puts both her hands on top of mine and gives them a really tight squeeze and says, "I am really your grandmother, not your aunt." Wrinkles form on my forehead with my eyebrows as my head slightly moves back and I'm thinking, 'what did she say? She's really my grandmother? Not my aunt?' Aunt Flora looks down at my hands, picks them both up and brings them to her lips and kisses the backs of them. She looks up, intently into my eyes and holds on tightly to my hands and says, "Angie, De Anne was my baby, not my sister, my beautiful baby girl. And you, you are my beautiful, smart and talented grand baby." Now she's crying and rapidly squeezing my hands. She's looking at my face as if my facial expression is telling her how I'm processing what she's telling me.

Her eyes are bouncing from my eyes to my eyebrows and I'm looking at her, thinking 'who is this woman looking like Aunt Flora telling me some crazy story about being my grandmother.' I stare into her eyes, maybe she took some drugs and she's trippin. But her pupils are normal. I started sniffing; is she high? Does she get high and that's why she doesn't come around the family? Nope, I don't smell any weed.' She says to me, "I'm not crazy nor am I high, I need to tell you the truth Angie; the real story." Uh oh, whoever she is, she can read minds! I sat there scared and unable to move so I listened to her story.

And a story she did tell. Her watery eyes still gazing into mine, she begins: "Daddy was in one of his moods. He would not come out of his room; he would go days and sometimes weeks eating very little and not talk to anyone. He just stayed in his bed, all day and all night. Mama had moved Daddy into Howard's old room a few days after Howard left for boot camp. His room was next to my bedroom down the hall away from her room or the big bedroom as it was called in those days. I had turned 16 two months earlier and wanted to go to my high school dance coming up in three weeks. A few weeks earlier I asked Mama if I could go to the dance with five other friends of mine. She said to me, 'I'll ask your father and if he says ok, then you can go.' You must understand; at school the dance was the only topic of conversation and every evening I would talk on the phone with my close friend, Carlota Hamilton and all of our conversations consisted of who was going to the school dance and every evening Carlota phoned me; she would ask if I had permission yet to go.

She liked Oscar Weeks, his best friend was Gary Fields and Gary liked Denise Tolliver and I had a serious crush on Brandon Stokes. Oh my gracious, he was so fine, so Carlota and I figured we could all go to the dance together as a group and our parents would think it was acceptable. You see, back then, good respectable girls did not go out with boys alone. Well, after 2 weeks of asking Mama every evening if I could go and she kept telling me 'your father hasn't decided yet.' As soon as my eyes opened that Saturday morning; I laid there in my bed and thought, 'it has been two weeks and going on three, today is it! I'm getting my answer; this has gone on long enough.' It was March 24th. After I washed up I passed Daddy's room headed to the kitchen, I could hear Mama in there humming. Daddy was still in bed, I was so mad. I thought 'he is not going to snap out of this mood of his until the dance is over' and I desperately wanted to go to that dance.

I marched into the kitchen and observed Mama seasoning a roast for tomorrow's dinner, so I stood there in front of the table and put my hand on my hip and me and my 16 year old attitude told Mama I was going to the dance and for her to let Daddy know it! Mama looked at me and asked who died and made me boss? I told her, 'Daddy is in one of his moods and I'm going to that dance, he wouldn't know if I were home or gone to the moon.' While I was talking to her she wiped her hands with her apron and moved slowly to stand in front of me, and as the last word left my mouth, she hauled off and slapped my face! She told me as long as I was black, I had better not ever think about talking to her like that again or my brothers and sisters would be buying black suits for my funeral! She pointed towards Daddy's room and said, "That man in there in one of his moods is your father, and you young lady had better not forget that as long as you live, which by the way just may not be too much longer!" She stepped back and told me to get out of her face before she slapped it again and the next time she saw my face; I had better have some respect!

I stormed out of the kitchen, went straight to my room and softly closed the door. I couldn't believe Mama was treating me like a child, after all I was 16. As I lay across my bed I wept like a baby. I stayed in my room for several hours, telling her off real good in my mind.

Later Carlota called and as soon as I said hello, with excitement in her tone; she started telling me her daddy said she could go to the dance. She was so thrilled and asked if I had gotten the green light yet, I told her my daddy was still in one of his moods. When she told me if I couldn't go she wasn't sure her daddy would let her go. She sounded as though I had let the air out of her balloon; she was so disappointed. She almost whined as she told me her mother and father didn't know Denise, and they might think she was wild and wouldn't let her go if I didn't. She pleaded with me to ask Mama again and after that conversation, all I could think about was; if I didn't go to this dance, no one could. Angie, I felt so much pressure on me, if Carlota didn't go, Denise wouldn't be able to go either. I had to figure out a way to go to that dance, even if I had to sneak out and go.

Somehow I had to get through to Daddy, so, after dinner I started thinking about what to say to him that would make him see the importance of this dance without him thinking I was wild. By night fall, I had a plan, I was going into Daddy's room and talk to him about school, and make him see how I was a good girl and this was the only time I would ask him to let me go to a dance. So I went and stood in the doorway to his room and started talking to him.

I was very soft spoken and respectful. I asked him how he was feeling. No response, so I kept talking. I told him all of my grades; I was an 'A' student. Then I told him about how Carlota, Denise and I wanted to go to the school dance and that some nice boys at our school would escort us and keep an eye out for us. He knows Carlota and her family, so I told him the nice boys were 'A' students like me and I could get their parents phone numbers and let him talk to them so he could see for himself they were good boys and come from good homes. Then I said, 'Ok daddy, do you want the phone numbers?' Again, no response so; I decided to enter into his room and I walked over to the foot of his bed and stood there. He was laying there watching me as I moved towards him, 'Ok daddy, do you want me to give you the phone numbers?'

I stood there staring at him; as he lay there staring at me, and I felt myself getting mad. How could he just lay there and watch me grovel, and beg. I glanced over to my right at his stump propped up against the wall; I thought, 'he doesn't deserve to stand up on two feet like a real man!' My father was selfish, mean and hateful to just lie there and listen to my plea for permission and not be moved at all. I said as softly as I possibly could, 'daddy can you hear me?' I stood there waiting for a response. He rolled his eyes at me and turned over on his side, putting his back to me. I felt my face get hot; I was so mad I blurted, 'You are a selfish miserable man and you don't care about anybody but yourself, I hate you!' And I spun around and ran out of the room, straight to mine and this time I slammed the door!

A few moments later Mama opened the door to my room. I was sitting on the edge of my bed socking the mattress; too mad to cry, I was fuming! She says,

'Flora, I heard what you told your daddy.' She was walking towards me as she talked. I twitched, bracing myself for her to hit me again and I didn't care if she did. I thought, 'she can beat me all she wants; I'm too mad to care.' She stops at the foot of my bed and says, "I have so much on my mind these days, I forget you still a child. You are right, you make good grades, you are not wild, and as long as you go to the dance with the friends you told your daddy about, you have my permission to go." I jumped up off the bed and ran to her, and we hugged each other so tight and I thanked her. She told me to give her the phone numbers by Monday so she could call the parents. Mama turned to leave my room and when she stood in the doorway, she stopped and while slightly turning her face towards me, she says, 'Flora, baby Mama's proud of you.' A few minutes later I heard her bedroom door close.

I was so happy she was letting me go to the dance, Hey, hey; hey I'm going to the dance! For hours I thought about how I was going to approach Brandon and let him know I had permission to go to the dance. Then around midnight I had this horrible thought. What if Brandon had already asked someone else to the dance because he thought I wasn't able to go? That thought kept me tossing and turning most of the night and I hardly slept.

7:45 a.m. Mama entered my room to wake me for Sunday School and church. I was so sleepy she had to call me again and hollered she was not going to call me a third time. I knew what that meant so I rolled myself out of bed and sluggishly prepared for church. She fixed daddy something to eat and as soon as I walked into the kitchen she told me to take it to him. I took the tray to his room and set it on the T. V. tray by his night stand, and said good morning to him and left the room.

While we were in Sunday school I yawned and stretched the whole session. During the break between Sunday school and 11 o'clock service, I walked the parking lot to wake myself. I'm telling you I fought sleep all through church; I wiggled and squirmed so much, Mama gave me a look. All the way home, all I could think about was taking a nap. When she pulled up in the driveway I told her I was going to take a thirty minute nap. "Okay, I'll put you a plate up and won't wake you,' she said. I walked in the back door and turned left headed down the hall to my room. Passing Daddy's room I gave a quick glance inside. I back tracked, I saw toast on the floor, I poked my head in the room, there was Daddy's breakfast Mama had fixed for him all over the floor. I heard the back door slam; Mama was now in the house.

I stepped inside Daddy's room looking for him, no wheelchair, where could he be. I went down the hall towards my room and glanced into the bath room, the door was open, where in the world is he, and why did he throw his food all over the room? Just then Mama let out a scream like I have never heard before. Something in her pitch went through me and gave me a chill; it was alarming but still couldn't prepare me for what I was about to see. I ran towards Mama's room and as soon as I stood in the doorway I saw pillow feathers and pieces of pillowcase fabric all over the wall and floor. Daddy had taken a pillow from her bed to use as a muffle and shot himself in the head. His note on her dresser simply stated, "Sorry it took me this long to die." By the time I entered the room, she was on the floor, clutching tightly onto Daddy's upper body while rocking him back and forth in her arms as though he were a baby, she was muttering; 'It's ok Roy, its ok Roy,' repeatedly.

I ran into the kitchen and called Brenda, no answer. I leave a message, "Come home quick! It's Daddy!" I called Shirley and left the same message, then Lester. No one was home, it was Sunday, and they are all on their way home from church. I dialed 911. The ambulance was there by the time I had pried Mama loose from Daddy. She was in shock and was acting like Daddy was just taking a nap. She kept looking at the clock and the paramedic asked her several questions until the police arrived and after answering each question; she would ask, "Is that all? I need to make Roy's lunch before he gets up from his nap."

Because she had blood all over her face, hands and the front of her suit and I had blood all on my hands and the front of my dress, the police asked us a thousand questions and right in the middle of her answering one of their questions she realized what had happened, what her husband had done actually sunk in and she hollered, "Oh god no, why Roy, why, why would you do something like this?" She couldn't stop crying and shaking her head.

She jumped up from the kitchen table and went to the sink and washed the blood off her hands. Still crying and shaking her head but now she is screaming, "Roy why? Why would you do this, Roy why?" After she dried her hands and turned around to face us, she propped herself against the kitchen sink, and crossed her left hand over her stomach then rested her right elbow on it as she closed her right hand to make a fist, and commenced to pounding her mouth over and over. Now the screaming has ceased but the tears; I have never seen tears flow so fast, ever. Lester walked over to her and grabbed her fist and guided her out of the kitchen into the dining room and sat her down at the table. We all followed them into the dining room. After helping Mama to sit down, Lester stood behind her and while he gently rubbed her shoulders to comfort her; he silently cried. Brenda sat to Mama's right; staring at her while she cried and repeatedly blew her nose. Inez sat next to Brenda crying and watching every move Lester made. Shirley sat at the other end of the table with one arm stretched completely out on the table as she laid her head on it; continuously screaming "NO, no, no" over and over while holding a wad of tissue in her other hand and pounding it on the table. Henry and Odell paced the room, both watching their wives. I sat on the left side of Mama crying and watching her and everyone else in the room; scared they would yell at me any minute for making Daddy commit suicide.

The police interrogated the rest of the family members and the neighbors to find out if anyone heard arguing or gun shots. It was a horribly long day for me and it was almost midnight before the police and coroner left with Daddy's body.

Shirley had us all spend the night with her, even though none of us slept. We stayed up asking each other questions like; did you think he would do anything like this, did you see this coming? Was he still taking his medication? What was the last conversation you had with him? How was he acting? Why didn't one of us see this coming? I screamed and sobbed something fierce when I told them what I had said to Daddy and I apologized to them for pushing him over the edge. They all told me it was not my fault but I thought it was.

Lester and Shirley told me Daddy had a dark side after he returned from the war. They both talked about remembering how Daddy acted before he left to go into the Army and how despondent he was when he came home. Brenda told me how loving and warm he could be and would turn cold towards you in a matter of seconds. Mama said he was a very loving and warm man when they met and married. He loved life and was a loving and protective father when Lester and Shirley were little. He had seen too much death in the war and he really didn't know how to process it and get his soul healed and he was mad at God and blamed Him for letting innocent people die. She apologized to me for not knowing the tender and loving side of him then she told us the beautiful story of how they met.

The next day Mama and Lester selected a funeral home and told them to speed up the process of Daddy's services because the family had a lot to handle due to the circumstances surrounding his death. The Funeral Director was very cooperative; we buried daddy in 5 days.

Daddy had four sisters and one brother. Aunts Maxine, Rhonda, Margarite and Serita, and they all drove to the funeral together and left the grave site returning back to Lexington, TN. Uncle Curtis and his wife; Aunt Beverly drove their car and they stayed for the repast at Shirley's house. Uncle Curtis told us that Daddy's sisters were hurt and needed to blame someone and they had decided since Gert didn't stop him; all the blame should be on her. We never heard from Daddy's sisters again after that, Uncle Curtis and Aunt Beverly sent Christmas cards but that stopped after three or four years.

Angie, you must understand; I was consumed with guilt for telling Daddy that he was selfish and that I hated him. I went completely wild, totally out of control on a downward spiral. I avoided Carlota, and started hanging out with the girls at school that smoked cigarettes, popped pills and drank whiskey. I skipped school and had sex with any boy that wanted to have sex with me. In my mind I thought my Daddy killed himself because of me and I should be punished, so acting wild and crazy was my way of hurting me. Mama was always on the living room sofa crying. She slept there and moved her clothes out of her closet into Daddy's room on top of his bed. She was so deep in her own grieving she had no idea I was drowning in mine.

Three weeks later, I was with my new friends and I drank myself sick; that was the night of the dance. We all took our drink and smokes and sat on the curb across the street from the school and watched the goody two shoes go to the 'square's dance.' When I saw Carlotta and Denise walk up to the door with Oscar and Gary, tears started forming in my eyes but I was determined not to shed one tear so I grabbed a bottle from someone and downed it. This dance was the reason I pushed Daddy off the edge; all for a stupid dance. I felt so bad, so I really got into making fun of the party goers. I got so drunk I began throwing up and a couple of the kids propped me up on their shoulders and walked or should I say dragged me home. They rang the doorbell and left me on the front grass where I had passed out.

Mama opened the door and screamed when she saw me lying on the grass; she told me later she thought I was dead. She called Lester and he came over and helped her get me inside the house. I was in the bed sick for two days I couldn't stop throwing up. After the throwing up stopped, I was sick to my stomach all the time. Almost a week later, after taking all the home remedies Mama could think of to help me feel better; she took me to the doctor and I found out I was pregnant.

We came home and Mama and I sat right here at the kitchen table and she asked me who the father was.

I told her how I had been drinking and having sex with any boy that wanted to have sex with me and had no clue as to who the father was. After her looking at me with unbelief for what seemed like 30 minutes; she said I would be disgraced and the poor baby would be labeled for the rest of its life. She sat there staring at me and when she finally spoke again she was the one to come up with the plan of hiding my being pregnant.

You see Angie, by me being hippy and with Mama being full figured, she told me, she would tell everyone she was having a 'change baby' and I would stay out of sight; you know, in the house until the baby was born. I could wear big blouses that went down to my hips, and she could wear Mu Mu's. Everyone knew how hard I was taking Daddy's death, so it was possible we could pull it off, it was worth a try anyway.

I was so out of it, it was as if my head was inside a cloud; it did not register at all that I was going to give life; all I could think about was 'I am the person responsible for what my father did; I spoke the last harsh words he heard.' Only when my body began to change is when it became hard for me to pretend nothing was happening to me. I stayed away from Carlotta because I would have told her I was pregnant. I walked around like a zombie until De Anne began moving inside me like a little flutter, it was then I finally let go of the guilt and responsibility I carried about Daddy's death and began thinking about life again; and being concerned about the baby I was carrying.

Mama and I became so close, she would tell me what to expect being pregnant and I would tell her every movement the baby made and how I felt and she would echo every word I uttered to Shirley and Brenda. Howard was away in the army and when he came home on leave, he stayed with Shirley and Henry but he phoned me and Mama every day. They all bought the idea that I was suffering a breakdown from Daddy's death and I stayed in the house and read most of the time I was pregnant, except to keep my doctors appointments. When I would get stir crazy, I'd go sit in the back yard for a while then it was back inside for us.

When school started again, Mama went to the principal and made arrangements for me to do home studies the first semester due to my father committing suicide. When I began to show I had to stay in my bed whenever anyone would come to the house. I was supposed to be terribly depressed and no one gave a second thought to me being in my room in the bed.

Sometimes Brenda would come into my room and sit on the foot of the bed and rub my feet while telling me to learn how to forgive myself. Lester and Inez would come into my room and ask if I needed anything and he would always pray for me to become healed emotionally. Shirley would bring her boney behind over and cry on Mama's shoulder about how she missed her Daddy, and every time she'd leave, Mama would be so distressed. Every time Shirley would leave, I would get on the phone and call Henry to tell him he needed to talk to his drama queen of a wife about coming over here and upsetting my Mama! The phone call would only work for a week or so then Miss Shirley would prance herself right back over here and perform all over again.

Preparing for the baby to come was just what I needed to start thinking again about my own life. We found out the baby was a girl and painted the room and made curtains and fixed Daddy's room up for De Anne. When I went into labor, Mama drove me all the way out to the County Hospital in Bartlett and she stayed overnight with me and the next day we came home with

De Anne then I called Shirley and told her Mama had the baby. Everyone thought I would take care of Mama and the baby; they thought it was the perfect therapy for me, so they didn't come over that often and our secret was safe.

The one thing that haunted me was I didn't know who De Anne's father was and that weighed heavily on my heart. I was so embarrassed and the best way for me to handle that was to tell myself, this was my sister, not my daughter. Every time I would pick my baby up I would have to tell myself 'this is your sister, this is your sister;' that way I wouldn't grab De Anne and say, 'Hey mama baby.' I told myself this is your sister so much, I believed the lie myself.

Her birthdays were the hardest for me because during the celebration I would remember the labor and the love I felt for her the first time I held her in my arms; that miraculous feeling you get holding your precious treasure for the first time. You know how Shirley is, always watching everyone's reactions when we all get together. I had to keep my facial expressions down to a minimum and I was terribly afraid I'd slip and say something about De Anne's birth, so I became this outsider from my own family; afraid something would slip out of my mouth and make them wonder if I were De Anne's mother and not her sister. This made me so angry and bitter inside. I was actually mad that my family had their lives and was close; and here I, had to live with this weighty secret, all because our father shot himself because of the words I spoke. Because of what I said to Daddy; his life ended, and that caused my life as I had known it to end. It wasn't until De Anne turned a year old that I realized the secret had me so bound, it choked the life out of me; I was living a lie.

Mama put the house up for sale but there had been a big write up in the local newspaper about the "War hero who killed himself," and we just could not sell it. Shirley and Lester put some money together and had the rooms in the house remodeled and that helped us be able to live here somewhat, but the memory of what happened in this house has never completely left.

Angie, it grieves me to tell this but; everyone thought Mama had dementia, she really didn't. She started recalling memories of Daddy being on the floor in her room and the blood being everywhere and she would sit and talk about it; some days all day. She would recall all of the conversations she and I had when I was pregnant. She was only reminiscing what actually happened in each one of her children's lives when their daddy ended his. She was... Angie she was.... just remembering the truth!"

Aunt Flora is crying now and she's trying to talk but the tears are gushing out of her eyes and she's unable to speak; she covers her face and 'boo hoos.' I lean closer to her and rub both her arms to console her. Being acquainted with guilt myself; I feel tears streaming down my face, after all; this is my grandmother crying and I can relate to her pain.

After a few moments she harnesses her emotions, grabs some napkins and blows her nose, and then she takes in a deep breath and continues talking. "Angie Mama was just remembering the truth and I let the doctors keep her medicated; I even gave the pills to her myself so she wouldn't tell what happened, me, me, the person she was protecting; I helped keep my own mother medicated so my secret wouldn't be exposed."

Now Aunt Flora is aggravated and shaking her head 'no' as she stands up with tears in her eyes looking at me, her forehead wrinkles and she continues, "Angie, De Anne would sit for hours and listen to Mama go on and on about what really happened and that made Mama feel so much better, you know; getting it off her chest. De Anne had no idea Mama was telling her about me and her; about how much I loved her and how she played a very important part in my letting go of the guilt I had about Daddy." Aunt Flora started crying again and reached over to get more napkins, this time to dry her eyes. I had to grab a few myself.

She slowly sits back down while fidgeting with the napkin in her hand and resumes, "When Mama died, I thought it was time for the secret to be revealed and I would get my life back. I had made my mind up to tell everyone the truth while we were all together planning the service, and the secret and lies would be over and done with. De Anne was still living here then, she had only been working at Slappy's Diner for a couple months. So I told everybody to come over here so we could all take part in putting Mama's obituary together and they all agreed. We were going through the boxes of old pictures and I remember getting up from the dining room table to come in here and get something when suddenly I heard loud glass breaking. I ran back into the dining room and De Anne had just stormed out of the front door. I asked what happened and Brenda told me De Anne never knew daddy killed himself.

She picked up a newspaper article about his death that was lying on the table and she just went off. She said just because she was the baby we had no right to keep something that important from her, and as far as she was concerned, we could all find a permanent address in the devils flames! And she threw her glass of water on the floor and slammed out of the front door.

She didn't come back for hours. We had just wrapped up everything when she walked quietly in the front door. We all sat still and watched her as she tip toed towards her room with her head purposefully being held down to keep from looking at us. She was so quiet, the silence made us all feel guilty.

It's not like we intentionally kept it from her, she was too young to understand how Daddy died and when she was old enough to understand, well, we had all forgotten she wasn't here when it happened. Suicide is something you just don't talk about; we never utter a word even though we all remember March 25th we never say a word." Now Aunt Flora. gets a worried look on her face and says, "De Anne was so angry about Daddy, Angie I just couldn't tell her the truth about me being her mother, it wasn't the right time. I wanted to be close to her, not push her further away from me. Had I told her then I was her mother, she never would have had anymore to do with me. She would have hated me for telling her a lie about being sisters and for keeping the truth about Daddy's death from her, so I had to keep my secret a little longer.

The day of Mama's funeral, De Anne refused to sit with us; she sat behind all of the grandchildren. When I saw her sitting so far from me, I realized she was all I had left in this world. When she walked up to view Mama's body I wanted to scream 'that's not your mother; she's your grandmother **I am** your mother.' It took every ounce of strength I had not to shout it out to her in front of everyone in that church. She was angry with me and there was no way I could tell her the truth without her hating me the rest of her life. I just couldn't bear the thought of not being able to have De Anne in my life Angie, I just couldn't bear it!

She drove her own car to the cemetery and before she left, she walked up to me and said, 'Flora I thought you of all people would have told me the truth about Daddy, but you are just as devious and trifling as the rest of them.' I reached my hand out to her and she slapped it away and told me to shove it. So all I could do was wrap my secret and lie a little tighter around myself, I had no choice but to keep pretending I never gave birth to De Anne and everything would be alright. But I lived in this house with my daughter angry at me for not telling her how her grandfather; the man she knew to be her father; had died, and that lie cost me dearly. De Anne slowly interacted with the family again but I don't think she ever truly trusted any of us."

Aunt Flora became watery eyed and her tone turned somber as she said, "When De Anne was sick and had to be hospitalized; I almost told it. I stayed with her in that little room and hugged and rocked my baby every chance I could. I wanted to tell her so badly she was my baby but I resolved to just telling her how much I loved her. The thought of her leaving this earth mad at me for lying to her all of her life, Angie please understand, I could not live with that guilt, so, I let her leave this world in peace....After she passed I was so grief–stricken I had to be sedated for the funeral. I could not trust myself to be quiet about my only baby being laid to rest. My beautiful baby who carved out a great portion of love from my heart was now taken away from me. I was truly reaping from my past deeds.

Even though I was heavily sedated for her home going, when you broke down, I wanted to run to you, hold you tight in my arms and tell you I was your grandmother and assure you we would get through this together. When I tried to stand up, I couldn't move. I had to sit there in silence, bury my baby and watch like a spectator as my only grand baby wept her heart out, Angie; I had to bury my baby who everyone believed was my little sister." Aunt Flora is crying again but she keeps talking. "When the family car drove from De Anne's grave site; I thought 'now Flora Bowen, you will go to your grave carrying the secret and lies with you. Will you rest in peace even then?'

Last night I accepted Jesus as my Lord and Savior. I realized I have been going to church all my life and have never had a relationship with Jesus, ever. I have been sitting in church and never once allowed the Word to get inside me until last night when Pastor Anderson preached on Matthew 11:27–30. You know when Jesus said: **"All things have been delivered to Me by My Father, and no one knows the Son except the Father…"**That caught my attention. I thought about my Daddy and how no one understood him, but the Lord. Angie, that sparked something in my heart and I started listening to Pastor Anderson with a different ear. Then he went on to verse 28 saying: **"Come to Me, all you who labor and are heavy laden, and I will give you rest. (29) Take My yoke upon you and learn from Me, for I am gentle and lowly in heart, and you will find rest for your souls. (30) For My yoke is easy and My burden is light."** Pastor Anderson told us to give Jesus all of our secrets, troubles and fears and for us to rest from carrying them.

I sat there and looked at Shirley sitting there with her family, then I looked over at Lester, Howard and Brenda, they were all there with their families and I thought, 'I have carried all the weight of a secret by myself, and it has kept me from my family. The family I was so close to before the secret and lies took root in me.' By then Pastor Anderson was saying to take on the yolk of Jesus and experience His liberty. I shouted, 'Yes

Lord' and sat there and cried so hard. When Pastor gave the invitation to accept Jesus as your personal Savior; I ran up to the alter. People were whispering but I didn't care. I know I have been in church since I was a little girl but I have never trusted Jesus to handle the day to day affairs in my life. I always thought 'I got this Lord, when I need you, I'll call on you.' Last night I repented of all my sins, secrets and lies. Now I need you to forgive me for lying to you for 26 years. You are my granddaughter and I want to have a granddaughter and grandmother relationship with you the way it should be."

Now she takes my hands and rubs them nervously and as she gazes into my eyes she says, "Angela, baby whatever hoops you need me to jump through; I'm willing to jump through them to prove to you how sorry I am. I know this is unbelievable and may be hard for you to take in at one time, but I hope and pray you don't hate me and will find it in your heart to forgive your grandmother for being so foolish." Aunt Flora stood up and kissed me ever so gently on my cheek. Then she stroked the side of my cheek with her index finger as if I were a small baby. I looked into her eyes and it looked to me like they were sparkling. I have never felt so much love and tenderness from her before. I sat there looking up at her as if I were seeing her for the very first time; this is my grandmother. I can't believe it! My grandmother, my grandmother's alive!

I sat there examining her facial features, and I could see Mothers nose and cheeks. Aunt Flora is my grandmother; I couldn't believe it. She knew I was dumbfounded, I guess she could see it in my eyes; so she pulled me up out of the chair, hugged me real tight, kissed my cheek and put my purse strap on my shoulder. Then, she put her hands on my shoulders and directed me towards the front door. She said for me to wait a minute and left me standing by the dining room table. I don't know why she thought I could move on my own. A few minutes later she walked up to me, pulled my arm out and put a plate covered with foil in my hand and guided me to and through the front door. As I stood there outside her front door; she told me to call her and let the phone ring twice and hang up when I get home; she would know I made it alright. She kissed me on my cheek, and told me she loved me dearly. I stood there unable to move and staring at her; I heard everything she was saying; I just couldn't move my legs. She stepped outside of the door, pulled me by my hand to my truck and opened the door and gave me a slight shove onto the driver's seat. I sat there a few minutes looking up at her and shook my head hoping to collect myself. I watched her as she walked into the house, closed the door and peeked out of the window at me.

I had to actually tell myself step by step what to do. 'Put your feet inside the truck, close the door, put the plate in the seat; take the key out of your purse; put your purse on the floor. Put the key in the ignition, put on your seat belt. Start the truck; take the brake off.' I had to tell myself all the way home what to do. 'Stop, ok you can go now.' After I pulled up in my drive way, I turned off the ignition and sat there thinking about what I had just heard. Aunt Flora is my grandmother!

CHAPTER THREE

Up Comes My Secrets!
Lord I need you now

As I sat in the driveway, my mind was going over what it had just heard and some things were starting to click about Aunt Flora's behavior. As if someone had inserted a computer memory stick in my mind; pictures began flashing of Aunt Flora's glances at me from the time I was a very little girl until now. She really did love me and now that I'm reflecting, she has never said an unkind word to me, everyone else but not me.

I remembered when I was little, every so often she would come over to the house and sit in the kitchen making Mother and me nervous because we couldn't figure out why in the world she would come to visit us, out of all the family members, why us? Mother thought it was because she and Aunt Flora were the last two girls at home and Aunt Flora felt it was her duty to watch over her baby sister or maybe the fact that Aunt Flora had no friends was why she visited us and no other family member; but now; tonight, I know the real deal. She was visiting her daughter and granddaughter; on the sly.

Whenever she would stop by the house to visit, Mother would ask her if she was alright and Aunt Flora would always respond the same way every time, she'd raise her voice and look back and forth at both me and Mother while saying, "Can't I visit my family without something being wrong?" We would feel like two-year olds standing there waiting for her to say something. Mother would stutter trying to make small talk like; so and so is doing this or oh, uh, have you heard about such and such. Err, uh did you hear about…. This would go on until Aunt Flora would get up and say, "I best be going; love you," and she'd leave never looking back to see us breathe a sigh of relief. Now that I think about it, it's funny, she was scared of us and we were scared of her. Talk about comical!

I remember her attending my high school graduation and after the pictures were taken she pulled me off to the side and gave me a card. Later that evening when I read the card, I was a bit confused as to why she had hand written on the left side; how very proud of me she was and, she had enclosed a check for $1,000.00. I never told anyone about the money because I thought she would hold it over me, threaten to take it back if I didn't do something she wanted me too. Oh man this is odd, now I'm remembering when I had a bad breakup with my first love, Elvin Jamison and I cried like a baby in church one Sunday and went up to the alter for prayer and right after service Aunt Flora walked up behind me and whispered in my ear, "No boy is worth all those tears. You wait on the one that's right for you." I thought it was her voice and when I turned around all I could see was the back of her as she walked away; I was so puzzled because I couldn't figure out how she knew I was crying over a boy. Now that I know she's my grandmother it all makes sense! I see the flash of headlights behind me and turn around to see Bobby Ray and Jimmy Lee. Bobby Ray has a key to my house and garage, this way I don't have to let them in when him and Jimmy Lee pick up to set up for our repeat events. I guess they had something to do after the luncheon and didn't drop off the tables and equipment earlier because I was still sitting in the driveway reflecting when they pulled up along side of me in the van. I still couldn't move and as I watched them unload the van, I wondered if either one of them had family secrets that would render them motionless.

After they unloaded, Jimmy Lee waved at me as he passed by going to the car they left parked in front of my house, and right behind him came Bobby Ray. Bobby Ray walked over to my truck, motioned for me to roll the window down and as he slightly leaned into the truck to ask if everything was alright; his eyes scanned the inside, then he glanced up at me to read my facial expression, I mustered up a smile and told him, "Yes I'm ok and I'll call you tomorrow." He turned around to leave and looked inside the back of my truck and as his eyes scanned my driveway I watched him in my side mirror as he walked away; he kept looking over his shoulder at me. I grabbed the plate Aunt Flora had given me and decided I had better get out of the truck because if Bobby Ray was suspicious something was wrong with me, or someone was bothering me, he would go home get his over & under shotgun and come back and check on me. So I decided to get out of the truck and as I did I waved him off before they pulled away.

When I hired Bobby Ray I knew he had a record so we made an agreement that he would work 30 days as a probationary period with me and if he was a good fit; he had the job permanently. Dora's Mom, Aunt Rose Marie taught Cosmetology and Barbering for year's downtown Memphis and when I told her I was going to hire a staff she volunteered to help me interview them; she is a very good judge of character and she gave me a lot of insight as to what to look for in a person in regards to their abilities for the position being hired for. As it turned out I hired almost everyone interviewed except for 3 other people.

Jimmy Lee Mason was first hired for transportation, he's built like a body builder but he has a very gentle spirit. Bobby Ray was the last interviewed and oddly he ended up being the most attentive to what was needed. Before leaving for a booking he would enlighten us on a few things such as; we might need extra extension cords and bricks to even out the legs on the tables when we serve outside, things like that he's a natural for. During the interview we picked him not just because of his strong upper arms, but because Aunt Rose Marie pointed out to me how he was very observant. So after his probation; I ended up making him supervisor and it just so happens, he and Jimmy Lee get along like brothers and their wives and kids all interact like family with each other also.

When I hired waiters Maynard Green was my first choice and only because his wife, Victoria or Vicki as we call her, was my first pick as a waitress. I figured if they could work together I would have no problems with them showing up. Maynard is a hard worker like the rest of them but he has a high energy level and can't keep still long so he's always working. Gregory Collins was the second waiter hired; he wears glasses, has a baby face and looks very professional in uniform. He's the one most people asks to get things for them because he looks the youngest of the group, sort of like a college student, but if the truth be known; he's the oldest of all the waiters. Jamal Black was the third chosen because he has good arms and is articulate and professional, not too talkative. Last was Willie Wilson or "W" as he's called, he has long strong arms also and has excellent manners. There's warmth about his persona that makes you feel as though you can trust him.

My waitresses are all beautiful women and fast thinkers. Vicki was first hired and what sold us on her was her easy outgoing personality and she has a photographic memory. Mattie Hall was second and is so beautiful inside and out; she can stop traffic if she has to and talk about street wise, she can spot trouble before anyone knows it's in the room. She has a tendency to be shy though if all eyes are on her. Miss Lula Mae Washington was third hired, she's a little dark woman five feet tall, soft spoken and can defuse the meanest biggest man around; there's a distinctive trait about her.

Once we were working a birthday party for drinkers and she talked this big strapping man with a knife in his hand down. He had too much to drink as did the other guy, and when we knew anything the big man was threatening to dissect the other man as he bent over, he put his hand inside his boot and came up with a stag horn handle switch blade. Lula Mae eased over to the table and stood beside the victim and talked to the big guy like he was a 2-year old. She softly said to him; "Now baby, let's think about this, you know you don't want to get in trouble; not tonight baby. Just put the knife down on the table like a good boy, come on baby." He laid that knife down on the table like he was giving her some money. I mean, she just talked to him and he went from beast to lamb right before our eyes. Everyone in that room saw first-hand how **a soft answer turns away wrath**. (Proverbs 15:1) The last hired was Wila Taylor, miss dark and lovely and she can be poster woman for hospitality, no one is a stranger when it comes to Wila; you feel as though she's family.

I thank the Lord for my staff; they are all good people, church goers, and hard workers. They get along well with each other and with clients and the only two times I missed a booking they worked it just like I was there and I pay them well so I can keep them.

As soon as I walk in the back door I plopped myself down in a chair at the kitchen table still stunned from what Aunt Flora had told me. All I can hear in my head is her saying, "I'm your grandmother not your aunt." I know in my heart it's true the way she treated Mother and me. Now my thoughts are switching to sympathy for Aunt Flora. I can relate to why she felt the need to keep her secret. I know what it feels like to realize you've done something stupid and how your mind tells you real loud not to tell a soul what you've done. I can't begin to imagine what it would feel like to have a baby and not know who the father is, but I do know that would make me lie, oh yeah now that I do know!

As a matter of fact, I'm not mad at Aunt Flora at all because I understand her shame and regret..... The more I think about it, I'm beginning to admire Aunt Flora's strength and her endurance, because when I was young, every time I was faced with my "love dilemmas;" suicide was the only option I thought I had. Now that's something! Tonight I find out why suicide had such a strong grip on me, my grandfather, no, I mean my great-grandfather's trait was passed straight to me, the one person in the family that didn't believe in family curses; huh!

Some of our Sunday dinners have good discussions about that morning's sermon and when my uncles went back and forth about the topic of family curses; I resolved there was no such thing, you simply reap what you sow. See, all of my uncles take turns teaching Sunday school, in most of their spare time you'll find them reading the Bible. Yep, if there's no game on, the Bible is out on the coffee table and a few other study aid books. Most of us pretty much have morning and evening devotions and will occasionally phone one another if a scripture leaps out at us, but when it comes to any subject in the Bible that I have a question about; I simply ask my uncles starting with Uncle Lester.

The Sunday they discussed family curses, my aunts were all involved and it was almost 5pm when we all left Uncle Lester's house. Uncle Odell would not change his opinion that Adam was the cause of being kicked out of the garden and having to work for what he needed to provide for his wife and family and; for the ground being cursed; because he was disobedient to God. In his opinion; Eve was deceived and therefore only disobeyed Adam. Uncle Lester and Uncle Howard said Eve was the downfall of Adam and that's why her sorrow was multiplied and pain in childbirth was put upon her. Oh I understand that because of Adam and Eve everyone is born into sin and must die; we don't have an option, but I feel once we are born again of the spirit; we are no longer under the sin influence, we are new creatures born of the spirit. I think Romans 5:18 & 19 explains that: "**18 Therefore, as through one man's offense judgment came to all men, resulting in condemnation, even so through one Man's righteous act the free gift came to all men, resulting in justification of life. 19 For as by one man's disobedience many were made sinners, so also by one Man's obedience many will be made righteous.**" I just believe we prefer not to walk in the spirit; but after our carnal nature; therefore we reap what we sow, that's just my opinion....

Tonight I believe my opinion may have altered in regards to curses. I understand curses enter a person's life through disobedience, however I didn't even know

Big Daddy had allowed a suicide spirit to take his life and yet; that same spirit had its influence on me just as Adam influenced death into the lives of every generation after him; geez, what an eye opener! Aunt Flora said Big Daddy was angry at God for allowing innocent people to die and he didn't know how to get his healing from the devastation he had witnessed. Suicide was his way of being free of the devastation; and I also perceived suicide as the ultimate remedy for my devastation; it was simply passed onto me, I didn't have to research it or question it, no, it just came to me so easily!

The first time I considered ending my life was after Elvin, 'the schemer' and I; maybe you could say, "Broke up." I was in the 11th grade and I loved me some Elvin Jamison. He was fine with all capital letters! My height, 5'7, built like a football player and was light skinned with a smile so sexy his top lip would slightly curl up on one side revealing his perfect teeth and he had big slanted dark brown eyes and thick corn rolls and talk about popular! He was a year ahead of me and had been the president of the senior student body.

We both had first period lunch and me and some other juniors sat in the lunch quad and watched the seniors so we would know what the buzz was on campus. I was sitting on the end of a lunch table talking to Jeanette and Valerie. I noticed the top on my drink didn't have a straw in it, I had forgotten to pick one up, so I removed the top, took a sip and hopped up real fast turning as I stepped away from the table; not knowing Elvin and a crowd of seniors were walking up behind me, and as I turned, I bumped right into Elvin.

Well you guessed it; no top on my soda, and bumping into Elvin caused the front of my sweater to get soaked. I looked up at him just as he jumped back to avoid me and he bumped into someone standing behind him and the drink he was holding at arm's length spilled on the front of his pants. It was so quiet for a few seconds and then everyone began laughing at us so he quickly stepped up to me and said, "Let's give them something to talk about, let me kiss you." Before I could say anything, he pulled me to himself and kissed me right in my mouth and closed his eyes. I stood there looking at him as I heard the laughter change into a loud "Ooh" from the crowd. He opened his eyes and loosened his grip from around my waist, and this giant grin appeared on his face as he said, "How old are you 15?" I said 16. He says, "16 and never been kissed. I want to take you out does your daddy let you go out?" "I don't have a daddy," I replied. His eyebrows slid up while he said, "Well, well, give me your phone number." I moved so fast scrambling to get my folder and I jotted my phone number down real fancy on a piece of paper and handed it to him. I was standing there gawking at him, showing all my teeth with the front of my sweater wet like a teething toddler. I was so excited Elvin Jamison was going to call **me**!

Later, while Dora and I were walking home from school, a lot of the kids walking past us were giggling and said, "Hi" to me and because Dora has second lunch period, I filled her in on what happened at lunch with Elvin and me. She told me he was bad news and I should stay away from him, but I was so in love; her words went in one ear and out the other as my heart kept beating to; "Elvin, Elvin." That night he phoned the house and we talked for over an hour. He asked me all about myself and like the naive little girl I was, I told him everything and he was taking notes. After a week of talking on the phone every night, he asked if he could come over to my house when my mother was at work and of course I said yes, he, he, ha, ha.

Well he came over and that night he taught me how to kiss with my mouth open. The second time he came over he taught me how to play "strip to the music," and the last time he came over he taught me how to play house, he was the daddy and I was the mama. The next day at school he acted like I was invisible and he never called me again. I thought when he told me he loved me; he loved me. My heart was not just broken; it was shattered into a thousand pieces. I couldn't figure out how he could love me and not talk to me again, what could I have possibly done wrong, I did everything he told me to do and he wouldn't even look at me; I was hurting really bad.

The following Monday when Dora and I were walking to school. She knew something was up with me and asked, "So you haven't mentioned Elvin for a couple of days and you're moping around what happened." I told her I didn't want to talk about it and she says, "Angie did you let him kiss you again?" I told her to drop it. She grabbed hold of my arm and asked, "You didn't do something you shouldn't have did you? I looked away from her, she stomped her foot and said, "Angie; I told you how he was, why didn't you listen to me?" Even though she had been telling me the whole time she heard all kinds of stories from different girls about how he was, and that he went around bragging to the guys at school about the girls he had at the school; I wasn't hearing a word and now she knows I wasn't.

After a few moments of silence I yanked my arm from her and started walking away, as I raised my voice saying, "He told me he loved me and since you've never been in love you just don't know how it feels." After a few more steps, I stopped, she walked up to me and we look at one another and I feel bad for not listening to her; I wouldn't be hurt right now had I listened, so I reach my arm out to her, she reaches for me and as we hug I started crying then she started crying and says in a quivering voice, "Well I hope you learned your lesson. Angie you are so gullible." I knew she was right but ooh I loved me some Elvin.

When Mother was at work and I would be home alone, I would think about Elvin and after almost three weeks of pining over him I thought I didn't want to live if he wasn't in my life. It was so difficult going to school knowing Elvin was shining me on and some of the guys at school were looking at me differently. I would catch them eyeing me up and down and when we made eye contact, they would give me a wink or smile and raise their eyebrows. After this happened to me several times I figured what Dora told me was true; Elvin had been bragging on himself about me and I loved him so.

That's when I realized he deliberately lied to me when he told me he loved me, and I felt so betrayed, cheap and manipulated. So, one Saturday evening I made my mind up to end my life tomorrow evening; that way I wouldn't have to go to school on Monday and be humiliated by the looks from the other guys and by Elvin avoiding me.

When Sunday morning arrived I was so depressed. I went to church thinking: 'this is the last day I will live; the last day of my life and I'm going to church to hear my last sermon.' It was the Sunday sermon our Youth Pastor, Pastor Jenkins preached from Psalms 147:3 **"He heals the brokenhearted And binds up their wounds."** He said there was two ways to handle our wounds. One way was to gather the pieces up and give them to Jesus, that is; if the wounds were fresh. The other way to handle our wounds was if they were old and scattered by the many paths we had taken, and the bad decisions we had made, those wounds were to be spoken too, just as Ezekiel had spoken to the dead bones in Ezekiel 37: 7; **"So I prophesied as I was commanded; and as I prophesied, there was a noise, and suddenly a rattling: and the bones came together, bone to bone."** Pastor Jenkins told us the wounds would come together just as the dry bones had, and become healed. Either way, Pastor Jenkins said; the Lord would heal our heart. During the whole sermon I cried and sniffled so much; it was as if Pastor Jenkins was preaching directly to me. As I walked up for prayer I told myself I had learned a lesson about liars and after my heart was healed I wasn't ever going to allow it to be broken again.

I'm sitting here at my kitchen table and can feel the pain, as it has once again emerged. I really don't want to remember this but, finding out this suicide spirit originated from Big Daddy is helping me to properly look at this so the root will be totally plucked up and out of me, this way it will never, ever pop up again!

I slowly slide my body down in the kitchen chair and lean my head back. As I close my eyes; Elvin's face appears, and tears are slowly dripping down mine. What makes some men purposefully set out to hurt women; to break their hearts, I wonder if their heart beats differently than other men, perhaps slightly slower. Lord I thought the part of my heart Elvin had destroyed was neatly tucked away forever by You. Now I feel as though there's a hole in my heart again, I really don't want to remember this right now. Oh why did Aunt Flora have to tell me this tonight?

As I lean forward in my chair, I cover my face with my hands, I can't deal with the pain....this is the pain that caused me to consider suicide in the first place, now it has resurfaced......Holy Spirit I need you to shield me as I walk through the memory of Elvin scheming me. I need to place healing and understanding at the root of the spirit of suicide and allow the All Consuming Fire of the Holy Spirit to forever consume this pain and impart healing in its place, in Jesus Name I decree it to be so, Amen.

After sitting for a few minutes allowing the Holy Spirit to minister to me, Isaiah chapter 54 verse 4 comes to my mind, it states; **"Do not fear, for you will not be ashamed; Neither be disgraced, for you will not be put to shame; For you will forget the shame of your youth, And will not remember the reproach of your widowhood anymore."** I remember memorizing that scripture and I'm surprised I can recall it tonight. I guess the Holy Spirit does bring all things to remembrance! Now I feel the warm, sweet presence of the Lord and finally, I'm able to get up from the kitchen table and with a smile on my face, I put the plate Aunt Flora gave me in the refrigerator and go take a long hot shower.

I crawled into bed and reached for my Bible on the nightstand but I know there will be no devotion tonight, I couldn't think about anything but the suicide spirit I had acquired from Big Daddy. I'm wondering why I never questioned how he died and why didn't I think it odd how none of my aunts or uncles has ever mentioned how he died.

As I lay my Bible down next to me in my bed, I realized every time love went sour in my life; I thought my only solution was to simply put an end to me. The second young man in my life was Derek Towns, 'the teacher.' I met Derek the second day I attended Memphis National College of Business. I had pulled up into the parking lot to park my Ford Escort. I was creeping, trying to find a space close to the building my class was being held in, when I noticed a space to my right in the next row over; I sped up to get it. Flying out of a parking space in front of me at about 40 miles an hour was this black Mustang with a wide, white stripe down the middle resembling a fast loud skunk and I almost hit it. I slammed on my brakes and laid on my horn to get the drivers attention. He looked my way, raised his index finger as if to indicate for me to give him a minute. Then he put his car in drive and drove back into the space and I thought 'Oh good he's coming out I'll just take this spot.' So I backed up to wait for the space. Why did this idiot back all the way out, completely straighten the car and pull right back into the space I'm sitting here waiting for! Geez!

I sat there while he gets out of his car and walks toward the building, totally oblivious to me sitting here. I slowly follow him just to see how long his head was in the cloud. He finally turned around and noticed there was a car behind him. I'm thinking 'STUPID!' Oh now he jumps as if he might get hit. I turn down the next row of parked cars and find a spot directly in front of his and I pull in.

When I was going to my last class I spotted him in the hall; talking on his cell phone. He was real cute, clean cut, preppy looking with glasses and all. When my last class was over, I walked to my car and he was standing at his car door with his keys in his hand, unlocking it. His cell phone rang and he stood there and answered it. I got into my car and it didn't want to start. I kept turning the key and giving it gas. He banged on the hood of my car and waved his hand at me. I rolled down my window and as he walked over to me, he told whoever he was speaking to; "I gotta go I'll talk to you later;" as he closes his phone he says, "Hey lady you're messing up your starter." I say to him, "So you know about the starter in a car but you don't know how to park one." He smiles and says, "Oh you're the two seconds to late driver." I'm looking at him as he's slightly bent over having his head partially in my car window while holding onto his cell phone with his left hand; he rests his elbow on the top of my car, now he lifts his right arm and rests it on my window.

He has the upper body of a football player and he is brown skin with real light brown eyes and a thin mustache. His hair is cut close and he has these long precisely thin trimmed side burns that go down the side of his face and connects to his mustache that is also precisely trimmed and connects to his close cut beard. Umm and he smells so good!

He looks inside my car towards the starter then back into my eyes and asks if I mind letting him try to start the car as he opens the door for me to get out. I don't reply I just get out and stand in the door holding it while he slides in. He bends over with his head in front of the starter and looks at my keys and says, "Ah, here's our problem, too many keys on your ring. Girl how many houses do you have all these house keys." I say sternly, "That's it! Get out of my car." He looks up at me and smiles. The words "No problem" slips out of his mouth with no sincerity whatsoever as he lifts both hands up as if I'm the police.

I roll my eyes at him as he gets out of the car. He stands there watching me get back behind the wheel and as I slam the door and look at him he says, "If you need to call someone you can use my phone." I try to start the car but it's not budging, not a click, clack, not a sound. Now I look back at him and soften my tone and say, "I would appreciate it. I need to call my uncle to come get me." While speaking to him I'm thinking 'Uncle Henry works for the City of Memphis as a mechanic and I know he is not home this early.' I guess the sigh and my speech combined with the look of dismay probably written on my face, was indication to him how I felt because he says to me, "Look, I'm not a serial killer or anything, if you need a ride someplace I'll drop you off." I tell him; "I would appreciate just being able to use your phone, thanks for the offer." He extends his hand out to me with the phone in it and asks if I know how to use it. Without attempting to take it from him, I ask if he would dial the number for me, he did and as soon as it rings he handed it to me.

My cousin A'letha, Aunt Shirley and Uncle Henry's baby girl, answered the phone and informed me no one was home, she was just dropping some papers off and was on her way back to her house. I told her my car wouldn't start and asked if she would call Dora and tell her that I'll be in the parking lot waiting for her or someone to pick me up. I gave him back his cell phone and sighed while thinking about the hours I would have to sit here. He offered again to take me where I needed to go. I declined his offer. He turned around and started to walk away. I watched him walk around my car to the passenger's side and he tapped on the window. I opened my car door and stood up looking over the top of my car at him and asked, "What in the world are you doing." He said he would wait with me because he couldn't leave me alone with no phone or anything and stranded. I unlocked the door. As he sat down he says, "Derek Towns." I said, "Angela Bowen." I was so disgusted with my car. He asked me what was I taking here at school and told me he was taking mechanics courses, he was 3rd generation mechanic. His dad had a shop and he was getting certified so he could help. By the time Uncle Henry arrived I knew Derek had a brother and two step sisters. And I knew everything about them except the numbers on their driver's license. Geez he can talk!

Uncle Henry came to pick me up in the City's tow truck and took me home. The next morning I drove Mother's truck to school; she was dating Mr. Maynard Ziegler at the time and he said he would be happy to take her to and from work for a few weeks. Knowing him, he was going to get breakfast and dinner out of Mother. He was not the kind of man to do anything without it benefiting him.

As I walked up to the corridor to my class, I noticed Derek standing in front of the doorway that leads into the classrooms. He was talking on his cell and looking around as if he were looking for someone. I walked past him and heard him say, "Ok, I gotta go bye, Hey Angela Bowen." I turned around and said, "Hello." He walks with me and asks, "What time do you take lunch?" I tell him 11:30 to 12:15 then he tells me to meet him here at 11:30. I kept walking thinking 'hope he's payin.' 11:30 I went to the corridor and he was there waiting for me. He tells me he wants to check this place out he's heard so much about but he doesn't like to eat alone and he would drive to save time. We go to this nice café a few blocks from the campus and after we finish eating, he looks at his watch and slides next to me and says, "Lunch is on me." And quickly leans in and kisses me, I am caught totally off guard and my eyes are open as I watch him close his eyes and he grunts. I push him away and tell him I'm taking a taxi back to school and I slide out of the booth grab my purse and walk out the front door. A few minutes later he comes running out behind me and tells me he's sorry and he'll take me back to school. I'm looking inside my purse for my wallet; I'm so nervous and mad at the same time. I'm mad because I really liked the kiss. He grabs me and kisses me again and this time I don't fight him, I close my eyes. We are both grunting now and when the kiss ends he grabs my hand and off we go to his car and he goes a block away to a motel.

It was 1:30 when I returned to my class. Derek had taught me a few things as he put it "about art." And on the way back to the campus he kept telling me I was an excellent student. I couldn't believe I had done something like that. I was feeling a rush and ashamed at the same time. When my classes were over I went to my car and noticed he was pulling away, and when he saw me, he honked. For the next 2 months we would meet at the corridor, go get something to eat and go to the motel.

Thanksgiving was approaching and that Monday before the break, while we were getting dressed to get back to school, he asked me what my plans were for the holiday. I was shocked because he never asks me any personal questions so I thought maybe he wanted me to spend Thanksgiving with him. I told him my family has a big dinner at my Uncle's home. That was the end of anymore conversation.

Thanksgiving morning I thought it would be nice to hear from Derek and it dawned on me I didn't have a phone number for him and he didn't have mine. That sparked uneasiness in my stomach. The idea of getting a phone number had never entered my mind. Through the week I'm doing homework in the evenings and on Saturdays I work with Mother at her events so the thought of getting his phone number never came up; anyways we saw each other Monday through Friday.

Thanksgiving afternoon, when the family was all gathered at Uncle Lester's; while we were holding hands awaiting the blessing to be pronounced, Dora asked me what was going on with me, why was I so jittery? I told her nothing was wrong she was imagining things. After we ate, Dora and I were the last two left washing dishes and she says to me, "It's that guy isn't it?" I had told Dora about him, not everything just about our meeting and seeing him at school and that we had a few lunches together. She says, "Why don't you just call him." I look away from her and she says, "Angie; don't tell me you don't have his number." I tell her; "No I don't." "Well maybe he'll call you." I look away again. Now she puts the towel down on the counter and turns me around to face her and asks, "Is he married Angie?" No! I shouted as I slap my towel down on the counter and walk back to the laundry room and she's right behind me. I close the door and tell her everything. "Angie you need to be filled with the Holy Ghost your flesh is way out of control." "Dora I want to be with him I can't explain it because I don't understand it myself." "Well I hope you have enough sense to protect yourself." "Oh yes Derek wouldn't have it any other way." I felt better telling Dora because I don't like keeping secrets from her but I still felt uneasy about not having a way to contact him, for some reason I was really bothered by that.

Monday, while I drove to campus I was determined to get Derek's cell number as soon as I saw him, yeah that's what I'll do, get his cell number. I drove to our area parking and didn't see his car anywhere. I thought he may be running late. At 11:30 I stood at the corridor and waited until noon then I went and ate. After class I looked for him on my way to the parking lot. 'I guess he didn't come to school today,' I thought as I walked to my car. Tuesday was a repeat of Monday and Wednesday was the same. By Friday I figured he had dropped out of school; I tried to think what could have happened to him but the only conversation we had was when he was giving me "art" instructions or when I asked him an "art" question, so I couldn't figure out why and if he was gone.

Friday evening I was going through Mother's desk to see what cakes she was making so I could make up some free hors d'oeuvres. I saw a card there for an estimate and I briefly looked at it and was replacing it back on the desk when I saw: "Mr. and Mrs. Towns" on the card where the names of the bride and groom to be were listed. I drew the card close again and sat down to read all of the information on the estimate card. Apparently Benita Williams had left a message about getting an estimate on a 3 tier wedding cake for Saturday, December 20th at the Hyatt Hotel and Suites downtown Memphis at 2pm, and Mother was going to phone her to get further details. I looked on the calendar to see if we had any other events; December is a busy month and already full so I dialed the number.

The phone rang 3 times then I heard a woman's voice, "Hello you have reached Benita and Derek; sorry we are not able to take your call at this time. You know what to do after the beep." Beep. I leave a message, "Hello this is Angela Bowen calling in regards to the estimate you requested for a 3 tier wedding cake on Saturday, December 20th. I am sorry to inform you we are booked however we do wish you the best in your new life together. Thank you for considering us, your business is very much appreciated." Click!

Derek was engaged all the time we were together! I was just the fling before the wedding. Now I'm feeling appalled, cheap and filthy. I began asking myself why was I so easy and what is it about me that men know it. I sat there and cried until I heard Mother pull up in the driveway then I went to my room and cried some more.

As I thought about Derek it became clear to me he never told me he loved me and never said anything to me to make me think he was serious about me. I really felt like a gull with all capital letters [GULL; a person who is easily deceived or cheated; hoodwinked]. I had totally submitted myself to him and for what; to demean myself; and to think I looked forward to it! How dense can I be? Geez Dora's right; I need to get my flesh under subjection.

For the next couple weeks I was so weepy I felt so slighted, I was a fool to give myself to a man that was committed all the time we were together; to someone else. I felt so stupid and real cheap as a woman; my life seemed very empty and meaningless I felt so used. Every time I thought about how much I looked forward to being with him; I would flush at the face being full of shame and humiliated. I couldn't concentrate on anything long I just wanted to cry all the time.

By the week before Christmas I was a crying mess. I was avoiding Dora all the time; I wouldn't return her phone calls. Sunday dinners I would eat and tell everyone I had a migraine then I'd go home to cry some more. Friday, December 19th I made my mind up tomorrow, after the booking; I was going home, help Mother with the clean up and take a bottle of pills and go to sleep forever.

Saturday December 20th, I got up and started making the crust for the pigs in the blanket. Mother was working Monday through Fridays then and she would shop early Saturday mornings for fresh buttermilk and eggs. I heard a car pull up in the driveway and looked out of the window to see the hood of Dora's car. My heart started racing; she can read me like her Bible and I was scared she would sense my late night plans. She walks in the door and stands there looking at me; I started crying and wiped the dough off my hands and ran over to her with my arms extended out. She closed the door behind her and extended her arms out to me. She grabbed me so tight, I began sobbing and she began praying in the spirit and rocking me.

The more she prayed the more I cried. I was picturing myself with Derek, as he was giving me instructions and I felt deep regret for putting myself in that position. I began to cry out loud, "Lord I'm so sorry, please forgive me." I kept repeating those words over and over. The more I said them, the more remorseful I felt and the more remorse I felt, the louder I became. I don't know if Dora had to get loud to hear herself pray in the spirit over me or if I had to get louder to repent over her. But we were both loud and in tears when Mother walked in the door and moved us out of her way. She put her bag down on the kitchen counter and joined in praying with understanding and in the spirit. After a while we all began leaping and praising God. We were all drenched with perspiration when we simmered down. I had repented of my sin and was forgiven; truly there is no greater love than a man who would lay down his life for a friend. That day was included among the days I will never forget! Thank You Jesus!

It's 2:20am and I am wide awake. I reset my alarm clock for 8am instead of 7 because I know I'll be up for a while longer. I realize I have secrets of my own, I love me some men and try to keep myself busy so I won't think about being with one. The last time I thought of suicide I decided to get filled with the Holy Ghost so I could have help like Dora tells me. She says when you get filled; you have an inner strength to rely on, sort of like having turbo inside of you. So I've been praying to be filled, some days more than others. As I lay here I realize Aunt Flora isn't the only one with a secret, and I thank God the suicide spirit is cast off and out of the family line; and not just me, in the name of Jesus!   Now I'm reminded of the last partner I had that left me wanting to end my life; Wiley Hawkins; 'MY student'.

Somehow even though I had repented; I never was healed.... I had become angry at myself; not for being an easy woman; no, I believed I was forgiven for that, but I was angry I had been "used.".…. However I didn't know I was angry; not until Wiley came into my path.

I had turned 19 a month earlier when one hot Sunday morning we had the Hawkins family of 4 join United Faith East; the "Bowen family church." Ester Hawkins joined and gave her testimony how she and her 17 year old son, 11 year old son and 8 year old daughter had just moved to Memphis from Arkansas. She had recently divorced and had family in Memphis but they were not church goers so she being a church going woman walked to the nearest church which happened to be United Faith East. Even though today was her first time visiting, she was certain she had found her church home. Her testimony was so moving; I really didn't pay much attention to her children the day they joined. It was when I went over Aunt Brenda's to take my cousin; her daughter, Kozette home from the DMV; that's when I noticed Wiley.

Aunt Brenda was still working at the Shelby County Clinic as an RN and I had bought my Chevy Silverado truck a few months earlier, so Kozette wanted to learn to drive using my truck. She had an appointment to take her drivers test that day and as soon as school was out I took her.   After her appointment I pulled up in front of her house where my cousins Kenneth, Karl, Ernest and SeBone were all in Aunt Brenda's long driveway playing basketball. There was this tall muscled, milk chocolate dribbler maneuvering the ball. I intended to drop Kozette off in front of the house, but after a glimpse of milk chocolate, I pulled up and turned off the ignition and as we walked up the driveway I was checking out this new guy. When Kozette and I reached the back door, we all said, "hey" and I followed her into the house. I stopped in the kitchen so I could watch the muscles in motion out of the window. As soon as I stepped up to the window to check out the new guy, here they all are coming into the kitchen. I turn around and stand at the counter and watch them all get glasses for some ice water out of the refrigerator. I ask muscles what his name was and he says Wiley. Kenneth and Karl go into another room in the house and Ernest and Se Bone' says they will check everybody later.

I stand there with my back slightly leaning on the counter and I began to grip onto the sink as my eyes become glued to the perspiration slowly running down Wiley's arms. Suddenly I realize we are alone, so I ask him, "How old are you." He tells me he's 17 and I immediately inform him, "I just turned 19." In my head I'm thinking he's not that much younger than I am. So I ask him if he has a girl friend. He says to me, "Ma'am?" I say, "Ma'am? I just made 2 years older than you, don't be ma'am'n me! Do you have a girl friend?" "No I don't." "Well, have you ever had one?" He starts grinning and looks around the room and almost whispering says to me, "no." I look at those arms again and notice how that wife beater he has on is clinging to him, and the urge to be held in his arms consumes me. I tell him that I will give him a ride home and ask if he's ready. He says yeah, then downs the remainder of the water in his glass, walks over to the sink and gently puts it down and he follows me out the back door. I yell, "Bye, I'm out."

I drove him straight to my house and he followed me into my room. This time I was the teacher and had a student. After an hour or so, I took him home and told him what time I would pick him up tomorrow. This went on for almost a month, then his mother found herself a job and he had to watch his brother and sister. The first day she worked I went over to his house; they lived with his mother's sister and family a few blocks from Aunt Brenda. I went into the house and introduced myself to his brother and sister and told him to show me his room. We went to his room and it had a twin bed and two sleeping bags on the floor so I asked where the bath room was and we went into the bathroom. His little sister started knocking on the door telling us she had to use the bathroom. Later, he walked me outside and I told him, "Tomorrow I'll pick you all up and take you to my house."

That Sunday right after service, I headed to my truck and had just stepped outside when his mother walked up to me and asked, "Are you Angela?" I said, "Yes ma'am." She steps up close to me and says, "You are not the type of girl I want influencing my Wiley. I want a girl like Dora to be with my boy." My neck jerked back, my forehead wrinkled as my left eyebrow went up and I opened my mouth to tell her Wiley was old enough to make that decision; but as soon as I opened my mouth, her hand flew up towards my face and she says to me, "keep it! I haven't been in Memphis that long, but I do know people go to jail for rape; you gittin me."

I felt like she socked me in the stomach, the wind left me as my jaw almost hit the concrete. She turned around and walked away. Just then I heard a car horn blow and when I looked toward the sound; there Dora was. In her car, at the corner street light and when our eyes met she rolled her window down and hollered, "Aunt Brenda made monkey bread, and you'd better hurry up." She drove off and I thought; 'rape? Am I a rapist? What have I done?' I drove to Aunt Shirley's but as Uncle Howard says, "I was as nervous as a cat in a room full of rocking chairs." I kept thinking there has got to be something wrong with me. What is wrong with me! I really like being intimate with men and now I'm choosing young boys, what is wrong, why am I like this? When I sit down at the table, of course Dora asks me, "what's wrong, why are you so fidgety?" I can't believe I'm so horrible and I don't even have a conscious, me a rapist! I can't eat so I tell everyone I'm not feeling well and excuse myself. Before I get to the front door Mother walks up behind me and puts her hand on my shoulder, when I turn around to face her, she asks me what's wrong. I feel as though tears are going to burst out of me and splatter every wall so all I say is; "My stomach." And I dash out of the door. I cried on my way home and when I entered the house. I slammed the back door and ran straight to my room and lay across my bed.

I was thinking; for as long as I can remember I have always been inquisitive about sex and once becoming sexually active, most of the time that's all I think about. I must be perverted and now I've become a rapist. I didn't deserve to live. I thought about why I chose Wiley and realized it was because I wanted to control him like I had been controlled. I wanted to be the one to decide when and if it's over. I was so intent on getting even; I never considered the idea of me hurting Wiley like I had been hurt. Not once did I consider his feelings. I wasn't fit to live because if I did, the older I would get, the more perverted I would become. What if I get desperate and start picking guys younger and younger! Geez, there is no way I should live and get more and more perverted, nah, Angela, you need to put an end to this; and right now! So I decided to get some of Mother's pills and end my life today!

I began crying as I got up and walked to the bathroom. As I opened the medicine cabinet thoughts of me picking up another young boy entered my mind. I know I'm crying loud, but I don't care because today is the last day I'll breathe, a pervert like me should... hey, wait a minute, there are no pills in here of Mother's just a few aspirin in a bottle and some liquid cold medicine. As I stood there in shock, I asked myself, 'Where in the world are her pills? Is Mother healed and no longer has to take medication? Why hasn't she said something? I'll go look in her room.' Oh what kind of mess is this; she gets healed and I turn into a pervert!' Now I'm sobbing so much, I can barely see. Why is her door closed she never closes her door. I turn the knob and open the door; my eyes are full of tears so I stand there in the doorway and wipe the tears away with the backs of my hands so I can focus, and when I do; I stop crying and gasp.

Mother has pills all over her room. There are pills on every wooded surface; both night stands and her dresser are covered with prescription bottles. I walk to the night stand closest to me and pick up a bottle and read the name. It's Mothers; I pick another bottle to read and its Mothers. I go through each bottle in that room and each bottle has her name on it and none of them have expired. I flop down on her bed and start thinking; 'she's been on dialyses now for what; 12 years. She couldn't possibly be taking this much medication. Let me get a writing tablet and pen and write down the dates on these bottles and see how many different medications she's actually taking.' I go get a tablet and pen from the kitchen and return to her bedroom and begin writing down the dates she filled the medications. After I had gone through both night stands the phone rings. It's Mother; she asks me how I feel and I say to her, "Mother, it's not about how I feel; it's about how you feel." There was silence on the phone. I tell her to come home so we can talk and she says; "Ok" And hangs up.

I continued writing all of her prescriptions down with each date of issue next to it and notice the dates are much older on the bottles on top of her dresser. I hear the back door close and turn around to watch as Mother enters the doorway. When she walked into her room she sat on the bed and silently began shedding tears. I turn to place the tablet and pen on top of the bottles and watch her in the mirror. She is sobbing, I turn around to face her and say tenderly, "Mother, why didn't you tell me you were this sick?" She just sat there with her head down, staring at her hands, as her upper body moves up and down, she's crying so hard she's unable to answer.

I walked over to the tissue box and pulled out some tissue, and then I headed towards the bed and sat real close to her. She kept her head down refusing to look at me and took the tissue from my hand, so I bent over real close to her face and nudged her to get her to look up at me, she grabbed me and hugged me so tight, I could barely breathe. She continued sobbing and I joined her. Her grip loosened then I hugged her tight as I thought; 'this is what I take for granted; LIFE! '

When we both collected ourselves, she told me she takes certain medications on certain days. Having the medications visible helps her keep focused on what really is important. She thanks God every morning and every evening that she no longer has to take the medications on the dresser. Mother kissed me on my cheek and told me she loved me so much and how proud of me she was. Then she asked me, when was I going to meet a nice young man and get married and give her some grand babies to spoil. We laughed and started talking and reminiscing about when I was younger and the times we spent together. She said she and Flora were the only siblings without grandkids, and she wanted to hold one of her grand babies before she left this earth. That night when I went to bed I thanked the Lord for allowing me to see what was really important; living! Then I repented of my control issue and I thought about how sick she is; and I made my mind up to dedicate the time she had left on this earth to making lasting memories with her; memories that would last me my lifetime; happy memories of Mother and me. I swore off men altogether, I'll keep my mind on other things like being happy with Mother. My devotion that night was from Psalm 26:7 **"That I may proclaim with the voice of thanksgiving, And tell of all Your wondrous works."** I memorized that scripture and every time something good happens to me or anyone I know; I pull it up from my memory file and bless the Lord, saying it while I lift my eyes towards heaven. I fell asleep that night thanking and praising the Lord because I wanted to wake up in the morning!

Right now, as I lay in my bed sobbing, I realize Aunt Flora has no clue her telling me about Big Daddy has given me understanding. I can cast that spirit of suicide back into the pit where it originated. Neither me, nor any other member of our family will be influenced by that spirit ever again, in the Name of Jesus! Thank You Lord for revealing the root of that spirit that used to taunt me! Hallelujah, glory! .... I got out of bed and danced my happy self tired! Thank You Jesus for deliverance!!!

Once I calmed myself, I thought about how I had sworn off men that night; the truth hit me square in the face! I became aware of my weakness for sex, and decided to apply some good ole common sense. That was to keep my, "Love me some good smelling, football looking men self, real busy!" I'm embarrassed now, thinking of how I used to be; actually how I would be now if I didn't keep myself busy, busy, busy!

Being in the catering business, I come in contact with a lot of people and some I know I won't see again because of the different circles we travel in everyday. After Wiley, I went almost a year without a man and one night at a wedding reception; I was serving a platter of champagne and came eye to eye with this football player looking, dark chocolate, 6 foot 2, bald, earring wearing man. The way he looked at me, I felt sparks and when I smiled my suggestive smile back at him, he asked if I could take a break. I said to him, "Sure, anything for you big man, lead the way!" He nodded for me to follow him, so I did, right out of the reception hall, to the patio area; where I rested my tray on an empty table; and switched my behind right behind him into the parking lot. I followed him right to the back of his long bed, tinted windows, truck. We were there for what seemed like over an hour.

I could hear the people as they were starting to leave and I knew I had to get back to work before I was missed. While walking back into the hall he asked me for my number and I told him I didn't give my number to strangers. He laughed so loud and said, "You got it twisted don't you?" I quickly turned to face him and the moment I looked at him; I realized he was right; I am twisted to do what I just did! Here I go again, feeling ashamed and cheap, lord I need to get this flesh under something besides a man!

I told Dora what I had done and she prayed for me, put oil on me and prayed in the spirit over me for at least 30 minutes. She told me very sternly, that I needed to be baptized with the Holy Ghost to get my flesh under subjection. She said for me to pray daily as she would for me and if need be; she would fast with me so I could get my baptism. That's when I included asking to become filled in all of my devotions.

The last time I went with a stranger was only 9 months ago and I remember that clearly! We were working a 50th birthday party for a Veteran at the West Memphis Country Club and man can those guys drink! I was manning the buffet table when suddenly this guy grabs me from behind and twirls me around and by me having a serving platter full of shrimp salad in my hand; the shrimp salad went everywhere. Here we go again with this tall light brown football playing looking man; apologizing very sincerely for the mess he's caused. I tell him not to worry and while I'm getting the food up, Mattie and Vicki comes and help me. After we get the food area clean, I go into the rest room and clean myself up as best I could. When I walk out of the restroom there he is waiting for me and he asks me to, "sincerely accept his apology." I thought he was drunk so I didn't want to upset him; some drinkers get violent and I didn't want Bobby Ray and Maynard to have to pull out their guns. So I smiled at him and said, "It's not a problem, mistakes happen." And kept walking away from him, he stepped in front of me, grabbed me by my waist and pulled me to himself and kissed me with the most passionate kiss and I heard myself moaning!

He leads me away as though we're dancing and we end up in the men's room. He locks the door and we were locked in there for a long, long time. When he unlocked the door he says "I hope my wife hasn't been looking for me." I stood there froze; 'did he say wife! Oh my, my, what have I done now?' I let him leave out first just in case she was watching him, then I slowly exited. My eyes were scanning the room to see who was watching. I saw Jamal and Willie glance my way and I felt my face turning fire engine red from embarrassment. Geez Angela! I hid back in the kitchen the rest of the night; talk about scared and embarrassed! Every time Jamal or Willie came into the kitchen I couldn't look them in the face and I was so scared the man's wife was going to come in the kitchen looking for me. Geez!

While cleaning and packing up to leave, I kept thinking what Dora is always telling me about needing to be filled to the brim with the "Holy Ghost Power" in order to overcome evil and temptation; and I almost started crying. Not because of what I had just done with a married man, but because I enjoyed so much what I had just done with a married man! His phone number would have definitely ended up on my speed dial if I hadn't found out he was married! These Memphis women carry knives to use on women just like me to protect their grits & biscuits! Dora didn't hear about that episode, I decided to keep myself real busy and not think about any more men period! Starting that Sunday and every Sunday service since, I have been going to the alter asking for prayer to become filled with the Holy Ghost; that last episode of sleeping with a married man was too scary.

Laying here thinking about this, I realize how I have always, for as long as I can remember; been attracted to men with muscles. I believe it's because I want a strong man in my life; the kind of man I can feel safe being in his arms. Wow, I feel the presence of the Lord; I think I understand the reason I yield to the men I have been with is..... Because .....I have never ever.... experienced being held securely in the arms of my biological father....... Wow, I realize now that when my relationships failed, I felt rejection AGAIN, from someone I thought would love and protect me, which summonsed the suicide spirit; ok Angela, just end your life! Wow, what a revelation.

After I meditated on that, I thought about Aunt Flora and how she thought she was freeing herself by telling me the family secret and lie; but, she has triggered my secrets to surface and now I'm examining myself, un be known to her. The Holy Spirit is allowing me to explore my soul and get to the root of the suicide spirit that was attached to me, and, reveal why I fall for the type of men I do. Thank You Holy Spirit; thank you, for revealing understanding; now show me how to become totally healed and please, fill me now as I yield to You. After waiting a few minutes for the Holy Spirit to fill me, I rolled over and slept like a baby.

CHAPTER FOUR

Meeting Nichols For The First Time
Who was that mystery man?

The phone ringing woke me. As soon as I reached for it the alarm went off. I said hello and pushed the alarm off at the same time. It was Dora, "So she didn't tie you up and keep you captive I see. What did she want with you?" Before I could say anything I heard her phone beep. She says, "Girl that's Aunt Flora, wonder what she wants with me. Oh I guess it's my turn to be tied up. I'll let her go to voice mail. Angie what did she want last night?" I tell her; "Dora I'll have to tell you later it was so much." "Angie you sound like it was serious. Is she ok?" "What makes you say that?" "Say what?" "That it sounds serious. What makes you think if Aunt Flora has something serious going on, she would tell me?" "Girl everybody knows you are her favorite niece. Oops, Angie I gotta go; call me later." As I hang up I'm shocked to find out my family has known all the time I was special to Aunt Flora. I wonder why I never caught it. I always thought Aunt Brenda and I are close. She has always been the one to tell me about Mother and my father and about the men in Mother's life, to me, Aunt Brenda is the one I'm closest to and besides she's cool.

After my conversation with Dora I had my morning devotion from Proverbs 17 and verse 27 really ministered to me today. **"He who has knowledge spares his words, And a man of understanding is of a calm spirit.** I meditated on the truth of the Word and how understanding is so powerful and calming. As soon as I read the last verse, the phone starts ringing, first Aunt Shirley. "Hey Angie how you doin; guess what, I got a call from Flora. She wants Sunday dinner over her house and she says it's important that everyone is there including the kids. I heard she had you over last night; what is she up to?" First Dora now Aunt Shirley, Aunt Flora is going to tell the whole family. I would make the same move, she must be my grandmother! "Aunt Shirley she's going to tell you Sunday." "Angie is it something serious? Tell me if my sister's sick. Or has she found a man? Oh Angie tell me something!" The drama was starting to rev up in her; my phone beeps. "I need to take this call Aunt Shirley, love you. Bye."

I click over, it's Aunt Inez, "Good morning Aunt Inez; how you doin today?" "Hey Angie, I'm good. Look I just got a call from Flora requesting we come to her house for Sunday dinner and it was very important we bring the kids. Do you know why she wants us all over?" "I know it's important and she'll tell you on Sunday and that's all I can tell you." "Angie she's not terminally ill or anything like that is she?" "Don't worry Aunt Inez; it's something Aunt Flora wants to share with the whole family. Look I have to go, I love you and I'll see you Sunday ok." "Ok baby, love you too." As soon as I hang up, the phone rings again, I say "Hello." "Hey Angie, it's your Aunt Brenda and you know why I'm calling." "Yeah, Aunt Flora's calling everybody. Well Aunt Brenda all I can say is she's not terminally ill she just has something to say to the family and wants to say it once. I have a busy weekend booked and need to start cooking. Love you and I'll see you Sunday ok." "Ok baby, love you too. Bye"

Ten minutes later Aunt Rose Marie called and while we were talking Bobby Ray beeped me. I told her the same thing I told Aunt Brenda and clicked over to

Bobby Ray, he just called to see if I was ok. I told him it was family stuff and I was going to get through it and I asked him to hold my family up in prayer. He told me he would, and that he and Jimmy Lee would be by later and we hung up. I got up and started preparing for tonight.

I have all of the cold dishes finished. This was one of the best fruit and cheese assortments I have done in a while because the Cantaloupes and the Crenshaw's were perfect. I attend all of my events as a worker so I can hear the comments of the guests and keep the tables full at all times. Presentation is what prepares the eyes opinion and smell confirms the goodness. That's something Mother taught me except not in those exact words.

She was a very loving person and always hugged and held me but Mother had her dark times. Now that Aunt Flora has told me about Big Daddy, some things are beginning to make sense to me about Mother. Even though he was not her father he was her grandfather and she definitely inherited his DNA; and apparently passed it straight to me. Thank God the Holy Spirit can break every fetter, the Anointing breaks every yolk and there is power in deliverance! Hallelujah!

While I'm cooking I'm thinking about how thankful I am for being delivered of a strong attraction to men and I'm remembering Mother and the men in her life. She would sometimes out of the blue give me some words of De Anne's wisdom. Say for instance we would be in the kitchen together, she would out of the blue start talking and stop whatever she was doing at the time and say something like, "Angie; a word of wisdom; now listen up; you have to watch out for certain kinds of men. Especially those 'Performance Men,' this kind wine and dine you and once you perform for them, poof, they're gone." Then she would go back to whatever it was she was doing. Her favorite De Anne word of wisdom was, "Angie, a word of wisdom; listen up now; always remember, men are selfish creatures, their number one priority is them! Yep, baby, always remember that, and you won't pick up the pieces of your heart after it's been stepped on." Sometimes she would be angry when she said; "always remember that!" When she was angry, I had to say, "Yes Ma'am" before she would continue about picking up the heart pieces. I knew she was angry at that time I just didn't understand until I became older; she was angry at the last man in her life. The last time she gave me words of wisdom was after she had been in her room for a few days crying. I could hear her late at night when she thought I was asleep.

This particular day is engraved in my mind because she came home from The Bottoms and I was sitting at the kitchen table doing homework. She was all bubbly and walked up behind me and grabbed me real tight and spoke into my ear and said, "Baby, the Lord is able to do exceedingly and abundantly over and above what you could ever imagine; even healing you from a heart that has been broken by a man." I thought, 'good, maybe tonight she won't be up late crying.' But I said, "Ok Mother, I'll remember." When she was in the hospital dying, she said to me, "Baby I'll be gone but remember the 'wisdom' talks we had; they'll save you a lot of heartache, ok?"

When I was little, I didn't understand why she would tell me the things she did, but as I became older, I figured it out. Every time she would stay home and not go out on a date, she had just "quit" her last gentleman caller. That always brought on a wisdom talk, so when I turned almost 16, I figured it out, and when the chance arrived, I would phone Aunt Brenda and ask her what was going on with Mother. Aunt Brenda always kept me informed about Mothers' men in her life. I have always felt as though I could talk to Aunt Brenda about anything and she'll always be truthful. I remember after we buried Mother, I asked Aunt Brenda about Mother's first love and we sat in her kitchen and over a cup of tea, she told me that Mother met a Mr. Dennis Mays when she was 19; shortly after Big Mama died.

Mother was working as a server at a local diner and they met there. After a few months of dating, they talked about marriage and he had an apartment near downtown so Mother moved in with him and they were saving money towards their wedding. Mother put every penny she earned from tips in a large container they kept in the kitchen. Aunt Brenda said every time she went over there the money was getting closer to the top and there were a lot of five dollar bills in the container. One Friday night after her shift at the diner ended, Mother slipped the key in the apartment door and found it completely empty. Mr. Mays had left her only a note with a smiley face stating, "It was nice knowing you." Mother was devastated and moved back home with Aunt Flora. She looked for another job because everyone at the diner knew she was planning to marry and she was too ashamed to go back and tell anyone what had happened to her. That's when she was hired on at The Bottoms and after several months working as a server there, she filled in a couple days for one of the cooks and the customers raved so much about her cooking she was quickly promoted to a cook. It wasn't until after I was born she became head cook.

The next man in her life was my father, Clarence Nichols who ate there regularly and when he noticed she was no longer serving he inquired of her and after being told she was promoted to cook and would not be back as a server, that same night he waited for her shift to end and introduced himself to Mother. After they talked, he ended up taking her home. He was a Probation Officer, and she was head over heels in love with him. Aunt Brenda said he was a fine specimen of a man, 5'9, had muscles like a body builder, dark brown complexion, wore glasses had a thin mustache and was extremely intelligent. Mother thought my father was the man of her dreams and it wasn't until she told him she was pregnant with me she found out her love was headed down a one way street.

When she told him she was pregnant he flipped all the way out. He did not want any children, he told everybody that would listen, because he worked with juvenile delinquents he was allowed to see first hand what was in store for Afro American youth in Memphis, and he did not want to father a child and watch it end up in the system. He told Mother to take care of the problem and she went crying to Aunt Flora and Aunt Flora called Uncle Lester and the two of them convinced Mother to keep me. Aunt Bernadine, my father's sister found out about Mother being pregnant and told their mother, Grandma Nichols that Clarence did not want the baby; and Grandma Nichols told my mother she would help her if she kept me.

Both Aunt Brenda and Aunt Shirley told me Mother was never the same after her and my father broke up. And how I was in need of no thing; everyone in the family bought whatever Mother thought I needed. With Aunt Rose Marie being pregnant at the same time, it helped Mother not feel so detached and dumped by Nichols. Grandma Nichols sent me gifts for my birthday and at every holiday when I was little but as she grew older and sickly, we stopped hearing from her. When I graduated from high school Aunt Bernadine came to my graduation and took a lot of pictures of me on her digital camera, but that was the last time I saw her. She was so amazed over my gaps, and kept shaking her head saying, 'My goodness you look just like my brother."

As long as I can remember Aunt Brenda has always told me the same thing, "Girl you sho nuff look like Nichols right down to his gaps." I have a gap on the top and the bottom front teeth. Most people with gaps only have them with their top teeth, not me. I remember when I brought home my school pictures; I must have been in the 2nd or 3rd grade, Aunt Rose Marie phoned Aunt Brenda and told her that I looked like Nichols with hair and she laughed so hard. When Mother came to pick me up, all of us kids were standing around almost in a huddle, watching for her reaction with anticipation as she pulled the pictures out of the envelope and stared at them. She took her index finger and gently moved it down the picture, starting at my eyebrows as she slowly sat down staring at the picture. When her tear softly dripped down her cheek, we all realized she was crying, she never made a sound. Aunt Rose Marie saw the teardrop and made all of us kids leave the living room and go into the kitchen to get us a cookie and we were to stay in there until she came to get us.

Being that young, I didn't understand Mother's reaction to my school pictures, back then I thought she loved me so much it warmed her heart to see me in a picture. I have never seen or heard from my father nor have I ever seen pictures of him. The only picture I have of him is mental. I thank God he gave my mother 2 brothers or shall I say uncles; Uncle Lester and Uncle

Howard and 2 sisters or aunts who married good men; Uncle Odell; Aunt Brenda's husband and Uncle Henry; Aunt Shirley's husband; because they all talk to me about life and treat me like I'm one of their daughters especially Uncle Howard because I'm always with Dora, so Mr. Clarence Nichols is never, nor has ever been missed by me, just Mother. Wow, Mother and her men!

Ok Angela, enough of that, tonight is Friday's booking at Memphis City Recreation Hall, where all of the City officials have their functions. The secretary to the City Council for the past 17 years is retiring and they are going all out, lots of food and only the best liquor tonight. There are usually a lot of big wig attendee's at these events and they can be pretty rowdy when the liquor flow gets past 3 hours so I'm praying for no drama tonight. Whew; I'm done cooking, now let me get showered and changed; Bobby Ray and Jimmy Lee will be here before I know it.

While driving my truck following Bobby Ray and Jimmy Lee in the van to the Recreation Hall, for some strange reason I began to think about my biological father, Nichols. I very briefly think of him on Father's Day; otherwise I never think about him at all. Maybe I'm thinking about him because last night I had a revelation; it's possible my weakness for men with muscles is because of him and today I've been thinking about the relationship he and Mother had. That must be it. Well we've made it to the Recreation Hall and it's time to hit it!

Its 8:15pm and everything is running smooth as silk. I'm going to check the table again. Yep, looks ok, the TOM's are low; I'll go into the kitchen to check the container and see how many are left.... Not that many and it's late enough to put the rest of these out. TOM's are one of the freebies I used to give away when I first started working with Mother. They are simple to make and very popular at these type events. I take two slices of fresh smoked seasoned turkey meat, lay it out on the chopping board and spread mayonnaise on top of it and place a fresh green onion on the end and roll it up tight, sprinkle lightly with red pepper; cut it into bite sizes and give each piece a small toothpick. TOM's are Turkey Onion and Mayonnaise. Easy and tasty!

I decided to go back out to the table and bring the dish into the kitchen and arrange the remainder of the TOM's on the dish. Now as I walk to the table to retrieve the dish; I notice this man is standing right in front of the TOM's so I stand behind him, at a distance, waiting for him to move. He turns around and stands there in my way. My focus is on the table so now I move to go around him and he extends his hand toward my arm and says, "Excuse me what is your name?" I look up and who do I see...Mr. Nichols standing here staring at me with his hand extended. I commence to stare at him. He is looking at my hair, eyes, nose and chin and he breaks out with a smile that reveals his gaps. I realize I do look like him with hair, except he's wearing glasses and is slightly gray around his temple. I feel as though I'm looking at my older twin brother; if that can ever be possible! He has my high thick eyebrows and long bountiful eyelashes, his eyes are exactly the same oval shaped, the nose is wide like mine, and even the heart shaped lips and chin is the same, or shall I say I have his! We stand here looking at each other; I'm standing here paralyzed watching his arm drop to his side. Wow, I do look like him with lighter eyes and hair, oh my goodness!

He says; "Well, well Miss Angela Elise Bowen; right?" I'm looking at him thinking: 'Yeah, right! And now I'm mad, the nerve of this man!' He extends his hand out to me again, still smiling, and before I know it; I slap it real hard and run straight to the kitchen. I stand at the sink trying to catch my breath and fight back tears I feel coming. The nerve of that man; if he had his way, I wouldn't be here breathing! He comes right behind me into the kitchen saying, "I only want to properly introduce myself." I turn around to face him; I can't believe he has the nerve to come into the kitchen. When I make eye contact with him; I roll my eyes at him and head for the back door. I shove the door real hard, I'm headed outside and he's right behind me saying, "Hold on Angela, I only want to talk to you." I walk a few steps, turn around and hike myself right up in his face yelling; "NOW you want to talk?" My neck is bobbing and my left hand is on my hip and my right hand is moving all up in his face as I proceed to tell him off, "Now after 26 years! There's nothing to talk about, get out of my face."

I turn around to walk away from him and he walks around me and positions himself a step in front of me and says, "Angela I want to get to know you." I stand there looking at him and I feel this heat and rage consume me and even though he's standing in front of me, I feel as if he's smothering me and I can't breathe. I reach way back and haul off and slap him as hard as I can, and almost lose my balance; I get my bearings so I can slap him again, and out of nowhere, someone behind me grabs both my arms around my shoulders. The way I'm being held makes my arms immobile so now I'm not just mad, I'm frustrated I can't beat the life out of him like I so desperately want to, so I start crying and kicking at him. I'm screaming, "Leave me alone! Leave me alone, I said! Leave me alone! I don't ever want to see your face again as long as I live. I hate you; you coward!" I'm raising my legs and trying to pull my body close enough to kick him real good; but I'm just kicking at the wind. Then I hear this Barry White sounding voice behind me say, "Mister I think you had better leave; I don't know how much longer I can keep her off you. Just leave man, please."

As Nichols stands there staring deeply into my eyes never once blinking; suddenly his eyebrows wrinkle, then quietly he turns to leave; walking towards the parking lot. While I stand there watching him the arms holding me, now releases me. I am so mad, I feel like my face is on fire. I turn around and look towards the back door and see all of my staff standing outside by the door watching me. So I shout, "I'm alright just mad but alright." Then it occurs to me; if all the staff is over there, who in the world was holding me? I turn completely around.

It has gotten dark and the street light is shinning down on this bald head, and I take inventory of this tall 6 foot football player looking, dark chocolate guy with big round dark eyes, wide nose and full perfect shaped lips. He looked like he might be African decent but when he spoke I didn't hear an accent. Now I'm embarrassed because he's a stranger so, as I adjust my shirt I say to him, "I'm sorry you had to see that." He chuckles and says, "See that? I was almost in that Angela; you have a lot of anger towards that man." Now I'm starting to get mad again, and as I place my hands on my hips my head automatically begins bobbing as I say, "Ok how do you know my name and who do you think you are telling me about my anger?" The volume of my voice has risen considerably. With calmness in his; he says, "Ok, let's calm down. I heard him call you Angela and your anger is obvious." Still yelling; I ask him, "What are you doing here anyway. Why are you even out here?" "I saw what happened at the table; I didn't hear what was said, I saw your reaction and I thought he was harassing you so I followed him out here. Are you ok now?"

There's something about him, and his voice; something in his voice makes me feel like he genuinely cares, but I don't know him and he sure doesn't know me; and for some reason a calmness comes over me. Now I straighten my bow tie and take in a deep breath to compose myself and say to him, "Yes I'm fine thanks. I just need a minute." He throws both hands up as a sign of surrendering, walks around me and says, "OK, goodnight." I turn and watch him as he walks past the Recreation Hall and towards the street. Who in the world was that man?

As we clean up no one is saying anything so when we are done, I apologized and told them my behavior was not professional and I would try and never let it happen again, and we all hugged each other bye. Bobby Ray and Jimmy Lee followed me home and unloaded the van. I was putting some things away, and they stood in the doorway to leave. Bobby Ray told me him and Jimmy Lee were concerned about me and asked if I was ok. I told them yes, it was family related drama that will soon pass. They looked at each other, then back at me and they say together, "Ok boss," and they left.

I took a long hot bath and thought about my meeting Nichols was not a coincidence. My meeting with Aunt Flora set off some serious memories. I thought about it being like disturbing a bee hive and provoking the bees to sting. You know, like everything in my past was in the hive handled, put away, done with and here comes Aunt Flora; stirring up the hive with some secret of hers, and now my old secrets are swarming around and some of them sting; I can feel the stingers stuck in my heart. Oh my goodness, don't tell me my thinking of Nichols before I met him for the first time in my entire life, was the Holy Spirits' way of preparing me. Holy Spirit was in this all the time! Now I feel so bad; knowing our meeting was predestined and I don't think I handled it too well. Geez Angela....It took some nerve for that man to just walk up to me, wanting to talk after all these years. "Well, well Miss Angela Elise Bowen," like he knows me and had an APB out on me for 26 years, ugh the nerve of that man! I think it was him calling me by my full name that set me completely off; like he knows me!

Now that I'm thinking the Holy Spirit orchestrated our meeting, I wish I had just paused for one minute to think about how Nichols had been on my mind; first last night, then today, and then I happen to run into him. If only I had thought about it, maybe I would have realized it was not a coincidence meeting him; it was the Holy Spirits gentle way of preparing me to meet him for the first time. Oh, I feel so bad now knowing how horribly I reacted to meeting my father for the first time in my life; I honestly didn't realize I had so much anger towards the man.

Holy Spirit; I am so sorry for reacting the way I did, I need You to fill me so I can walk in Your Wisdom, please, I've been asking to be filled with the Holy Ghost for some time now; with the evidence of speaking in tongues, but it has not happened yet. I want to live my life pleasing to you Father and not keep making situations worse, I need Your Power working inside me, please fill me, please!.... I cried and begged the Lord for another chance until the water in the tub turned cold.

After my bath I seasoned the meats for tomorrow and went to bed. But again I couldn't sleep; seeing Nichols face to face for the first time in my life tonight, made me think about some things. As if my mind were a jute box player, up pops this record of my childhood memories and they began to play.

Like when I was real little Mother would pop some Pop Corn and sometimes rent an animated movie and watch it with me or just the two of us would sit for hours and watch cartoons. But after we would spend a long time together she would sometimes turn what I call "dark" on me, it was as if she would detach herself from me. At that time I thought I had done or said something to her to make her mad at me. The older I became, and the more I listened to my aunts and uncles talk about how they had to learn to deal with Big Daddy suffering from depression, I figured Mother was a lot like her daddy, and suffered from depression also. I learned to just leave her alone and after a couple hours she would always snap out of it. However, tonight I think I know what she was dealing with; I look just like the man.

I'm thinking about Elvin and Derek and about the possibility of me having a baby by either one of them and not being loved by them, having to look at my baby every day and my baby looking exactly like its daddy. Being reminded every day of the rejection and humiliation every single day, every time I hugged or kissed my baby, wow, I wonder how I would react to my baby. Whenever I spent a lot of time with the baby I loved and carried for 9 months, would I turn dark whenever I thought of being told, "I don't want you or the baby, get rid of it." Would I turn dark?

I remember when I was about 17 or 18 and one Saturday morning Aunt Brenda came to the house to pick up a cobbler Mother had baked for her. While they talked I spilled some egg whites on my pants. I took my apron off and left it on the table. I went to my room and changed into some clean jeans. I already had on a big white Tee shirt. Before returning to the kitchen I decided to pin my hair up in a ponytail before putting my cap back on. When I entered the kitchen, Mother stared at me so long; Aunt Brenda stopped talking and looked at me to see what had mesmerized her. I stood there wondering why they stopped their conversation and said, "WHAT!" Aunt Brenda told me to come take the cobbler to her car. While we walked she told me because I looked so much like Nichols it was very difficult for Mother to totally forget him; but I should always remember Mother loved me with all the love a mother can have for her child.

Right now considering Nichols did not want her to keep me; maybe I was a reminder of why she wasn't still with him. Yet I never doubted she loved me, and now that I've met Nichols... I can understand her pain. Having to choose me over him knowing she loved us both really pricks my heart. I began to wonder; what if I had given my baby up to keep the man I loved and afterwards; would I be able to live with myself. Or, would I do as Mother did and give up the man for my baby and be constantly reminded of my choice every day looking at my baby who looks just like my man. Tears began to flow out of me and my heart ached with so much pain. The more I thought about Mother's situation the harder I cried. I wish she didn't have to make a choice; I wish she could have had us both, she might have lived longer.

Why is it that Nichols is still living, and my dear sweet mother is gone? He gets to breathe and make others miserable. I wish I had never met him. I hate the fact that I know what he looks like. I hate him, I hate him!..... Why am I crying over him when I hate him so much....... Every time I say I hate him, I feel a tug at my heart....I really don't hate him.... I want to hate him.....I should hate him because of the way he treated my mother and me. He's got some nerve trying to talk to me after he didn't want anything to do with me for almost 27 years. If it were up to him, I wouldn't even be here living and breathing, the nerve of him; wanting to get to know me!

Now that I've met him why can't I continue to automatically not think about him, why can't I just hate him; he wronged me and Mother? ......Now I'm crying uncontrollably; Lord he's my father and I don't want to love him.... But.... I do. It's just not fair! He deserves my hatred after what he did. I know I have to get this un-forgiveness out of my heart, help me Jesus. Mother was never the same after he broke her heart. How does he get off scot free for what he's done?

As I dry my eyes I hear this tiny still voice ask me, 'Who said he got off scot free? He might be miserable for what he did to you both.' Then I thought, 'yeah, didn't he tell me tonight he wanted to get to know me? He wanted to talk. Maybe if I had listened to what he wanted to say, I would know where his head and heart is. Maybe that's why the Holy Spirit prepared me to meet him, so I could receive what it is he has to say. Maybe he is sorry for what he did'....

Oh Lord I wish I had listened; I was so angry I didn't want to hear anything he had to say, I wanted to hurt him like he hurt me, like he hurt Mother...... Holy Spirit please, please, help me, heal me, please! I need you to comfort me oh Lord, let my cry be heard in your ear, don't hide Your face from me, please answer my cry Lord, heal and comfort me Please! ....this pain... Oh such pain....Lord I surrender all of the hurt, bitterness, hatred, un-forgiveness and any other negative emotion I've been harboring against my father. Take it, remove it and replace the emptiness with love and understanding. Create in me a clean heart and renew a right spirit within me, you have my permission to do so, Holy Spirit; I trust You, I love You, make me clean, and fill me Lord...... Amen.

Hallelujah! Thank You Jesus! When I finally fell asleep I slept good last night. I realized I have been carrying a ton of hurt around like weights. I was hurting for Mother and myself. In a way; I'm glad I ran into my father last night it opened my eyes to see the anger and un–forgiveness I harbored against him. The weight I carried was so heavy and what makes it so strange is; I didn't realize it until I came face to face with the man. Because I never thought of him; I had no idea how much animosity I had for him. I had carried it for so long, I had gotten used to it, now it's lifted and I feel so liberated! I'm going to continue to cry out to the Lord and allow the Holy Spirit to wash that wound that has been opened until it's completely healed. Glory!

My devotion this morning was from Ecclesiastes 7 and verse 7 caught my eye, **"Surely oppression destroys a wise man's reason."** I thought how true it is because last night I totally acted without reason even when I was warned by the Holy Spirit, oppression surely had the best of me. Verse 9 states: **"Do not hasten in your spirit to be angry, for anger rests in the bosom of fools."**

I realized my anger overshadowed all of my reasoning and I acted a total fool! Heavenly Father, I am so sorry for allowing my anger to overtake me. I sincerely want You to create in me a clean heart so I may serve You by walking in the Spirit and doing what is good and acceptable in your sight. I want to decrease that You may increase in me and my actions. I ask to be filled with the Holy Ghost that I may be endowed with power to do the right thing; the upright thing that will bring me wisdom and peace and give glory to You. I am sorry for the way I treated my father and I ask for Your forgiveness and please Lord, allow me another chance to ask him for forgiveness and listen to what it is he has to say to me. In the name of Jesus I pray, Amen.

Lord I worship and adore You. I give you Honor and Glory; You are so worthy of all Praise and Adoration! Hallelujah I worship You Most High! Hallelujah, Hallelujah! .... After I worshipped I renewed my mind with more Word. I studied for over an hour and lay in the presence of the Lord for a good long while.

CHAPTER FIVE

The Mystery Man Revealed
Family secret; bared to the family

I was so renewed; I went to the store and kept thinking about how badly I want to be filled with the Spirit. I came home and cooked up everything for tonight's booking; a friend of Colonel Melvin Whitmore.

I met his wife, Abby at a booking we did over 3 years ago at the Mound City Dodge Dealership. She took one of my business cards and later that week phoned and had me cater Colonel's 50th birthday party a few months later and believe me when I say I've gotten a lot of business from her and her friends; let me just say that's putting it mild! Abby loves to entertain and most times she and Colonel have parties at their home for their friends, like tonight. Colonel has a friend who has just transferred to Memphis Marine Base and is turning 30 years old, so they are throwing a party for him at their home.

I called Bobby Ray and him and Jimmy Lee will be here soon to pick up the foods. As I lock up the garage and walk into the house, I realize I'm a little edgy about the party tonight. After Nichols appeared like that out of the blue; I'm wondering if he could show up at any other events now. I really want to handle it right the next time I see him. All these years and last night I run into him, wow.

Colonel and Abby have a beautiful home, perfect for entertaining. We set up in the same spot all the time. Abby knows exactly what we need and she's told me more than once that we clean up better than we find it. Because they entertain so much they have adequate equipment and furnishings so I never have to charge for any chairs or tables and that allows me to give them a nice discount. Tonight we should be able to clean up by 9 and hopefully we'll be walking out by 9:30. I hope Aunt Flora's dinner meeting goes well tomorrow I'm starting to get nervous when I think about it. Maybe that's why I'm so edgy; I want to get tonight over with.

We have everything set up and the guests are expected in 20 minutes. I don't know why I'm so nervous! When we work the Colonel buffet events we have our routine. Wila keeps hot dishwater going and washes the dishes as needed while helping me with the tables. She really hides in the kitchen because sometimes someone will ask her about an ingredient in some of the foods and she gets nervous answering. I am really very comfortable with the questions people asks, it's flattering to me in a way; when someone wants to know what's in a dish. I take it as a complement!

Bobby Ray and Jimmy Lee keep the floors clean and the trash emptied. Maynard and Gregory tend the bar while Lula Mae, Vicki and Mattie keeps the empty drink glasses cleared and the ash trays and rest rooms cleaned.

One hour later:

Jimmy Lee is gathering the trash to take outside and we can hear the noise getting louder which is an indication of a lot of guest; so I go out to check the table. I start at the end closest to me which happens to be at my left tonight. I'm scanning the table and get to the end and out of the corner of my eye, I see something in the corner, the whole time I'm glancing over the table whatever it is, hasn't moved. I know it's not a plant or statue because I know Abby's furniture placements so I glance over to see what it is. It's that man who held me down last night. He's standing there chewing and his head is slightly down as his eyes are glued to mine. It's as if he's been standing there waiting for me to make eye contact with him.

I walk over to him and ask sternly, "What are you doing here?" All of a sudden I hear this loud, slurred, "Hey Chapman, happy birthday man." I turned slightly to my right and see this staggering, obviously inebriated man put his hand out toward the man standing in the corner. The man who kept me from beating up my father last night; his name is Chapman and this party is for him! Now my mouth has fallen open and I feel so embarrassed asking him why was he at his own party!

He turns and responds, "Thanks man." As they shake hands the loud man turns his attention towards me and says, "Hey, hey baby!" He drops his hand shake and reaches both arms out towards me and takes a step my way like he's going to hug me and before I can blink, Chapman steps in front of me and says, "Look man you just got here and don't know this is my lady. You need to back off." "Ah man I didn't know. You know Donna left me right?" I turned quickly and went back to the kitchen, straight to the sink and stood over it thinking, 'what just happened, what's going on.'

'I saw him last night at the Recreation Hall and now he's here; this is his party! What was he doing at the retirement party last night, I am so confused.' I shake my head as if to clear my mind as I think, 'Ok Angela; you have entirely too much going on right now to be worried about this. Get yourself together.' My heart is beating so fast, I turn and look at Wila and ask her to watch the table for me I'll be outside getting some air. I go out the side door where the trash cans are so I can be alone. I start praying: "Heavenly Father I ask for your understanding and peace right now. You are not the author of confusion; I command understanding to come now and for the peace that passes all understanding to flow through me right now, in the name of Jesus." ....

I walk to the fence and try to think on some scriptures about peace. The Holy Spirit begins to minister to me, **about** me and I break like melted ice. 'Why do I even care about that Chapman guy being at the Recreation Hall last night? He's big and strong like the men I always fall so hard for and why in the world has our paths crossed again tonight? ...... After a few minutes I realize I don't have issues with Mr. Chapman, I have issues with men period. I don't trust any of them and I am afraid to be around this Chapman fellow because he matches the description of Angela Bowen's kryptonite. I have kept myself from being around men altogether ever since the "married man." I've been keeping myself busy so I don't have to deal with the core of this issue. I really do need to be filled with the Holy Ghost, I can't keep alienating myself from men and I need to get the victory over my flesh; bottom line! There, I've admitted it, and I feel so much better too. Lord please, please help me!'

I feel relaxed and at peace with myself; hey, the truth really does free ones self! As I think about me having a weakness for big strong men, I find myself crying and realizing Aunt Flora told me the truth about her being my grandmother and my father just pops up in my life last night, now, tonight this Chapman guy has me out here trying to make sense out of why I care so much about him. I don't want to end up in his bed only to be dumped. I'm old enough to have a handle on this;

is that why he's appeared in my little space? Is it time for me to grow up? Not just in this area, but become who the Lord made me to become and stop running and start living single and holy? Lord please help me get an understanding about what's going on in my life right now, it seems the truth is hitting me in the face everywhere I turn. Lord, help me please! .... Umm, I realize I want help; I don't want to yield to temptation! My heart is crying out for deliverance, thank you Jesus! Finally I'm able to mature, especially in the area of lust; I **want** to mature in this area.

After walking around singing worship songs in my heart, I'm able to return to the kitchen and I start drying dishes and I keep myself busy in the kitchen cleaning up. I'm keeping my mind on the Lord and He is keeping me in perfect peace, man the Word works!

Before I realize it, everyone is bringing empty trays into the kitchen and it's time to clear the buffet table. Abby comes in the kitchen and hands me a check. I ask if everything went well and tell her I appreciate the business. She asks me if I met the man of the hour. I tell her yes. She says, "Colonel found out you had a party yesterday and gave Chapman the address and directions. It was so cute; he told Chapman to go sample the best food he'll ever eat in Memphis, for free and the best part is the same caterer was catering tonight. Today Chapman phoned and thanked Colonel and told him he was right; the food was excellent. Angela I think you have another client!" She was so animated thinking the Colonel had done me some business. She continues, "Alright now, I have to get back to my guest. Thanks again." Off she goes. So that's why he was there last night, getting a sneak preview, ah ha and a freebie at that, he must be cheap.

We get everything packed up and I head to my truck when I hear a loud deep, base sounding, "Angela." I recognize the voice from last night, it's Chapman, and I stop and turn around. He's walking towards me and starts; "Are you ok?" "Yes thanks." I turn to leave and he continues, "Sorry about that little scene in there, his wife just left him and he had way too much to drink." Quickly turning to face him, I cut him off, I raise my hand and say sternly, "Thank you good bye." Again I turn around to leave and he says, "Angela" I stop, he walks up to me and stands in front of me so now I raise my voice, "LOOK" I put my hand on his chest and give him a push but he doesn't budge and I say in a controlled loud tone, "You don't know me. I don't care about you or him I'm tired." Just then Bobby Ray pulled up and rolled down the van window. "Boss you ok?" Before I could answer him; he put the van in park and opens the door to get out. He is looking, no staring Chapman down, so I say, "Yeah, hey Bobby Ray wait for me, I'll follow you." I walk towards my truck and glance back at Chapman and roll my eyes at him.

As I drive home I began to cry; why am I so mad at this Chapman guy? And I go over what happened with that loud guy in my head. I remember Chapman moving so fast and then I thought about how fast he subdued me last night. To be such a big man he sure does move fast. Then I thought about my father and how big and strong he looked and that thought took me to Mother and how she died too young.

She was diagnosed with diabetes while she was pregnant with me. She was only 20 years old; almost the age I was when we found out she had been on dialysis too long; her kidneys had began to slowly shut down. She kept working and never told anyone how sick she was. One Thursday morning Aunt Flora received a phone call from Mother's boss that the ambulance had just taken her to Regional Medical Center; she had fainted in the kitchen. By the time I had arrived at the hospital, she was in intensive care; hooked up to all kinds of machines.

She was comatose for three days and when she came out of it she was spaced out. I was the only person she remembered and she only referred to me as, "my baby," then a few hours later she gradually began to call everyone by name. My aunts and I took turns staying with her at the hospital after the doctors told us her body was gradually shutting down and she only had days to live. The night I stayed with her she kept telling me that she loved me and I brought her so much happiness while I was growing up. Some times she would wake from being heavily medicated and she would talk to me as if I were Nichols. She told me/him that she forgave him for not being able to love her and Angie. My heart ached because I couldn't hug her; there were too many tubes coming out of her. So I just kissed her on the forehead and cheek and I held and rubbed her free hand.

We buried my mother the weekend before Memorial Day; less than 2 weeks before I turned 20. She was only 40 years old and was she a gorgeous woman, strikingly beautiful. Five feet, six, real dark with thick shiny beautiful hair; her eyes were pale brown, almost grey and she kept her eyebrows arched in a shape that made her eyes look as though they were always on display and when she colored her hair auburn, her eyes would be the second thing noticed when she walked into a room. She was hippy like all of us Bowen women, but she had a brick house shape and wore clothes to show it off.

She loved her some sweets and I was always telling her not to eat what she baked and that she should eat the sugar free pastries but she would always say, "And who's the mama you or me?" And don't let one of her siblings tell her to watch her sweets intake, she would tell them, "I might be the baby but I'm not a baby, back off me now!"

Now that I'm thinking about this, she didn't look anything like the rest of them. She was built like Aunt Brenda and Aunt Flora; small waist and busty but that was the end of the family resemblance. All of my aunts are five feet three, and my uncles are all 5'6 or 5' 7. Mother's coloring and eyes were totally different than the rest of them and, no one else in the family is that dark or has light eyes nor does anyone else in the family have diabetes. I wonder if I'm the only one that's just figured this out. Dora told me I was Aunt Flora's favorite niece and it was news to me. The meeting tomorrow is going to be real interesting. Yeah I do believe it will be!

I get home and while Bobby Ray and Jimmy Lee unload the van, I wash the bowls and pans. After I lock up I walk in the back door and the business phone is ringing. I glance at the clock on the kitchen wall, 10:34 pm, who in the world is calling about a booking this late? I answer, "Taste and See Catering, Angela speaking." "Hello Angela; Malik Chapman here. I was calling to make sure you were alright." Geez; let me set this man straight right now! "Mr. Chapman, this is my business phone and I only conduct business on this line. I don't have time to play are you alright games with you. And how did you get this number anyway?" "Colonel gave me your card and I don't play games. Last night a man hurt you and today a man tried to disrespect you. I'm concerned about you Angela."

I stand straight up like at attention and ask, "Who told you that man hurt me last night? I never said he hurt me." "I saw it on your face. I didn't hear the dialogue, but the look on your face told it all; you were deeply hurt." I went totally silent. As I stood there holding the phone, I was thinking: 'I just realized I was hurt, so how could he see it.' Mr. Chapman breaks the silence, "You ok?" My tone has softened some, and I answer, "Yes, thank you. I need to go please don't call me again, I'm serious about this being my business phone." Brief silence, I start to hang up and he says, "Hey wait up; I'm new to this area and I'm looking for a church, do you know of one I might be able to visit?" 'What does he think I am, 411?' "No I don't Mr. Chapman. Try the yellow pages." Almost cutting me off he says, "You mean to tell me you don't attend church?" Now he's gotten me irritated and almost yelling I say, "Yes I do!" "Well what's the name of the church you attend?" With an attitude I say, "United Faith East; now Good bye Mr. Chapman!" And I slam the phone down, ugh that man!

After I showered I get into bed, and I go over my Sunday school lesson. One of the scriptures used as a reference is; Proverbs 18:1 and boy did it jump out at me; **"A man who isolates himself seeks his own desire; He rages against all wise judgment."** If that scripture wasn't on time for me! Wow, I needed that. I thanked the Lord for giving me a Word, and pray to be filled until I fall asleep.

I woke up on my own at 6am. I laid there and thought about my meeting with Aunt Flora Thursday and all of the emotions I went through and now that I know what she has to say to the family I'm beginning to feel nervous for them and for Aunt Flora. She must be really worried having to reveal the family secret to the whole family. I must admit telling it once is the same move I would make. I know Memphis' personal drama queen; Aunt Shirley, will find a way to steal the spotlight from Aunt Flora some kind of way, how interesting this is going to be.

I read Psalm 51:10 **"Create in me a clean heart, O God, And renew a steadfast spirit within me."** I really meditated on it and prayed until 7:30 am, and then I phoned Aunt Flora to see if she needed me to bring a dish; and to feel out where her head is.

"Hello Aunt Flora." "Its granny now Angie, call me granny." "Ok, granny I was wondering if you need me to bring a dish for dinner today." "That's so sweet of you dear; but I'll be just fine. I knew my family way before you did. As long as the drama queen gets her time everything will go fine." "How did you know I was calling about the meeting?" "Angie you're my blood and we do think alike. To tell you the truth I'm glad to get this over with. I miss being around my family we have always been close." "Aunt Flora what are you cooking?" "Granny dear, call me granny. I have a prime rib of beef roast, baked lemon pepper chicken, scalloped potatoes, fresh grilled asparagus, broccoli I'll steam and butter, fresh grilled sliced carrots, a tossed salad, potato rolls, iced tea, lemonade and for dessert; a 7up and a lemon cake." "I see you keep the 2 green vegetable rule also. It sounds like you have everything under control. I'll see you at church, Aunt Flora, I love you." "Its granny dear, and I love you too. Bye."

I ate breakfast and was ready for Sunday school with time to spare. Even though I talked with Aunt Flora I still felt uneasy about her facing the family alone I wished I could stand next to her and hold her hand; something to let her know I support her. I just couldn't shake the uneasy feeling I had.

I arrived at church early so I went into the sanctuary where a few other early birds were and waited. When Dora came in she looked surprised to see me and came and sat next to me. After we exchanged hugs she asks, "So; are you ready for the revealing of the big secret?" I didn't want to go there so I said, "Nice outfit is it new?" "Ok, I get the drift cuz." Mother Evans and Sister Rosen came in and talked with us about the church anniversary until it was time for Sunday School to start. It was very good; we looked in depth at Colossians 2: 6-15.

Mother Howard taught us that we have received Christ Jesus the Lord, so we are to walk in Him, take a stand for holiness and be rooted and build ourselves up in Him and watch our faith become established. She encouraged us to abound in thanksgiving to the Lord and read and get an understanding of the Bible for ourselves so no one will be able to cause us to trip or fall by enticing us with the philosophy and traditions of men, because in Christ dwells all the fullness of the Godhead bodily; and we are the body of Christ, therefore we are complete in Him, who is the head of all principalities and powers. She broke down the importance of us being buried with Him in baptism, both water and spirit which both reminds and renews us as we allow the Holy Spirit to put this flesh under subjection to the Spirit. Every time we put flesh under subjection, we disarm principalities and powers, triumphing over them just as Jesus did. We were all so fired up after she taught us Dora and I stayed in our seats talking about the class.

Big Mama started attending here after she and Big Daddy were married and our family has made this "The Bowen family's church," and, we all have our set in stone places to sit and our families always sit together on their appropriate pew so let me tell you the exact seating chart.

I always sit with Dora on Uncle Howard's pew; that's the 5th row from the front on the right side of the sanctuary; if you are entering from the rear. I sit on the end of the pew because Connie, Dora's sister sits next to her then Connie's husband Paul, their 2 kids Lamont and Adrian then its Howard Jr., his wife Roslyn and their son Howard the 3rd or HJ as we call him, then sits Aunt Rose Marie and Uncle Howard sits near the isle. Right behind them on the 6th pew sits Ernest, Dora's baby brother, right behind his father, and then it's Kozette, Aunt Brenda's baby girl along with some of the other youth in our church. Aunt Brenda's pew is the 4th row in front of Uncle Howard's however Aunt Brenda and Uncle Odell sit on the end in front of Dora and me not near the isle. Next to Aunt Brenda sits Melissa and Micah her grand kids by Karl and his wife Lauren who sits next to Micah, then sits Karen; Kenneth's wife and Tamala sits between her mom and dad and Cousin Kenneth sits in the isle seat. Uncle Lester's pews are the 2nd and 3rd pews in front of Aunt Brenda. He sits near the isle on the second pew with Aunt Inez next to him then it's Bernard, his wife Cassandra and their son Michael, Cousin SeBone and his wife Essie then Sonae', the baby of their three kids. Quincy and Eboni sits on the third pew behind their parents with Rufus and his wife Desiree' and their daughter Pamela and then it's Eunice and her husband Tyrone and their two sons David and Paul.

Now Aunt Shirley and Uncle Henry sit on the left side of the sanctuary's 4th and 5th row pews from the front with all of her family. Uncle Henry sits in the isle seat with Aunt Shirley next to him then its A'letha, her husband Walter and their four kids; Va'Trice, Jaquem,

Reynard and De'Ron. The fifth pew is Wanda Faye and her husband Ronald and their two sons Ronald Jr. and Rodney then next to Rodney is Cousin Roderick and his wife Della and their three kids Summer, James and Camille. Aunt Flora sits on the 7th pew at the end not on the isle side on the same side as Aunt Shirley.

Everybody knows where the Bowen's sit and know better than to sit in our seats and the ushers know better than to sit someone in our seats. Not a pretty sight in church to mess with the Bowen's seats!

After the 10 minute break between Sunday school and 11 am service, the pews start to fill up then we open with prayer. Pastor Anderson; our Senior Pastor walked up to the pulpit and we all stood for opening prayer. While he's praying and all heads are bowed, this whispering begins and I look up to see Aunt Brenda is hitting Uncle Odell trying to get his attention and is pointing her thumb towards the rear of the sanctuary. By now everyone has their head half bowed and is looking towards the rear of the church and is slowly turning back to face Pastor Anderson. I keep my head half bowed and turn around to see what the commotion is about just as Dora is hitting me trying to get my attention. Who is standing at the door waiting to be ushered to a pew but Mr. Chapman!

Now we all say amen and sit down. I turn around to see him pointing at me and he sees me looking at him and gives me a nod and smile. Dora hits me on my thigh, leans towards me and says, "Girl you know him?" "No, he stopped me from kicking my father. I'll tell you about it later." The usher is now standing at our pew and extends her hand for him to sit next to me. Dora tells Connie, "Move down some." And she moves away from me and pats the pew for him to sit between us. Oh boy! Mr. Chapman is dressed to the bone!

He's wearing a celery green Alfani silk blend suit with a tan and light green stripped silk shirt and tan shoes. This man has a diamond stud in his ear that makes the shine on his bald head take a 2nd. He is carrying a custom made dark tan leather Bible holder that looks like it's been utilized.

I realize just this second that I have never seen him in daylight. He sits down and crosses his leg and I notice his socks are silk and tan like his shirt and he smells so good. OK ANGELA! Aunt Brenda looks at me out of the corner of her eye and turns back around facing the front. When I look around the sanctuary everyone is looking at Mr. Chapman. Aunt Brenda puts her arm up on the back of her pew and slides her hand down and I noticed she has a piece of paper in her hand and she shakes the paper at me; it's a note. I grab it from her and put it on my right side and open it. "Who did Dora bring to church?" I look up at Aunt Brenda and hunch my shoulders. She turns around and looks at Aunt Shirley and hunches her shoulders. The rest of them sit back in their pews and relax. I laugh to myself, Dora with a man; geez; give me a break!

After I laughed about Dora I got mad at Mr. Chapman for tricking me into telling him where I went to church. Then I got mad at myself for not catching the play. When the choir got down on the song, "I Am Souled Out," Mr. Chapman stood up and clapped and raised his hand right along with the rest of us.

The sermon was on Philippians 4:8, **"Finally, brethren, whatever things are true, whatever things are noble, whatever things are just, whatever things are pure, whatever things are lovely, whatever things are of good report, if there is any virtue and if there is anything praiseworthy–meditate on these things."** Pastor Anderson went through each whatever and gave references to each one and tied the scripture with pulling down strongholds and laying aside every weight that easily besets us. During the sermon I noticed Mr. Chapman had no problem finding the scriptures and his Bible was marked up with different color highlighters. I also noticed his Bible had 2 different versions; a New King James and the Amplified.

The alter was full of us seeking to become filled with the Holy Spirit so we can walk in the Word we had just received. I went up for prayer and while Pastor Anderson prayed, I remembered Aunt Brenda telling me when she was filled; she heard a stammering language in her inner ear, so she repeated it and that was how she was filled. As I stood there while Pastor had his hand on my head, I heard a strange language in my ear so I repeated it and, **I spoke in tongues!** I was so excited! Finally, I'm filled! I leaped and jumped and spoke so loud. I felt like I was floating in the air! What an awesome feeling, I am filled! Oh, thank You Jesus! I spoke all the way back to my seat, I was so excited. I sat down and picked up my purse, retrieved my tithe and offering envelope and was rocking and singing in my seat. When the offering basket came to us I noticed Mr. Chapman had filled out an envelope and put a hefty amount of cash in it and I wondered if he was trying to impress somebody. Oh well, if he is, I am not the one impressed!

When we were dismissed, I hurriedly stood up to try and leave. My intent was to leave Mr. Chapman since I didn't invite him, he found his way here and he can find his way back from where ever he came from! However; Aunt Brenda's whole pew swarmed around me and I couldn't move an inch. Dora's end of the pew was blocked also; everyone was introducing themselves to Mr. Chapman. Uncle Howard had to walk all the way around the sanctuary and Bo guard his way through the crowd, and when he shook Mr. Chapman's hand he said, "I'm Dora's father, nice to meet you." Mr. Chapman said, "Nice to meet you sir. I'm a friend of Angela." Uncle Howard said, "Angela is my niece but I love her like my daughter. You get my meaning son?" "Yes sir." Now that the crowd knows Dora doesn't have a man caller, they spread the information among each other and the crowd suddenly thins.

The three of us are left standing; Dora, Mr. Chapman and myself. Dora says to Mr. Chapman; "I'm Dora; Angie's cousin and I want to apologize for the family assuming you were here as my guest." Now Dora is chuckling as she continues, "But I must admit it was entertaining to me. Especially watching Aunt Brenda pass that note to Angie; it took all my strength to keep from laughing out loud. And Mr. Chapman, you played it off very nicely." As Dora and Mr. Chapman laugh, Aunt Flora walks up and says, "Hello young man I'm Flora Bowen and you are?" He extends his hand to Aunt Flora and says, "Hello ma'am, I'm Malik Chapman, Angela's friend." Aunt Flora says, "Oh well, you will be coming to dinner today won't you?" I shake my head NO and butt in, "Aunt Flora." She blurts, "Granny dear, granny." I continue, "He's not able to come." I grab her arm and guide her body to turn around as I start walking with her out of the sanctuary. I glance quickly at Dora and notice the puzzlement on her face.

I walk Aunt Flora outside and she tells me, "Angie bring your guest with you, I have plenty food." I tell her, "He's not my guest he's not even my friend. We don't need company at the meeting we're having; company is not a good idea." She looks at me and strokes my cheek with her index finger and says, "Angie it doesn't matter he'll find out sooner or later." Now we are standing outside the front door of the church and Dora and Mr. Chapman are standing behind us listening. I tell her to get to the house; everyone will be there before her, she agrees and take a few steps to leave, then stops, and turns around to tell Mr. Chapman, "It was nice meeting you. Have Angie bring you by sometime." Dora steps up alongside me and says, "What she mean granny; Angie is she alright? Is that what this meeting's about?" I pull her away from Mr. Chapman and say; "Dora she's fine, go on to her house I'll meet you there, go on." I give her the eye towards Mr. Chapman as I slightly lean my head his way like I have some business to attend to. She raises her eyebrow and says, "OH ok, see you in a few cuz." She turns and smiles as she waves at Mr. Chapman and walks to her car.

He takes a few steps to stand next to me. I get a real mean look on my face and say to him, "Mr. Chapman that was not cute or funny. I don't know which one you were trying to be. Don't you ever." I put my finger up in his face. "Ever pull a stunt like this again or I'll embarrass you so fast you'll wish you were never born. You get that?" Very calmly; as if he didn't hear a word I said to him he says, "I would like to spend some time with you and see you not get mad." Now I'm almost yelling, "Man; are you retarded? Don't you get I don't want to be bothered with you?" "Angie, do you have a man in your life?" I haul off to slap him and he stops my hand in mid air. At first his grip is strong, he's holding my wrist. And in a few seconds, he loosens his grip but my hand is still stopped. My eyes got so big and my mouth flew open as I stood there staring at him. I couldn't believe how fast his hand moved to stop mine. I thought about how fast he held my arms down after I slapped my father and I wondered if he was some kind of karate expert.

While staring into my eyes he calmly says, "Remember Friday night, I do. You slapped that man. Angie I don't play games and I don't believe in violence. Promise me you will behave and I'll let go; promise." I say with a tone, "Promise." He let my wrist go and says, "I'm sorry if I hurt you Angie, all I want to do is talk to you." I blurt "You don't know me, stop calling me Angie and I don't appreciate you telling everybody today you are my friend." "Woman why are you so angry? Who hurt you so badly you can't have a conversation with a man without getting angry?"

I stand there looking at him and he's looking at me waiting for an answer, but I don't have one. I turn around and walk to my truck. 'Lord why does he make me so mad? What is it about him that upsets me so? And why is Mr. Chapman springing up now in the middle of all the mess going on in my life, why now? See, that's nobody but the devil; I get filled today and here comes the devil to steal all of my joy! I need to get to Aunt Flora's before she tells everyone.' As I pull out of the church parking lot I start praying for peace, I need to be calm for this meeting so I pray for the presence of the Lord to be in control of our meeting; or at least be in the room!

When I enter Aunt Flora's living room I close the door and stand there with my hands behind me holding onto the door knob as I face everyone in the room; I'm taking inventory. All of my cousins and their families are sitting around on the couches, wing back chairs and at the dinning room table. Aunt Flora has mixed matched chairs from all the rooms in the house, desk chair, side chairs, folding chairs and patio chairs everywhere; there is only a small pathway to the kitchen. You can hear a pin drop in here but there are a lot of voices coming from the kitchen. The tones are light and the conversations are short and polite. I can tell they are all thinking why are we here? And let's just cut to the chase and find out. But no one dare to say that to Aunt Flora. Well, maybe Aunt Shirley but she hasn't been here long enough.

Kozette asks, "Angie who was that mystery man?" Connie says, "Yeah where you been hiding him?" Dora says, "Come on Angie out with it." I walk over to the couch and squeeze myself between Dora and Connie and take in a deep breath and tell them, "We met by accident. I had a booking Friday night, he was there, a situation occurred and he helped me. The booking I had yesterday was for his birthday party." "How old is he?" asks Kozette. I tell her, "It was his 30th, anyway; he ended up helping me again last night and today he shows up at church. I had no idea he was coming. I was just as surprised as everybody else was." "Ah ha, and I have some swamp land to sell anybody buying Angie's story," says Dora. "What is it you find so hard to believe?" I ask. Dora says, "Well for one, why would he help you and it's his birthday party. And for two, you had to tell him where your church was. Angie why is it so hard for you to admit you like him?" Agitated, my voice rises as I say, "I don't even know him Dora, and how can I like someone I don't know." She grabs my hand and looks me in the eyes and says, "Now Angie; would you be this upset if you didn't like him?" I look down on the floor because again, I don't have an answer. Once again there was silence just like it was when I made my entrance.

Dora is very smart; she went to College the same time I did however she took Computer Programming and Business Administration. She has a real good paying job for the District Attorney General. She has a very logical thinking cap and I think she sees life as a big giant flow chart; everything flows together at some point, it all comes together for her brain. I'm used to her asking me questions; I just don't have the answers today.

Here come my aunts and uncles walking behind Aunt Flora as if she's the lead duck and they are all her ducklings. My heart begins to race and I stand up to let them have a seat. All of us sitting on the couch and the two winged backed chairs; we are all getting up to give them our seats out of respect. Aunt Flora walks straight to the fireplace; she steps up on the bricks and lifts her arm up on the mantel as she watches her sisters and brothers being seated. Uncle Lester, Aunt Inez, Uncle Howard and Aunt Rose Marie all sit on the couch. Aunt Shirley and Aunt Brenda each sit in the winged backed chairs with their husbands standing behind them. While they are all being seated I walk over to Aunt Flora and ask, "Do you want me to stand beside you?" She strokes my cheek again with her index finger while smiling and looking me in the eyes and says, "No Angie, I got this." I back up and stand next to Uncle Odell. Aunt Flora begins.

"I invited everyone here today to reveal a family secret. Now I know this will be difficult for some of you to handle but I have carried the burden of my secret since I was 16 and my next birthday I'll be 61. When daddy died I was consumed with guilt because I told him he was selfish and I hated him the night before he shot himself." A few gasps are being heard, mostly from my generation of cousins. "I went completely wild and started hanging around with the girls that smoked and drank. Then I started skipping school and having sex with any boy that wanted to have sex with me." Now the gasps are coming from my aunts. She tells the events of that Saturday before Big Daddy shot himself just like she told it to me, and then she says, "Try and see where I was at 16. I thought Daddy killed himself because of me and I should be punished. Acting wild and crazy was my way of hurting me.

Lester, I don't know if you remember the night when you came over and helped Mama put me in my room after being passed out drunk on the front grass; the following week Mama had to take me to the doctor and I found out I was pregnant." Almost everyone gasps, she continues, "Mama was the one to come up with the secret. She said she would tell everyone she was having a 'change baby' and all I had to do was stay in the house until the baby was born. Everyone would think I was taking Daddy's death hard and it worked. The first 3 months I walked around like a zombie and when De Anne started moving in my stomach, that's when the guilt left and I began thinking about life again. Mama and I became so close, every day I would tell her every movement the baby made and she would tell one of you." She looks at her siblings and takes in a deep breath, then starts again.

"When I went into labor, Mama drove me to the County Hospital in Bartlett, and stayed with me until we bought De Anne home. I felt real bad not knowing who her father was. I was so embarrassed and the easiest way for me to deal with it; was not too. So I told myself this is not your baby this is your sister." Aunt Flora reaches up on the mantle and takes a piece of paper from between the candlestick and the last family picture of the 5 of them. She unfolds the paper and passes it to me. I take a look and see its Mother's birth certificate with Flora Bowen as the mother and I pass it to Uncle Odell. She's still explaining, "After a few years, I believed the lie myself. Because I was afraid I'd slip and say something about De Anne being my baby, I separated myself from my own family. Separated myself from my big sister Shirley who taught me how to dance. And from Brenda who taught me how to wear my first bra. And being the little sister, I missed my oldest brother Lester who always came to my rescue when Mama was fussing at me. Howard is only 2 years older than I am and you were my big brother that taught me how to drive a car. Truly I missed being around you all and having alienated myself from my sisters and brothers and your families, and all because of a secret and a lie; I was only giving power to the lie by keeping the truth hidden. I love you all and want to become part of the family again and the only way that can be is if I expose the truth.

Almost everyone here today attended Wednesday night Bible study last week and you know I finally gave my life to the Lord." Almost everyone says, "Amen." Aunt Flora continues; "Now I need to ask you, my family, for forgiveness. I have allowed a family secret and lie to cause division in the family for too long." Uncle Lester shouts out; "Flora, you're our sister and we love you; of course we forgive you baby sis and I speak for all of us." Now the room is full of sniffles. She blinks back tears and says, "Thank you, thank you all. Now does anyone have any questions for me?" The room was silent as Aunt Flora combs the room with her eyes looking for a question.

Having the same story told to me Thursday evening, I decided to help, so I start, "I have a question for the family. Mother didn't look like any of you so my question is did anyone ever wonder why?" Aunt Brenda says, "I questioned if De Anne was daddies for that reason but I couldn't see Mama cheating on him she loved him so much. Now that Flora has told us the truth; it makes sense." Uncle Howard speaks: "When I knew I was coming home for leave, I called home and told Mama, and she talked me out of staying here in the house. She told me the room had not been cleaned because she couldn't stand to go back there and she was having a hard time keeping Flora from feeling guilty; so I didn't stay here. At the time I thought it odd she didn't want a man around the house but now it makes sense." Uncle Lester spoke up, "I thought De Anne looked like Mama's mother. I remember her having light brown eyes. And we all know Afro Americans can have any color child, so I thought nothing of her being darker than the rest of us."

Aunt Shirley stood up and said with an attitude, "I can't believe you wouldn't tell me your big sister what happened to you." She's pointing to herself, takes a step forward as the drama queen is revving up; her eyes are rolling around and her voice is beginning to tremble. "Flora you are my baby sister and to think you went through all of that alone." Now she's working up tears. "I just feel so bad for you, Oh Flora you poor thing." She covers her face with both hands and plops down in her chair, but touches just the end of it, and, as she slides slowly down to the floor, the sound of her knit blouse next to the plastic on the chair; sounds like a giant whoopee cushion. A'letha and Kozette burst out laughing and Uncle Henry who was standing behind her, extends both hands, as if to catch her, and when she hits the floor, he burst out with a loud laugh and, as if his laughter was a bell to start room laughter; everyone in the room is bending over with loud bouncing off the wall laughter. Even Aunt Shirley herself is laughing so hard she has tears running down her face.

After the laughter simmers down Aunt Flora goes into the kitchen and all my aunts follow her. Dora calls me and walks to the couch, sits down and pats the cushion next to her. I answer her summons and sits down. She starts, "I want to hear everything, start with Friday and lead me up to this morning." I start, "There really isn't much to tell. My father shows up to the booking I had Friday evening." Dora's shocked; "Shut up! Nichols was at one of your catering jobs?" "Yeah girl, wanting to 'talk' and I was definitely not going for it. I went outside to get away from him, he followed me and before I realized it, I slapped the taste out of his mouth and out of nowhere, some kind of way these strong arms locked mine; to keep me from slapping him again. Dora, I really acted a fool. I should have handled it better than I did. I had to repent and I actually understand now that I was hurt and angry at him, but the Holy Spirit ministered to me that I love him because he's my father. I don't mind telling you, Dora that hurt, me admitting I love him; really cut to the core of my soul.

Anyways, yesterday the birthday party I had at the Colonel's ended up being for Mr. Chapman but I didn't know it until the party was well on. I was manning the table and saw him standing there parked in a corner by the food table and chewing like a cow. Along comes this drunk guy walking up to Mr. Chapman all loud, saying happy birthday Chapman and that's when I found out it was his birthday. Oh wait, I forgot to tell you, when I saw him in the corner, I asked him what he was doing there. Girl when I heard that man say happy birthday then his name; I was so embarrassed. Dora I was mad at the man for being at his own party! I had to go outside and pray because I realized... I don't have an issue with just my father, but with men period. That revelation humbled me tremendously, I felt so small. I stayed in the kitchen the rest of the night. After I arrived home, Mr. Chapman calls me on my business phone and in a sly way asked me if I went to church and which one; that's how he knew where I attended church. Girl I had no idea he was going to show up, I was just as shocked as everyone else."

Dora smiled and pulled her head close to mine and said, "No, I beg to differ; did you see the look on Aunt Shirley's face when Aunt Brenda hunched her shoulders? I got such a kick out of that and on my way over here I thought about it and got insulted; do they think I can't have a man call on me? They better recognize; I can catch them I just throw back. If he's not interested in the kingdom of God; I keep moving. Anyway I just might have someone sitting next to me in church real soon, anything is possible! " I ask, "Dora, do you think we will ever get married? Will we be old maids like Aunt Flora?" She replies, "You mean granny don't you?" We put our foreheads together and laugh. The 'dinner's ready' call comes from the kitchen and like the sound of a herd, we are all filing into the kitchen for the blessing to be pronounced.

The order to Sunday dinner has always been all the aunts warm up the foods and during the sermon discussion, all of us nieces clean up, then we leave the Aunts and Uncles to the rest of their discussion. Today, after we finished the dishes, instead of going home I stayed with Aunt Flora. I hugged her then grabbed her by the hand and we walked into the living room and headed for the couch. Wanda Faye and Connie were still here and when they noticed us coming towards the couch; they got up and let us sit. I told Aunt Flora I thought the meeting went well and she said, "Yeah right down to Shirley's grand finale; she has always had to be the last act. But I love her anyway. Angie, tell me why didn't you bring that fine young man with you to dinner?" "Aunt Flora." She interrupts me, "Granny dear, granny." "Granny, now you know I'm going to need some time to remember to call you granny, don't you? For 26 years I've called you Aunt Flora so I need more than 26 hours to change. Ok?" "I know Angie, I love you grand baby." She reaches over and kisses me on my cheek. It feels odd, yet good to have her love on me. We are all affectionate and all of my aunts hug and kiss me and each one of them tells me they love me, but having my own grandmother makes me feel almost complete in a strange way.

I tell her, "He is not a friend; he is someone I met at a booking and asked about a church. I had no idea he was going to show up today." She puts her hand on mine and tells me, "Angie the way he looks at you; he thinks he's more than someone you met. Be careful baby ok?" "Ok I will. Aunt, Granny, do you need anything before I go?" As I stand up I watch sadness become her expression. She grabs my hand and starts swinging it from side to side and asks, "Do you think De Anne would have forgiven me?" I sit back down and hold on to her hand and say, "Aunt Granny, Mother would have forgiven you and then baked you a cake!" She smiled as tears ran down her face and says, "Yes she would wouldn't she." While she breaks out with a full smile, I give her a long hug and tell her I love her. I found my purse and left for home.

CHAPTER SIX

Mr. Chapman's Sad, Sad Story
Can we just be friends?

I went in the house and changed my clothes. I need to go in the garage and do inventory so I can go grocery shopping for this week's events. After I make my list, I go into the house to see what events I have so I can complete my shopping list from the menus. I go to the desk to pull out my calendar, and notice there is a message on the business phone. The first thought I had was, 'if that Mr. Chapman dialed this number again I'm having it changed.' I push the button. "Hello Angela Elise Bowen, the best caterer in all of Memphis. You made your mothers petite lemon cheesecakes better than she did. Man could that woman cook, and judging from what I tasted Friday evening, you are just as good or better. Angela, I want to talk to you face to face and apologize to you. Since our eyes are the mirror of our soul; I need you to see all of the sincerity I have in my heart when I tell you how sorry I am. I don't know if you are aware of the fact you turned out to be my only child, and now that I am approaching the age of 50, I want to get to know my only heir.

I asked Councilman Richardson for your business card, he invited me to Carmen's retirement party. He also informed me your company does all of their catering.... Angela, I will leave my phone numbers on this message, and I pray you return my phone call. I really am sorry for being so selfish and for any deficiencies you may have acquired as a result of it. My home phone number is 901-555-1212 and my cell phone number is 901-555-1213. I am optimistic of your call bye." I don't know why, but tears began streaming down my face as soon as I heard him call me by my full name. I pulled the chair out and sat down. I thought, 'he is sorry for not wanting me to be born, now that he's older and wiser. I can relate to that; considering the mistakes I've made in my youth! '

The phone rings and before I realized it was my business phone, I picked it up hurriedly and spoke as if I were rushed, "Hello, I mean Taste and See may I help you?" "Yes you may." I recognize the voice, its Mr. Chapman. I sniff up the tears that were streaming down my face and wipe my eyes so I can tell him off. "Angela, are you alright?" I spew out, "I'm mad thinking about how much money it's going to cost me to change this number Mr. Chapman. I told you this is my business phone and I don't have time for chit chat!" By the time I finish talking I'm hollering at him. "I heard what you told me and I'm calling in regards to a catering job." I didn't know whether to believe him or not, so I thought I'd ask a few questions to find out. He says, "Hello, are you still there?" I answer as softly as I can, trying not to let the aggravation be heard in my tone. "What day are you interested in?" He says, "Two weeks from yesterday." "Just a moment please." I check the calendar; I'm booked. "Sorry, that Saturday is booked. Please remember us for any future celebrations."

"Wow, you are very professional. How long have you been catering?" I knew he was up to no party; now I really have to change this number. "Mr. Chapman I don't have time for you and your games." He interrupts me, "Angela one thing I don't do is play games. I want to talk to you; you seem to be going through a rough time and I think I can be of some comfort." "Now how do you think you can be of some comfort to me and you don't even know me Mr. Chapman, and quit calling me Angela like you know me, man!" "I know you're hurt... Angela, I know hurt when I see it." I felt like he could see me through the phone; this is the second time he's said this to me, how does he know.

"What makes you think I'm hurt?" He replies, "I went through the yellow pages like you suggested and found a coffee shop on Brewer Street, it's Café La Mode,' meet me there and I'll tell you." "Mr. Chapman." "Angela; bring your Bible and is that far for you? Or do you know of a place we can meet publicly and share scripture? "No, it's not far for me and besides; you wouldn't know how to get anywhere I suggest anyway. Give me 20 minutes ok?" He says, "Ok, see you in 20 minutes." Click.

I pull up in the parking lot on the side of the coffee shop and see 4 guys drinking out of brown paper bags and remembered a friend of Ernest was shot here a few weeks ago. I guess Mr. Chapman doesn't know this area, I sure hope he's here already. Just as I stepped from the parking lot to the sidewalk he pulls up tooting his car horn. I stopped and waited for him and watched him get out of his Dark Titanium Metallic Chrysler 300. With his Bible in hand, he's walking towards me, but his eyes are taking in the guys standing next to the building with their paper bags. When they notice him he gives them a nod and looks at me. He walks up to me and turns around and faces the parking lot and glances at the young men standing next to the building. His eyes are watching everything around us as he says to me, "Are you comfortable being here, I didn't know this was the hood." He's talking to me but his eyes are all over the place. I tell him, "If you want to follow me I know a place we can be comfortable." He looks me in the eyes and says, "Ok I'll follow you." He walks me to my truck and I wait for him to follow me to the Rib Shack; a few blocks from Uncle Lester's house.

There wasn't that many people there when we arrived and he selects a booth for 4 that's up against the wall facing the door and the counter. He puts his hand out for me to have a seat where my back is to the door, and before he sits he says, "Angela you want something?" "Yeah we better buy something. Get me lemonade please." I watch him walk up to the counter looking at everything around him. I'm thinking, 'He sure is observant of his surroundings; as big as he is I know he's not scared. What's with him?' He comes back to the table with 2 lemonades, sits down, and slides himself on the bench over against the wall. I watch him as he slightly turns his body to prop his back up against the wall. I put my Bible on top of the table and look up into his eyes.

He's got a real serious look on his face and pulls his Bible towards himself but he doesn't take his eyes off mine. For some strange reason, I feel as though I'm in trouble and he's going to teach me a lesson. I say, "Mr. Chapman don't give me that 'I'm gonna give you a whipping' look. You may be a big man and all, but you don't scare me and my uncle lives right around the corner." As I speak I pull my cell phone from my purse and slap it on top of my Bible. "Angela; I'm a Marine, I do special operations and when I get serious I make some people uncomfortable. I'm not trying to scare you and if I did; I apologize."

He continues, "I just transferred here from Bethesda, DC less than 2 weeks ago." He is looking me directly in the eyes and his eyes are piercing but his tone has gotten soft, almost to a whisper so I scoot towards him and lean in to hear. "I was married for 7 years to a marine, and during that time my wife,

Theresa, had 4 miscarriages. The last pregnancy, she was 5 months along and we were so happy, we thought she was going full term that time. I had been on a mission, and as soon as I walked in the door she ran up to me all excited about a sale on baby beds, and, she wanted me to go look at them with her. I told her I was too tired and she said she would drive; she was so excited, so I agreed to go. We walked out of the house, I was right behind her, she was so happy, we were finally getting to buy a baby bed; we had never gotten that far before because she always lost the babies in the first trimester.

She sat in the driver's seat while I was headed to the passenger side and I thought I had better go ahead and drive; so I turned around and headed for the driver's seat. I opened her door and told her I would drive; she gets out of the car and I was so tired, I just slid in the front seat watching her walk around the front of the car to get in the passenger seat. I watched her as she slipped and fell on the concrete, face down." Mr. Chapman looks away from me, towards the wall. When he focuses his eyes towards me, he clears his throat and says, "Excuse me." He clears his throat again and continues. "I rushed her to the hospital, but she lost the baby; it was a boy. She damaged her back when she fell and was on pain medications for a good while. She stayed in the bed a lot but I thought that was her way of handling her grief from losing our 4th baby. After 6 weeks she went back to work and I thought she was going to get back to her old self, but she became distant towards me and after a few months I started noticing things like jewelry and appliances missing. Around the fourth month after she miscarried, I was called in to see my commanding officer, and was told she had failed her random drug test and was being put on leave pending investigation.

I left his office and went home; she didn't come home that night at all. Three days later I came home from work and there she was, and, she acted like nothing had happened, like she had never left. We argued almost all night and she apologized and explained to me she was still experiencing pain and was taking medication and that's why her drug test came back positive, then she promised to clear up everything by having her doctor fax the information to her commanding officer and she told me her disappearing would never happen again; she was afraid to come home after being put on leave without pay. She stayed home four days and left again and just like before, she came back home and acted like nothing had happened. I knew then she had a drug problem, but I loved her and wanted to believe her. After that she would be gone from the house for days or weeks at a time and every time she came home, it was the same routine; we'd argue all night; the next day she would take something and leave. Then she would come home; steal something and leave, she wouldn't wait for me to come home. This went on for almost a year and there wasn't anything left in the house of any value so, for 11 months she never came back. I started volunteering for missions so I wouldn't be alone, even though deep down in my heart; I always hoped she would be home when I arrived. Last year in August, I was summoned by the DC police department, to the coroners division; to identify a female body that fit her description.... I had to confirm it was her. She died of an overdose."

He takes a deep breath and looks down at his hands for a few moments. I just sit and watch him; he seems to be controlling himself. Now he looks up at me and starts talking again "I went to therapy and started going to church. Therapy would open me up, but it only made me angry to know how I felt, and frustrated not knowing what to do with all the anger I had. I couldn't figure out why I wasn't getting farther along in the sessions than I was, and one Wednesday night Bible Study, I heard a sermon on prayer, and how we can empty ourselves when we pray and as individuals, we must develop our own personal process on leaving our burdens, anger, hurts and fears at the foot of Jesus. That night I gave my life to the Lord and I felt a lot better. I started praying to become filled with the Holy Spirit so I could talk directly to God and empty my emotions without telling everyone my business.

You see I realized I was full of guilt and, I was tormenting myself about her losing the baby. I kept thinking, if only I had assisted her as she walked to the passenger side of the car I could have caught her and stopped her from falling. Then regret began to set in about how I should have helped her deal with the baby's death. I should have taken time to listen to her or perhaps forced her to talk about losing the baby. I should have done something or said something to stop her from being depressed about the miscarriage. I was consumed with guilt and I had a real bad case of the shoulda, coulda's. I even thought she blamed me for changing my mind about driving, and then I regretted changing my mind. Over a year of living in that house with the memory of Theresa, I decided to move to another barrack and I just happened to be in the office putting in my request to move when Colonel phoned a mutual friend in the office.

When I took the phone, Colonel told me he had heard about Theresa and asked how I was doing; I told him I was moving, attempting to make steps forward with my life, so he suggested I move here, to another state. That's why they had the birthday party for me. He and Abby are trying to help me get settled here. We served in DC together for a while and we always keep in touch. Anyway I volunteer for missions because I'm not married and they keep me busy, I need to keep busy. Tuesday I went in the office to pick up some paperwork and Colonel told me to sample the food from the caterer hired for my birthday party, it was free and he gave me the address and directions.

Friday night I was sampling the food, and just like Colonel said; it was good. I looked up right at the precise moment you were looking at that man; Angela it was as though I was looking in the mirror at myself. I saw anger and hurt on your face and I couldn't believe my eyes." Now Mr. Chapman is pointing at his stomach and saying, "Eyes of the soul." All of the therapy I had, and one look at you and the light came on. I need to stop being busy; and let go of the hurt! When I saw him walk out after you, I followed him to make sure he didn't assault you, but, as it turned out; I ended up protecting him from you." Mr. Chapman pauses, gets a look of puzzlement on his face and asks, "Are you with me so far?" "Yeah I follow you."

"Angela, now don't freak out, but when I went home Friday night I pulled out my Bible to have my devotion and the Holy Spirit revealed some things to me about me, and after crying and accepting the truth; my healing was finally made complete. All of the guilt and hurt I carried over Theresa is gone and you played a big part in that and I want to share some scriptures with you on healing. I think that's the least I can do. Will you just allow me to return the favor?"

I feel sorry for him, but I feel like, if I say yes I might be biting off more than I can chew. I have a lot on my plate right now. He's sitting here looking at me as though I'm a judge getting ready to tell him what his sentence is. It's taking me too long to answer so he says, "Angela; I won't hurt you or manipulate you, I will be honest, just as I've been thus far. I told you, I do not play games, I would like to get to know you and allow you to get to know me, and, if we can't be friends, then we won't be friends, ok?" He slightly bows his head, and purposefully directs his eyes precisely into mine, as if he wants to tie my eyes down, like he's demanding my full attention.

I let out a sigh as I say, "Mr. Chapman." He interrupts me, "Oh so I'm Mr. Chapman not a friend." "Let me finish; I was saying I have a lot of stuff," I put my fingers up in the air as if making quotation marks. "Going on right now and I am very busy, actually occupied with it all." He makes his eyebrows wrinkle and his eyes bounce around as if he's thinking and he says, "Ok, ok, I can work with that. So do you eat?" "Yeah I eat." I snap at him, thinking, 'what a dumb question!' "Then why don't we meet when you have time to eat and we can talk then, so you can still have your stuff time huh?" He gives me a quick smile and I take my eyes away from his because I don't know what to tell him. My heart is racing, I'm scared and don't understand why. I look past his head at the wall and I need to answer him but I don't know what to say.

I feel as though I'm in the 3rd grade and my teacher has just asked me a question on a test and I don't know the answer! Why can't I answer him? "Angela have you ever had a man friend?" I sharply direct my eyes towards his, raise one eyebrow at him and say, "Why would you ask me a question like that? You tell me this sad story and then you say something retarded. What is your problem?" "Answer my question Angela." He says this in a deep voice like with authority and I sit straight up and say, "Yes." Just then I realize; he is big and strong and I have a weakness for big strong men. They always put me in a submissive role and I'm not letting him take me there so, I squint my eyes at him and with a stern low even tone I say, "Mr. Chapman I don't appreciate you treating me like a child. Don't order me around like I work for you because I don't!" He slightly nods and softens his voice and says, "Ok Angela I won't and since we're going to be friends, call me Malik." He raises his eyebrows and extends his hand out for me to shake; I shook his hand while I rolled my eyes around in my head. "Now, do you have a pen and paper? Oh, I'm sorry; I sounded like I was telling you what to do; didn't I?" We look at each other, he's smiling and that makes me chuckle. That causes me to relax, I can't figure out why I'm so nervous. He opens his Bible and says, "I really do have some scripture for you and I know personally they will help." I found paper and pen in my purse and as he gave me several scriptures on healing, I wrote them down to study later.

He pushes his Bible next to the wall and says, "It sure smells good, have you eaten here before?" "Yeah and it's pretty good." While staring into my eyes he asks, "What do you recommend?" I say, "I don't eat a lot of pork I get the chicken." "Ok I'll get us a combo the chicken for you and the pork for me; I'll be right back." As he slid to the end of the booth, I was thinking about how easy he made my decision for me. When he walked away; I was trying to figure out if I wanted to be mad at him and I thought about how he says he does not play games and wondered if I could trust him. I was thinking all this when he put his hand on my shoulder and I jumped. "Are you ok, I've been calling you and you didn't hear me?" "You scared me I was in deep thought." "What sides do you want?" I told him and he went back to the line that had formed.

He came back to the table with the ticket number in his hand. He slid back against the wall and watched the people in line because it has gotten real crowded in here, so I began looking around the room. He started tapping the ticket on the table and when I turned to watch him he was looking at me. I say to him, "Are you nervous or something?" He slides towards me and says, "I don't want to seem invasive, but are you comfortable with telling me why you slapped that man?"

For a split second I was going to say none of your business. But he looked so innocent, like he could be trusted so I leaned forward and started, "He's my father." I watched his eyes and facial expression to see how he would react but he never flinched, he just kept looking at me, waiting for me to continue, so I did. "27 years ago he was dating my mother and she ended up pregnant with me. He told her to get rid of me; she didn't, he left and Friday was the first time I have ever laid eyes on the man. He wanted to talk; I didn't and I slapped him; end of story."

He sat there motionless as if he was waiting for me to continue. I felt relieved telling someone what happened but as the words left my mouth, I felt this pain in my heart and I felt as though I was going to cry; so I turned my face towards the counter blinking back tears. I felt his hand on my arm and when I turned to face him he had some napkins in his hand for me to take. I grabbed the napkins and the tears poured like a facet. A number was called and he said, "I'll be right back."

I wiped my eyes but the tears kept coming and I had to get more napkins. I want to let the tears flow, but being here, in a public place, I really don't want uncontrollable tears to start; the owner may think I need a strait jacket. Mr. Chapman walked up to the table and placed the food down in front of me; it was in a "to go" bag. He quickly slid himself to the end of the bench and gathered up both Bibles and my cell so fast. The next thing I knew he was standing behind me tugging on my arm, so I glanced up at him and he gave me a 'come on, let's go' nod. I stood up and followed his lead. I put the strap to my purse on my shoulder, grabbed the bag of food and he grabbed my free hand and started walking towards the door. Just as I imagined the parting of the Red Sea; every step he took forward, people moved back to give him a clear path.

He walked me to my truck and asked, "Angela can you drive or shall I call you a cab?" Trying to hold my composure, I say in a trembling voice; "I can drive; just give me my Bible and cell. I'll be alright." I burst out sobbing and turned around to lean on my truck and I hit my head; THUMP! I spun back around towards him to give him the bag; unaware he was leaning down stepping towards me and we bumped heads. Both of us say, **"ouch"**; at the same time and burst out laughing while rubbing our heads. When our laughter simmers down we are looking at each other and I find myself thinking, 'man he's good looking, ooh, those lips!' His expression turn serious and he says, "This is why we must keep our time together public ok?"

I'm thinking, 'thank you Jesus' because had he reached for me I would have kissed him. He says, "If you unlock your doors I'll put your things in the truck for you." I go into my purse and get my keys and unlock the door. He hands me my cell and opens the door to my truck and puts my Bible in the passenger seat. I hand him the bag with the food in it and he says, "You take it I'm not hungry now. I'll call you to make sure you get home safely in what 10, 15 minutes?" As he walks away, he slightly turns towards me, looking directly into my eyes. "Thanks Mr. Chapman, but I'll be alright, I don't stay far." He stands still and turns completely towards me, slightly tilts his head and says, "Its Malik and 15 minutes." Then he turns completely around headed to his car. I'm standing here, truck door open like my mouth, eyeing him up and down. Wow! Mr. Chapman is FY I EN! (FINE)

As soon as I started my truck, I thought, 'what just happened? I almost threw myself at him what's wrong with me. Why do I keep falling for these big strong men? I thought I was delivered after Mr. Married. One minute I was crying my heart out and the next I was laughing and then I wanted to kiss the man! Angela Elise Bowen you have got some soul searching to do! ..... That's what my father called me on the message he left me. I was talking about him when I couldn't stop crying like a fool, outside the front of the crowded Rib Shack and in public! Mr. Chapman must think I'm crazy, Holy Spirit, I need some understanding; show me what is crooked inside my soul and give me the wisdom to be still long enough to allow you to make it straight!'

I pulled up in my driveway and as I walk to the back door the phone is ringing, it's my house phone. I hurry to catch it and its Aunt Flora. "Baby did I wake you?" "No Aunt Flora", "Its granny dear granny." "No I just walked in the door." While I head to my bathroom to wash my face, I listen to Aunt Flora. "Angie everything went well today. After you and all the kids left; Lester, Inez, Shirley, Henry, Brenda, Odell and Howard, we all sat in the living room and talked about everything. The Lord blessed our conversation and now, oh thank the lord; I have my family back. Angie, I am so glad I gave my life to the Lord and took His yolk and found out first hand His burden is truly light. Baby the truth really does make you free. I just wanted to share that and tell you that I love you; Angie you hear that, sounds like a phone is ringing." "Aunt Flora, that's my business line." "Well I'll let you go, bye baby." Click.

I go into the kitchen and lift the receiver, "Hello" I answer. "You made it home without any problems?" "Yes Mr. Chapman, look, I am so sorry for the way I acted." "It's Malik, and no apology is needed. You are hurting and need to release; Angela hurt and anger can easily lead to un–forgiveness and un–forgiveness is not limited towards others; it can be harbored against ourselves too you know." I softly say, "Thank you Mr. Chapman." He says, "If you want to talk about how you feel about your father, I'll listen." I sigh and tell him, "Honestly I don't know how I feel. I just met him Friday and after I came home is when I realized I was hurt and wanted to hate him but deep down I don't... and... that makes me mad because he deserves to be hated and that's why I'm so confused!" Now my voice is trembling and I'm fighting back tears. "I'm listening"

"Well....I love him because he is my father, and I do look just like him; right down to that double gap. I couldn't believe my eyes; for as long as I can remember I have been told I look like him but with hair and now that I've seen him, I can't do anything but agree. I think my looking like him is what makes me not want to hate him because looking exactly like him is what makes me realize he is my father and I am from him. To hate him would be like hating myself. But the way he abandoned my mother and me while he lived his life with all the responsibility of raising me on her; well it makes me want to slap him again! Then I think about he was trying to reach out to me.... and I feel ashamed because I really should have handled it better." I sigh again and say, "Now do you understand why I'm confused?" "Are you? You know what you need to do to free yourself and it seems to me you are facing the truth. Where are you confused?" "I want to forgive him for hurting me and Mother all these years but... I want him to hurt like he hurt us." Now I'm crying again.....

After I have a good long snot cry, I realize Mr. Chapman is still on the line. "Mr. Chapman, you still there?" Very tenderly he says, "Yes I am and I'll be here as long as you need me." Oh I wish he were here so I could just lie in his arms. OH NO, that's not good, I shouldn't be thinking like this; don't go there Angela! "Ugh, thank you Mr. Chapman for lending me your ear. Talk to you later." Click! 'See, this is why I can't have male friends. My libido is too high for a single woman. How did I get pulled into this again? Angela you are going to have to back off before you end up hurt and alone again. Let me get my Bible and meditate.'

I go to get my Bible and see the scriptures Mr. Chapman gave me and I can't get out of my mind how he came into my circle of life. I think about how he stopped me when I slapped my father then how he protected me from that drunken guy at his own birthday party and how he came to church. Hey, I tried to slap him when he reminded me of my past associations with men. He asked me a simple question and I got so mad at him. I have never really found a way to interact with men and keep my flesh under subjection; I just stay away from them. Now here comes Mr. Chapman and I'm faced with the same old issue. Maybe I like him because he's big and strong; after all he does fit the profile for the type men I'm attracted to. And why has the Holy Spirit allowed him to come in my life now; precisely at the moment I could have physically hurt my father?.......

Ok my father wants to get to know me now and says he is sorry for not being in my life and, that I ended up being his only heir. Heir; interesting he used that word. I know I inherited his looks but I don't know what else from him I inherited. It might be worth meeting with him so I can get more answers about who I am. Aunt Flora told me about Big Daddy having a suicide spirit on him and I was able to receive healing and understanding about the spirit of suicide being on me. Realizing I wanted to end my life was my way of running from the rejection I did not want to face, now, am I running from my father because I don't want to face forgiving him. Am I a runner? My father ran from us. I just faced the fact I want my father to hurt and if I forgive him somehow I think he won't get the hurt he deserves..... I should forgive him and allow the Holy Spirit to deal with him so I can have a relationship with my father; the man who has a major role in my being born. Wow this really hurt...oh these tears....

Mr. Chapman is right, I need to forgive. What did he mean un-forgiveness can be towards oneself? What could I possibly have not forgiven myself for.....?

As I blow my nose I start praying; Heavenly Father I choose to forgive my father for not wanting me and hurting my mother. Oh God...help me as I choose to forgive my father, Lord help me let go of this un-forgiveness...I forgive him for running away from what he feared; being responsible for Mother and me. I want to love him and know who he is, regardless of his faults, and, I will allow the love I have for him to cover the faults I see....oh Holy Spirit, strengthen me when I weaken and reveal the right way for me to handle my feelings toward him. I surrender; I surrender to your healing and delivering power in Jesus Name I pray, Amen.

After I prayed and cried, I remembered I was filed today and I began to pray in my heavenly language; WOW what a boost! When I looked at my clock forty five minutes had passed and it seemed to have only been ten; lord I love being filed! It is the ultimate in being in the presence of the Most High God! I was so fired up I put on some gospel music and danced before the Lord with praise. I tired myself out and turned the music off and sat down then I decided to read some of the scriptures Mr. Chapman gave me.

I remembered his Bible had the Amplified version so I went into the other bedroom and pulled out my Amplified Bible and crawled into bed and went over all of the scriptures and had revelation; my running hinders my healing.

I fell asleep thinking about how there was a similarity in me running from my father and running from Mr. Chapman and I had a dream. In my dream I was running in what looked like a tunnel and I was crying out loud; "where is my answer; who has my answer?" Then I ran into Mr. Chapman and he asked me, "Angela why are you running from me, I have the answer." I woke up panicked and sat straight up in my bed. I calmed myself and lay back on my pillow and my elbow touched my Bible. I reached over and turned my light on and looked at the clock. It was 4:38am; I turned back towards the Amplified Bible and noticed the page was open. The scripture looked as if the letters were in 30 inch font, Acts 9:5. The red letters leaped out at me. It read: **"I am Jesus whom you are persecuting. It is dangerous and it will turn out badly for you to keep kicking against the goad [to offer vain and perilous resistance]."** I read the whole chapter turned off my light and laid there allowing the Holy Spirit to minister understanding to me.

As if I were watching a movie, I saw my childhood flash before me. I saw myself listening to all of the comments being spoken by my aunts, in regards to my father and mother and their relationship. And it became apparent to me, as if I was combining dry mixture with liquid to make a crust; the picture of how I formed my view of relationships for my life began to come together.

Understanding my fear of relationship became clear as a bell. I actually recalled how I felt and, the conclusion I sketched in my mind about my mother and father's doomed relationship. Looking like my father and having my mother's eye color, I began to think I would be like Mother and not have a man to love me. I know this is dumb; however this is the mind of a child. A child without her father because he didn't want her or her mother. I'm surrounded by aunts and uncles loving and tender towards each other, except in my house with my mother; there was the absence of a loving husband!

I assumed all men would leave me broken and if I didn't please them; I'd end up lonely the rest of my life. I never knew how to engage myself in a dating relationship; how two people interact, give and take between each other, I thought whatever the man wants, make him happy and give it to him. That's why the two relationships I had; I did whatever they wanted me to; in hopes they wouldn't leave me. But when I do that, all I'm doing is allowing my self respect to be measured by someone who doesn't care about respecting me; because I don't respect me......

Once I experienced intimacy, I liked it; and not putting a value on myself, I seemed desperate, and no man, not even a doggish man likes desperation, so he takes advantage of the situation, after all if the woman's inclined, so the man will always be.

Then I realized having my uncles' love me as a daughter is excellent; however, me having a father alive somewhere here in Memphis, only left a longing inside me to be validated **by my own father**. Being loved by my own father, supported by him is what I need and not having that; I gave myself to men that I considered to be strong; symbolizing the security and protection a girl needs from her father. Had Nichols been dead; that would be different, but knowing he never wanted me to be born....well, now I understand where the desperation came from.....

Now that he wants to be in my life, I need to let him so he can validate me, that way I will be able to have a healthy relationship with a man.... After lying here allowing tears to flow and cleanse; I decided I would call my father later today and agree to talk with him perhaps pray with him so we can mend and connect.

CHAPTER SEVEN

Validated At Last
Breaking bread with Dad!

MONDAY:

I awakened at 7am and told the Lord how much I love him and began praying in the spirit; I am loving this! For my devotion, I studied I Corinthians 14: 1-6 **"Pursue love, and desire spiritual gifts, but especially that you may prophesy. For he who speaks in a tongue does not speak to men but to God, for no one understands him; however, in the spirit he speaks mysteries. But he who prophesies speaks edification and exhortation and comfort to men. He who speaks in a tongue edifies himself, but he who prophesies edifies the church. I wish you all spoke with tongues, but even more that you prophesied; for he who prophesies is greater than he who speaks with tongues, unless indeed he interprets, that the church may receive edification. But now, brethren, if I come to you speaking with tongues, what shall I profit you unless I speak to you either by revelation, by knowledge, by prophesying, or by teaching?**

Knowing that when I speak in tongues I speak to God directly makes me feel as though what's in my heart is known to Him, and knowing He cares; that encourages me, how awesome!

I remember when Dora and I were about 7 or 8 years old and her grandmother Elsie; Aunt Rose Marie's mom, came to spend a month with them while she recuperated from hip surgery. Every time I went over

Dora's she would be in her room talking with Nana as we all called her; and one day Nana was telling Dora about the Holy Spirit and how we can talk directly to the Father by speaking in an unknown tongue otherwise referred to as speaking in tongues to church folk. Aunt Rose Marie came into the room and asked Nana if she thought we were too young to understand what she was telling us and Nana said the more you speak in tongues; the more you would understand. She told us that she was baptized in the spirit when she was 15 and the more she spoke, the more she began to see in the spirit what she was praying.

Dora asked her what did she see and Nana told us some of the experiences she had and after our talk with Nana, Dora told me she wanted to speak in tongues so she could see in the spirit. I was scared; I told her to go right ahead and whatever she saw; keep it to herself! Now I'm remembering the conversation on that day and I'm not afraid of seeing anything. I just love the way I feel while speaking, it's like; I'm in His presence and there is so much love. When I'm done, I feel so fueled; I am truly loving this!

After devotion, I ate and cleaned up the house, and then I listened to the message my father left me and wrote his name and numbers down in my phone book and called his cell. He answers: "Nichols here." My heart pounds so loud I can barely hear myself speak. "Hello this is Angela." Silence ..... "Angela, my heart is warmed hearing your voice; I am so glad you called, I'm almost in tears. I prayed you would allow me the chance to prove how much I regret not having you a part of my life, Angela when can we meet?" My heart is aching knowing his is hurting, so I say as tenderly as I can, "Anytime, my schedule is flexible Monday through Thursday after that I'm usually booked." Silence again.

"I'm sorry." He says, "I can't believe I'm talking to my daughter, thank you Angela for giving me a chance to repair the inexcusable circumstances I caused in both our lives; thank you, (sigh), how about tonight for dinner, my treat?" Now I'm getting excited knowing I get a second chance to handle seeing my father again; "That sounds good where?" "Let's do a buffet that way we can both eat what we like, wow I get to find out what my daughter likes to eat, wow." He's just as excited as I am, so I say, "The one on Overlook Drive is good what you think?" "Perfect, 4:30 good for you? I like to beat the crowds." "Yeah, I'll see you then...Dad." Short pause; "Yeah, bye." Click. I realize I'm smiling; I like the sound of Dad rolling out of my mouth.

I put a load of clothes in the washing machine and decide to get the scriptures Mr. Chapman gave me. I took my time and looked up some of the words to get an understanding. I allowed each scripture to penetrate my heart and I feel myself embracing healing; then I pray in the spirit specifically to build myself up like Jude verse 20 states. **"But you, beloved, building yourselves up on your most holy faith, praying in the Holy Spirit."** I can't describe the confidence I feel after praying in the spirit, I understand now why Dora loves to do it.

Later as I dress to go have dinner with my "Dad," my business phone rings and I let it go to voice mail. Before leaving out the back door, I listen to the message. "Hey Angela Malik here, I'm calling to see if we could have dinner, I'll treat anywhere you pick; the yellow pages don't work too well for me. Give me a call when you get this message; my cell number is 901-555-1219, later." Click. I hit save and think about the similarities in both dinner invitations I received today.

On the way to Overlook Drive I'm praying and thanking the Lord for my father wanting me to become included in his life and for some strange reason I feel as though this is going to help me understand myself and I'm looking forward to it.

I walked into the doors of the buffet and spotted my father sitting in the waiting area. He saw me and waved. As I get closer to him, he stood up and stuck his chest out and smiled so wide; geez, I look just like him with hair! When I stood in front of him he hugged me so tight I thought he was going to smother me; I realized I was holding my breath. What stunned me was his cologne; he smelled so good. When he loosened his grip he took a step back as if to examine me and I stared at him unable to move. He was smiling at me with our gaps and his smile fell; he leaned in toward me and said, "Am I embarrassing you; because that is not my intension I promise. I am so proud of you Angela you are a beautiful woman, an excellent cook and you are my daughter; my daughter." He rests his hand on his chest and he's smiling again and I'm still dumbfounded.

My father is exactly like the men I have had in my past, men I have fallen with desperation for; searching for validation from, validation I just received. Whew; Holy Spirit You are awesome! He puts his hand in my back and directs me to the line. He smiles real big and tells the cashier as he hands her the money, "I'm having dinner with my daughter!" She stands there smiling politely but her eyes were saying, "AND!" We get our plates and sit down at a small table for two.

He grabs my hand, bows his head and began to bless the food. While saying "amen" he looks up at me and says, "Bern always told me I would live to regret not wanting children and she was so right. It was humbling for me, but I told her she was right; you see Angela; over 7 months ago I gave my life to the Lord. I repented of all the wrong knowing and unknowing I've done. I have since joined a church that teaches the Word with understanding and I have developed a relationship with the Lord, and in doing so, I spend intimate time in prayer and study and lately I'm learning how to listen to the Holy Spirit. I'm just realizing He is a person and I need to get to know who He is, it's amazing, knowing the Father, knowing the Son and knowing the Holy Spirit; just amazing.

I was praying a few weeks ago and the Holy Spirit prompted me to pray for my daughter and I have been praying for you every day since. When I saw you Friday, I was both amazed and happy. You look like your pictures but you haven't aged that's why I asked about your name. I couldn't stop smiling at you because the Lord put you in my path and I never prayed for that; just that you would be blessed and not damaged because I shut you out of my life. The scripture says the Lord will do way more than you could ever imagine and that became true for me Friday. Angela... I want to get to know you. Can you forgive your father and grant me that?" The sincerity in his eyes confirms it all; I smile at him and say, "Yes Dad, I can do that. Can you forgive me for the way I behaved Friday; I am ashamed of the way I handled meeting you for the first time?" "Yes I have. Where is your friend tonight?" I'm puzzled, "What friend?" "That man who kept you off me as he so politely put it." I thought, 'Why does everybody think he's my friend?'

"Oh Mr. Chapman; he's not my friend or anything he just happened to be at the retirement party and thought he was coming to my rescue and ended up at yours." I chuckled but he had a serious look on his face.

So I get serious and ask, "What?" He leans in and says, "Angela I'm a man so hear me; no man protects just any ole woman. He either likes you or he wants something. I don't want to give the impression I want to control you because it's obvious you have done very well for yourself without me telling you what or how; but I'll say this; you have a great business and some men are attracted to women in business. So be careful, and I will continue to pray for you. Ok?" I don't want to get upset over Mr. Chapman being a gold digger so I let it roll off my back and just say "Ok."

"Angela tell me about yourself, where did you attend college and how did you get in business." I told him about my courses and how Mother helped me get started. He was saddened when I talked about her but he didn't say anything. "So what are your goals?" He asked... For a moment I felt like I was in the 3rd grade again. I told him; to keep my business running and live peaceable; I do not like drama in my life. He says, "I mean do you have aspirations for marriage and a family." I must have looked puzzled because he put his fork down and looked very seriously at me as I spoke. Feeling as though I gave the wrong answer; I said, "I have never really thought about it. All of my cousins except 3 are married and have kids, I have never thought about it, all I want to do is cook and go home for some peace and quiet." He leans in again and asks, "Angela, you're not gay are you?"

A loud burst of laughter spews out of my mouth and I quickly put my hand up to muffle the noise, I'm laughing so hard. He's still looking at me with the serious face so I put my hand down and lean in and now my laughter is down to a chuckle as I say, "No, I am not gay." I was still chuckling when he says, "Oh praise the Lord. I want grandkids you know, to love and enjoy; kind of experience what I missed with you. I want some grandsons and I'll take a grand daughter or 2 but I want to see them take their first steps and watch for the first tooth. Hey, maybe we'll keep the Nichols gaps going." I interrupt him, "Aunt Bernadine doesn't have a gap." "You're right; all the Nichols men have gaps. A few women have them but all of us males have gaps; it's our signature. You are all I have kiddo; my only hope of becoming a grandfather is in you." Now I feel scared; I'm an only child and if I don't produce heirs for him there just won't be any, geez talk about pressure!

We finish eating in silence and as we both take in the fellow buffeters, he began to fiddle with his napkin. I look at him and ask, "What is it; what do you want to tell me." He almost jumps out of his seat as he turns towards me. Squirming, he leans in closer and almost whispering says, "Angela, I really loved your mother, I was young and stupid. For years I kept telling myself, had De Anne placed a demand on me to commit to her I would have. After I became born again I had to face the awful truth; that is I was too selfish. I went through women like they were clothes; get tired of wearing this one; just go get another. Now that I'm approaching 50 I realize family is really all you have. When you sit and think things over; really and truly, only what we do for Christ and our seed is all there is. Angela I don't have anything of value to show for my life but you. And I regret with my whole heart never wanting you in my life, baby I truly regret that." He starts to blink back tears and I'm sitting here watching him as tears are streaming down my face. Maybe because he looks like me; but sitting here watching him as he opens his heart to me; for the first time in my life I was afraid; afraid of being old and lonely.

I gave him my cell and home numbers and as we stood up to leave, he reached over and hugged me again so tight and told me he loved me and thanked me for having a forgiving heart. Then he closed his eyes and started praying, "Heavenly Father I thank you for blessing and keeping Your Hand over my daughter, my seed. Father I pray you mend our relationship and bless her with a good man so the fruit of her womb will be blessed, In the Name of Jesus I pray; Amen." I told him that I loved him and fought back tears because I meant it, I really did mean it!

We walked out together and he walked me to my truck and kissed me on my cheek and said, "Love you!" My response was, "Love you too Dad." I was smiling so big and when I sat down in my truck I fought back tears, I'm 26 years old and heard my father tell me for the first time he loved me and I knew I was validated.

Thank You Jesus! I am on the road to healing! Then the thought of 'for who' came to mind and I became scared; I actually felt myself tremble. I'm a long way from being ready for a relationship. My cell phone rings and its Dora. "Hey Angie, where you at?" I responded, "I'm just leaving the Overlook Drive Buffet; I had dinner with my Dad." "Shut up! He's Dad now; that must be good. Angie I'm glad for you. Are you on your way home now?" "Yeah, what's up?" Dora mysteriously says, "I'll be there in 10 minutes. Bye."

As I walk in the back door I hear a car pull up so I leave the door open for Dora. She comes in and slams the door yelling, "Angie I got a problem." I yell, "Come in my room." As she's coming she's talking, "You are not going to believe this, your cousin Dora," she steps into the doorway of my room, with her hands on both hips saying, "Has man troubles. Can you believe it; me, with man troubles?" "Dora you're lying; girl, sit down and do tell!" As I change into some shorts; she sits on the edge of my bed and starts; "Well it all started Friday; we had some testing to do, so you've heard me talk about Parker right?" "Yeah I remember Parker, the smart quiet guy right?" She sighs and says, "Right. Well, we were in the conference room eating dinner; me him and Ms. Garner and when Ms. Garner left the room he clears his throat and says to me, "Dorinda, I would be honored if you will accompany me to the movies tomorrow evening."

I was chewing on my sandwich while reading a computer magazine and being completely shocked, I jerked back; and, my chair being on rollers; began rolling back. I leaned forward to try and stop myself from moving and as I did, I quickly inhaled the food in my mouth, and it went straight to the back of my throat. Now, I'm unable to breathe so I started rocking back and forth desperately trying to gasp for air and mentally praying the food in my mouth would supernaturally move away from the back of my throat. Girl, Parker jumped up and followed me in my chair with this confused look on his face. Suddenly, he jumped behind me and stopped my chair. I jumped up out of the chair still choking. He grabbed both my hands and was trying to pull them up in the air; I had no idea what he was doing and I began fighting him off me and in walks Ms. Garner. She stood there eyes bucked wide and staring at us. Parker lifted both my arms up in the air and my food moved from my throat.

Angie I have never had that many thoughts go through my mind at once in my life! I was embarrassed, scared I was going to die at work in the conference room and, shocked Parker asked me to go anywhere with him. I ran to the table, grabbed some napkins and spit my food in it. Then I grabbed everything on the table where I was sitting and calmly walked over to the trash and threw it all away. I could feel their eyes on me, so I ran out of the conference room to my desk and thought about what had just happened.

Here Parker comes with the magazine I was reading while I was eating. He lays it on top of my desk and desperately tries to un- crumble it. I turned my head away from him and looked straight ahead, I just couldn't look him in the face I was too embarrassed. He lifts up the magazine and stood there looking at me. I slowly lowered his hand to the desk. I kept my head down, Angie; I was so embarrassed. I just kept staring at the magazine. He says to me, "You mistakenly trashed this; Dorinda will you go to the movies with me?" I couldn't even turn my face towards him, I sat there and directed my face straight up and as I stared at the wall, I shouted "NO!" He stood there a few seconds and asked, "how about next Saturday, is that day good for you?" I slammed both hands on top of the desk real loud as I stood up, turned and looked him in the face and told him real slow and calm, "Parker, I don't date coworkers."

Angie would you believe he says, "Well what if I quit?" My eyes bulged and my mouth flew open as I stood there unable to answer him. He stood there staring into my eyes, waiting for an answer. Without taking my eyes away from his, I slightly bent my knees, pulled out my drawer and slowly reached in and pulled out my purse, then quietly walked around him and left the room. I was so way past embarrassment. I stayed in the bathroom most of the afternoon, avoiding Parker. I questioned myself why was I so shocked, why did I react the way I did? The conclusion I came to was he is the first man to come at me like he did. Angie, I was so embarrassed, I didn't want to think about it and with all the talk about this meeting at Aunt Flora's; I just completely erased Parker out of my mind. But today;" Now Dora is wobbling her head back and forth.

"When I went to work this morning he saw me at the downstairs elevator and waved. I felt my heart beat so fast, I dashed into the ladies room to avoid him. As soon as I stepped into the restroom, I looked directly into the full length mirror, and Angie; I looked at the expression on my face and... I think I like him. I never noticed him before, I mean you know, not like that; I mean, I always noticed he was nice but I always saw him as a coworker not as a man and now when I see him; I see a man. He's cute and so smart; he reminds me of daddy. I thought if I brushed him off I would be alright, but Angie," Dora starts to cry and we reach out for each other as she continues, "I think I like him, I can't stop thinking about him. Oh Angie, tell me what to do."

As I rub her back I say to her, "I can't tell you what to do, lord knows I'm the last person you want to copy; but Dora why are you afraid to like him?" I can't believe that came out of my mouth! She gets up and gets some tissue off my dresser and blows her nose. "Angie I have never thought about boys like Connie and you; after she got married all she ever says to me is "When you gonna settle down: you tryin to be the next Aunt Flora?" I have been content with my good job, my condo and Volvo; I have always been content; now he comes and asks me out to the movies and I freaked out. I know he knows I have never been out with a man before and I'm scared he might try and take advantage of me. But I like him; why am I scared of him?" "Dora I think you just answered your own question. Let's look at this; tomorrow do you think you can you walk up to him and tell him you will go to the movies with him if he promises to be a gentleman because you have 2 brothers and 6 male cousins that would hunt him down and put him in the hospital if he tries anything disrespectful? You think you can do that and see how he reacts?" Her eyes light up and she says, "Yeah I can do that! Thanks Angie, I knew you would know what to do. I have been so uncomfortable around him; and driving home today I realized I can not get any work done hiding from him and I have butterflies in my stomach. Angie I just never thought I would like someone the way I like him. We have worked together for almost 2 years and I never knew he liked me; I'm just a nervous wreck. How did you handle this feeling when you realized you liked Elvin?"

"First of all Dora, Elvin never loved me and I didn't deal with it logically like you are. I went with whatever he wanted, hoping he would love me. If Parker is willing to quit his job for a date with you; he's serious." We look at each other and I start laughing but she has a serious look on her face. She says, "That's what I mean Angie, was he really serious or did he just say that to get me to go out with him; that's what I need to be sure of." "Dora you've worked with this man for what, 2 years; has he given you the impression he's a dog?" She looks worried now and says, "But that's what I mean about not knowing, I never looked at him like I had to trust him, I just worked with him." I stand up and say, "2 years, you get to know a person Dora; you get a feeling about them. Why weren't you afraid to be left in the room with him when Ms. what's her face left?" "I was reading my magazine; yeah I was comfortable around him before."

I can tell by her eye movement she's thinking so I say, "go on" she says, "I guess I'm the one uncomfortable because dating is new for me. I'm afraid of the unknown; I'm afraid because I like him, Angie I really do like him and I have never liked a man before." Now she's smiling as I say, "He won't hurt you Dora, he probably knows about your brothers and if he knows you have a father he definitely won't hurt you.

What are you going to do tomorrow when you see him?" She turns around and starts walking towards my mirror hanging over my dresser and as she looks at herself, she gains confidence and her shoulders get straight as she lifts her head high and says, "I'm going to tell him that I have thought about the movie invitation and would consider going with him. I'll say, 'your invitation caught me off guard and I apologize for taking so long to give my answer.' Now the confidence has left her face and she turns around towards me with a questioned look and says, "You think he still wants to go?" I start laughing, "Dora if the man is willing to quit his job; yeah." She starts laughing and we meet each other in the middle of my room and hug. I tell her I never would have dreamed she would be coming to me for man advice, nev–er!

My business phone rings while Dora and I are still laughing. I started to let it go to voice mail then I thought it might be Mr. Chapman, so I tell Dora I need to get this and I run and pick up the phone and answers, "Taste and See, Angela speaking. " It's Mr. Chapman; "Hi Angela, I called earlier, I guess you didn't get my message." I remember my father hugging me and telling me he loves me and a smile covers my face as I say, "I'm sorry, I had a dinner date!" Silence, then I say, "Hello; Mr. Chapman you still there?" "Uh...yeah; did you say a dinner date?"

"Yeah, with my Dad; it was really good, he apologized, I apologized and we talked, it was great." Dora comes into the kitchen and says, "I'm gone I'll call you tomorrow; thanks cuz, love you." We hug and out the door she goes. I realize he's been silent the whole time Dora talked so I sense something is up with him and say with a concerned tone; "Mr. Chapman, are you ok?" "Yeah I just wanted to see you." "Well is something wrong, why do you want to see me?" "Angela, can we have lunch tomorrow my treat. I have to go on a mission tomorrow evening and I won't be back until Saturday." I answer, "Well, yeah, but can you tell me what the meeting's about." "I just want to take you to lunch; spend some time with you." He sounds so sad and serious, I'm wondering what's wrong so I say, "Ok Mr. Chapman, but are you sure you're ok? You know you helped me a lot last night and I want to return the favor; so if you want to talk now, I'll listen," Silence. Then, very tenderly he says, "Angela...... I'll tell you, but, I'm not sure you're ready for what I have to say." "Alright Mr. Chapman, I'm ready; shoot" He replies, "Oo Kay, here goes...

When I met you Friday, I went home and couldn't get the hurt look you had on your face out of my mind. I thought about how I carried hurt and guilt around in my soul and before I realized it; I found myself praying in the spirit and completely emptying myself. You see my spiritual eyes were enlightened and I realized I haven't thought of anything or anybody but my job and church for over 2 years. I had focused on keeping myself busy with my work and studying the Word until I no longer interacted with someone unless it was absolutely necessary. When I awakened Saturday, I felt like I was alive again; I was excited about my birthday party.

Saturday evening at the Colonel's; I was standing by the table eating some of your little crust with the meat and cream inside when you walked out of the kitchen. That was the moment I knew why I was so excited about my party." Now he lowers his voice and says almost whispering; "So I could see YOU again." More silence, "Angela you still there?" "Yeah" "I thought you might hang up on me. Angela I like you. I haven't thought about or looked at a woman since the last time Theresa went missing; when I saw you at my party I knew why I felt alive again."

I'm thinking real loud to myself, 'You are not the only one Mr. Chapman.' But I say, "Well I'm glad to have been able to help you because you have helped me, so can we say we're even and don't owe each other anything?" Silence.... "Angela I like you." "Mr. Chapman, can we just be friends and leave the emotion **like** out of the equation?" "Woman, why are you afraid to tell me how you feel?" "Look man! Why are you pushing me?" "Angela, let me explain; I am in the Marine Corps. I go on missions that are deadly and may not make it back. I don't have time to play games; life is too short. I really like you and I think you like me too so why can't you say so. I haven't hurt you have I?" "No you haven't." He almost whispers, "Well tell me how you feel about me." "Mr. Chapman" "Malik, Angela; call me Malik." I make a long sigh and then I say, "Well Malik, I really don't know you, but I guess you're a nice guy." Quickly he says, "Ok, ok, I'll take 'a nice guy,' now please; tell me you'll have lunch with me tomorrow. My treat but you have to pick the place; my yellow pages skills aren't that good." He laughs then I laugh thinking about the guys with their brown paper bags at the Brewster Street coffee shop. Then I thought about when we left the Rib Shack and how I wanted to kiss him. Alright, if I'm going to overcome this flesh; I can not keep running. So I say, "What time?" I can hear him smiling as he says, "One thirty good for you?" I reply, "Perfect, how about the Rib

Shack, maybe this time we'll get a chance to eat." "Great, Angela thanks, see you tomorrow." "Ok, bye."

I sat there thinking about him telling me that he likes me and wondered if I'm attracted to him because he's big and strong, um I wonder. Then I started mentally rewinding my dinner date with my Dad as I finished my laundry. While waiting between loads, I went through my events calendar and did some paperwork before I showered and crawled into bed to have my devotion.

I read Colossians 3:1-7 **"if then you were raised with Christ, seek those things which are above, where Christ is, sitting at the right hand of God. Set your mind on things above, not on things on the earth. For you died, and your life is hidden with Christ in God. When Christ who is our life appears, then you also will appear with Him in glory. Therefore put to death your members which are on the earth: fornication, uncleanness, passion, evil desire, and covetousness, which is idolatry. Because of these things the wrath of God is coming upon the sons of disobedience, in which you yourselves once walked when you lived in them."**

I pulled out my Amplified bible and read it again. Verse 5 really ministered to me because I know I must put my sexual immorality to death; I have kept this secret of mine too long, it must be dealt with now. I can not keep avoiding men like Mr. Chapman; I must face the truth and put my flesh to death in order to live a balanced life that's pleasing to the Lord. Now that I am filled I have the power I need to fight and defeat my flesh! Thank You Jesus!

I thought about my father and how I felt safe and relaxed with him at our dinner together. There was a confidence I have never felt before; like I was very unique and valuable, as if I was wanted and my life means something to my Dad. I keep seeing the smile on his face when he told me he was proud of me. How his chest was poked out and his big smile!

I'm remembering how fearful I was of being old and lonely as I sat across from him in the restaurant and I realize I need to allow the Holy Spirit to heal and deliver me of lustful relationships so I will be able to embrace a healthy lasting one. I don't want to become old and lonely and full of regrets.

I'm feeling like an animal trapped in a cage, as I remember how I felt when my Dad made me think past the moment; how he made me take time to consider what I want for my future and how Mr. Chapman made me look inside my heart, to examine why I am so angry.

Maybe that's what the dream meant; him telling me in the tunnel that he had my answer. Maybe that's it! Mr. Chapman has entered this chapter of my life to somehow help me face and deal with my anger towards my father and fear of sleeping with men I find attractive period. That's why they both entered my life at the same time! I projected my being tossed aside by my father into every relationship I've had; thinking I would end up being tossed aside like an odd sock; unwanted, not loved or needed. Mother didn't help by being an example for me when it came to forming a healthy opinion about relationships with men, the way she kept her men friends away from me; she never allowed any of them in the house. You know, I never really saw her interact with a man and I only know of her being serious with only 3 of them, no, 4 including my father. However, she went on a lot of dates.

All my life I have observed my aunts and uncles interact with one another and my married cousins, but being affectionate is part of being married, so I can't really use them as a measuring stick when it comes to how single people are to act in a relationship; seeing someone in a relationship that is not married and not sexually active; that I have not observed, ever! Oh I've watched couples living together interact but a couple not sexually active and having a wholesome relationship.... I don't think...no, I don't recall anyone.... No wonder I lack balance in the interpersonal intimacy department; there has not been a godly example of being single and wholesome for me to pattern after. Mother was very secretive of her men friends, maybe she had high raging hormones like I do; I wonder why she was so evasive around me with her dates.

When I became a teen I thought she didn't want me to get close to her men friends for fear I would get attached to them and she was protecting me because each month there seemed to be a new friend in her life. Now that this has come to my mind, it seems as though she was almost scared to let a man near me.... wonder why she made sure there was distance with me and her dates? She made them always sit in their car in the driveway and wait for her. Most times I would walk her out to their car and have a short; "how are you," conversation and she would tell me when to expect her home and that was it. Usually while she was getting dressed to go out she would tell me where her and her date where going, otherwise she never made conversation about them. The few men she dated a while were always introduced to me at Sunday dinner. Wonder why ...now my curiosity is stirred... I'm going to talk to Aunt Brenda, she knows about Mothers' men friends and she has always told me the truth, what time is it; 8:35 pm let me call her.

"Hello Aunt Brenda, are you busy? I need to talk." "Hey Angie, I'm not busy what's up?" "Well I have been doing some soul searching these last few days, and realize Mother was very cautious about letting her men friends come around me, do you know why?" Silence; I can hear the T.V. in the background, now she's breathing as though she's walking and as the volume in the background disappears, I hear a door close, then she says, "Angie, I was talking to Flora earlier today about De Anne and I'll tell you what I told her; De Anne was a loner and naïve; she wasn't street wise at all. You know when you consider how Flora was when she carried De Anne; it makes a lot of sense.

After daddy died Flora was cautious of speaking her mind so the fear, and insecurity she harbored in her heart, she imparted onto De Anne. By Flora being so promiscuous; De Anne had that same trait. When she met Nichols she was head over heels in love and in the beginning of their relationship; he acted like he was too. Truth is Nichols had no intensions of marrying De Anne and she was too naïve to see it and you would think after Mays, her guard would have been up. After you were born she put all of her energy into saving to buy a house for you. While she spent her last days in the hospital and was able to talk; she told me she bought the house close to the family because she knew she wouldn't live a long life with diabetes so severe, and she wanted you to grow up around us so when she left, we would be your support, and not some man.

Angie after Nichols ....baby you have to understand for almost a year after you were born your mother was in a dark place emotionally. She phoned me almost twice a week talking about ending her life, about how she felt like a failure and her life was meaningless without a man to love her. She was so desperate for love.....she started sleeping around a lot; trying to find out what exactly was wrong with her, you know, why men walked over her heart. She said, she would, what she called "interview" the men she slept with looking for a common statement but sadly, she found none. She confided in me all the time for two reasons. One because she said Flora was so inexperienced at matters of the heart and wouldn't understand her and would probably judge her actions. The other reason was, I was a Registered Nurse at the County Clinic and she would call me to get tested after she had unprotected sex and I would always make sure she was seen as soon as possible. After all she was my baby sister and a diabetic so in my book she was definitely a priority!

Baby; you are grown now so you can handle this, when you were about 7or 8, De Anne met a man by the name of Grant. Now mind you he was the first man she loved after Nichols and again, you would have thought after her experience with Mays and Nichols; she would have taken notes but she just went gaga over tall strong men. I think she never had Daddy to hold her like me Shirley and Flora did and she jumped; no, she leaped into the arms of the first man that paid attention to her. Anyway, she dated Grant for a few weeks and invited him to Sunday dinner so we could all meet him. She was so eager about the family meeting him, I mean she was all animated; she thought he was "the one;" anyway all of us women were in the kitchen warming up the food. When the doorbell rang, she almost jumped out of her skin running to the front door.

We were at Shirley's that Sunday for dinner and Henry went to answer the door and De Anne told him

Grant was her friend and she had invited him to dinner. Well, Henry said all of you little ones went running to the door and was standing there watching the new comer as he entered and jokingly Mr. Grant said, "De Anne you didn't tell me you had so many children." De Anne replied, "Oh Mr. Grant I only have one tax deduction, this one is mine, her name is Angela. Say hi Angie to Mr. Grant." Mr. Grant takes a step towards you and bends down and says, "Hi there little Angie." Now Henry said the man looked at you like a dog looks at a bone and he looked at De Anne and she was looking at you, not Mr. Grant so he yells for Lester, Odell and Howard to come to the door and tells all of you kids to go to the living room and sit down. Mr. Grant stood up and looked at Henry and knew Henry saw the look on his face and started backing up, out of the house.

By the time your uncles all made it to the front door, Henry had stepped outside following Mr. Grant and was yelling at him, telling him if he ever saw him in the neighborhood again, it would be his last day to live. When Henry told Howard about the look on Mr. Grant's face, Howard ran up to Mr. Grant's car and yanked on the door handle yelling at him to open the door. Mr. Grant tried to back his car up and leave but by then Lester picked up a stick and was banging on his window. Odell went to his own car and got his gun, and by this time De Anne had walked out on the front steps and was screaming and hollering she had no idea what had just happened.

By now all of us ladies were at the front porch and I ran and pulled De Anne up onto the porch with us. Mr. Grant hit a few cars parked, and finally took off. After all the guys walked up on the porch Henry told us what happened. De Anne called Henry a liar and said

Mr. Grant would never harm you. Howard said he could spot a pervert a mile away being a teacher, he's seen his share and; what had just left was definitely a pervert. He told De Anne if he caught that man anywhere near her or any child in that house; he was going to jail because he would kill Mr. Grant dead. De Anne ran in the house and grabbed her purse and was going to leave and I grabbed her and held her in my arms and told her it was not her fault. Henry was mad, he loved children and his anger was at Mr. Grant not at her. She cried so hard in my arms and told me she really liked him and she was a terrible judge of character; first Mays then Nichols and now Mr. Grant. After that De Anne brought every man she was serious about to Sunday dinner with the family first, and then she dated them.

Angie a few years later we saw Mr. Grant on the news, he was being arrested for child molestation. De Anne phoned her brothers and brother in laws and apologized to each one of them because she would be in jail had Mr. Grant done anything to her baby. When she was in the hospital she told me she thought about taking her own life several times especially after Henry made her feel so stupid and small about Mr. Grant. She really loved Mays and he robbed her, she loved Nichols like she never knew anyone could ever love, and he left her pregnant and she really liked Mr. Grant and he was perverted. She felt like she would never have a good man in her life and thought about just ending it right then. She didn't take her meds for a few days hoping to never awake again.

What stopped her was you; she remembered how angry she was finding out Daddy had taken his life and the hurt she felt so deeply-seated; and oh the guilt and humiliation attached to a family member after suicide;

she didn't want you to feel the pains of it, so she made up her mind that the men she would meet from then on would have to succumb to Sunday dinners with her family because she didn't have enough discernment when it came to matters of her heart.

You know she called me after her and Ziegler broke up. She told me that Flora casually mentioned to her while leaving church one Sunday that she had been worried about her and asked if she was doing alright. De Anne said she was tired of Ziegler never contributing anything to whatever they did. The movies, ice cream, gas in the car; he never volunteered a penny and she was opening her eyes to his antics; when Flora asked her if she was alright she said that was the confirmation she needed to end their relationship.

Our next Sunday dinner she told him in the front yard of Shirley's house to leave and never come back she'd had it with him. She said he looked at her and said; "OK" turned and walked away. The very next holiday after she broke up with Ziegler, we were all together and I pulled her aside and asked why she didn't have a date and she told me after Ziegler she realized she didn't need companionship that badly and made up in her mind she would be single in every sense of the word; and she was, from that day on. She told me once her mind was made up to be content with singleness; she was fine. She prayed and asked for strength to stay single but it never was a struggle after her mind was made up. You know I just remembered when she was in the hospital and it was my turn with her; I asked her if she had any regrets about her life and she told me she wished she had more children because you were a blessing to her."

As Aunt Brenda was talking I was envisioning Mother saying and doing all of the things she was talking about and tears were dripping down onto my pajama top; I missed my mother so much. I thanked my aunt for taking time for me, and then she told me that everybody was doing some soul searching after Sunday's dinner. We all need to get an understanding of not only what happened; but why. Aunt Brenda prayed for me over the phone and when she commanded I surrender to the Holy Spirit as He instructs me on becoming whole and complete, so that I may be found by my husband; her words leaped in my heart. After I thanked her, I told her how much I appreciated and loved her before we ended our conversation.

Her words about me being complete were ringing loud in my mind. I sat there and began to think..... Now that I know Mother was fighting to keep her own flesh under subjection and my Father now regrets not being in my childhood; I feel as though I need to take responsibility for who I am. I have been running for a long time and now I'm willing to trust the Holy Spirit who I claim lives in me; to have his way. I must allow Him to instruct and direct me as to where I need to grow.

I thought about the school system and how we are tested to see what areas we need to study more; for us to improve in. Then I thought the Holy Spirit teaches us the same way. The Word of God we hear abides in us and must be tested so we will know where we are weak and pray for strength and understanding, then, when we are tested again, hopefully, we pass. Thinking about it this way seems doable to me; yeah, I can do this! I can do all things through Christ.

I am so glad my father has come into my life now; deep down in my heart I want him to be a part of my life. I love my uncles and really do feel as though they took the place of my father while I was growing up, but

I like the feeling that came over my heart when he called me "daughter." And to think I can talk to him like Dora does Uncle Howard, and how protected she always feels when it comes to her Daddy; now it's my turn to have that same comfort in knowing my Daddy has my back. Lord I thank You for my healing! I'm going to call him tomorrow just to see how he's doing.

I feel the presence of the Lord so strong, I began praying in the spirit and I read from the Amplified Romans 8:1 **"Therefore, [there is] now no condemnation (no adjudging guilty of wrong) for those who are in Christ Jesus, who live [and] walk not after the dictates of the flesh, but after the dictates of the Spirit."**

I fell asleep knowing I was blessed to be loved by God, my Dad and my family. I went to sleep with a smile on my face and woke up with a smile; I felt so renewed.

CHAPTER EIGHT

Taking "The Test"
You go Dora!

TUESDAY:

After my morning ritual I went shopping for Thursday Friday and Saturday's menus. I didn't get back home until after noon so I put up everything and left for the Rib Shack to meet Mr. Chapman. It was 1:20 when I stepped out of my truck and as soon as I closed the door; up pulls Mr. Chapman right in front of me, next to my parking spot. He gets out with Bible in hand and I was trying to remember if he told me to bring mine or not when he says, "Good afternoon Angela, how are you today?" He was smiling so big I thought he had something up his sleeve. As I walk towards his bumper, I tilt my head and I peer at him and ask, "What's up Mr. Chapman? What exactly is this meeting about?" I stopped at the foot of his car and he walked up to me, still smiling and says, "Angela why does something have to be up; can't I be happy to see you?" He puts his hand in my back and guides me into the Rib Shack. I keep my eyes on him and he is almost laughing at me. I know something is up and, I'm sure to figure it out if I keep watching him.

We entered the Rib Shack and he looks around for a table facing the door and counter just as before. He spots a booth extends his hand out towards it and says, "After you." I sit and hold onto my purse in case I have to leave suddenly; he's acting strange. He sits across from me and starts laughing as he puts his Bible on top of the table. I ask, "What's so funny, share the punch line!" He leans in towards me and says, "Angela, you still don't trust me do you?" I don't think that's funny and say, "You think it's funny I don't trust men I don't know Mr. Chapman?" I raise my eyebrow and give him a look. He gets serious and says, "I am sorry if I gave you that impression. I don't think it's funny, I think it's very cautious of you. Please, do accept my apology." I nod and say to him, "Apology accepted." We sit staring at each other and he breaks the silence saying, "Angela you look nice, I like that color on you." "Thanks Mr. Chapman." "Can you call me Malik? This is the second time here; can we make it official that I'll be Malik? Huh, can we do that?" He smiles and I think, 'he is so fine, and why does he have to smell so good!' ....I look at his thick arms and began to eye him and think, 'Ok, this is the test Angela, let's pass it.' So I say yes, but my heart is racing so fast I am afraid he'll end up hurting me.

He asks if I know what I want to eat. I tell him the chicken lunch and lemonade. He gets this real serious look on his face and says he'll be right back. I felt like I was in trouble again; I don't know why he makes me feel like I'm in trouble. I'm sitting here trying to figure out what it is about him that intimidates me; he returns. He slides back up against the wall and looks at me again. Ok I've had enough so I blurt; "Mr. Chapman, you said you don't play games so what's with this making me feel like I'm in trouble." I lean in towards him and get a little loud because I'm irritated, and I continue, "Let me tell you again, you're not going to make me feel intimidated just because you are a big tall man; I'm not afraid of you, you got that!"

As if I never said anything, he tilts his head a little and says, "I thought we agreed you were going to call me Malik." He leans in towards me and continues, "Look Angela, I honestly don't want to intimidate you that is not my intension." "Well Malik, just what are you trying to prove?" He scoots in real close to me, never taking his eyes from mine and speaks, pausing after each group of words and says, "That you can trust me... (Pause) ... that I'll never hurt you... (Pause) ...I will always protect you... (Pause) ...and... (Pause)... I'm in love with you." My eyes got so big and my forehead automatically went to wrinkles; I sat there and stared into his eyes to see if he was joking, but his look was so penetrating, I felt as though he could see right through me.

He didn't blink nor move and I felt as though we were the only two people in the room; then I felt uncomfortable because I desperately wanted to be held by him. I throw up both hands as I shake my head no and say, "Man you don't know me. Are you crazy Mr. Chapman do you go around telling women that line all the time? Are you just looking for some stupid desperate woman to jump in bed with you?" He sits there, staring at me.

Then I thought 'what is it about me.' And I leaned in towards him and asked, "Mr. Chapman I want to ask you a very serious question and please, please be honest with me, please." He shakes his head yes. "What is it about me that make you think I'm easy?" I look directly into his eyes to watch for any indication of a lie. He never moves or blinks and says, "Angela there is nothing about you that reads easy." I start sliding out of the booth to leave and say, "If you're not going to be honest with me Mr. Chapman; I'm out of here." "Angela... I think the question is; why do you think you're easy?" I was almost standing up but I halt in mid air. I turn my head to look at him. He's looking in my eyes and I feel as if he can read me; look right at my soul.

I remember the dream; the part he asks me why was I running, he had my answer, and I sit back down and feel tears coming. I swallow and blink back the tears and slide on the bench towards him. He slides up close to me and here comes the waitress with our order. Never taking his eyes from mine, he thanks the waitress; I'm sitting here again feeling like I'm in the 3rd grade. As I blink back tears I decide to tell him the truth. "Mr. Chapman, I have poor judgment when it comes to men and relationships. I end up in their bed and then left alone." I'm trying to read his face and I'm holding my breath waiting for a response. He bows his head and blesses the food and as he reaches for his plate, he says to me, "How do you feel now that you've told me the truth." I look down at the table trying to find the emotion I feel, I no longer feel like crying so, very slowly I say, "I feel good, now that I've told you the truth, and yet, I'm not sure I can trust you." Then I look up at him to see his reaction to what I just said.

I keep looking at him. He has started eating a rib and when he looks up at me I move my eyes away. Not wanting him to see me looking at him, I slowly peek at him out of the corner of my eye. He's licking his fingers and glances around the room, and then at me, so I ask him point blank, "Do you think I'm cheap now that I've told you the truth?" He chews what he has in his mouth, wipes it and grabs my hand and says, "Angela, I think you are beautiful, passionate and can cook your butt off. I never see or think of you as cheap or easy." I'm looking at him intensely and can not determine any lying. He's looking directly at me and gets that serious look again, the look that intimidates me, and he lets go of my hand. I point my finger at him and say, "There, that look right there, why do you look at me like that?" He puts his elbow up on the table and makes a fist with his hand and lightly pounds on his mouth a few times and his eyes are bouncing around on the table as if he's contemplating what he's about to say to me. He clears his throat and removes his hand from his mouth and leans in close to me, looks me in the eyes and says, "Angela [pause] I am a man. You are very sexy and that's all I'm going to say. Ok" ... It took me a minute to compute what he meant. Now I'm embarrassed and he leans back pushes his plate away and looks around the room.

Now I'm looking away from him. I hear him as he unzips his Bible cover and I turn towards him to see what he's doing. He says, "I made up my mind last night I was going to tell you today that I'm in love with you, and when I saw you in the parking lot I was so happy today was the day; I couldn't stop smiling. I didn't mean to upset you." He looks at me, smiles and says, "Angela I'm happy," He hunches his shoulders and continues to say, "I'm in love." He pulled out a sheet of paper from his Bible and held it up between two fingers and says, "Now I want you to read these scriptures while I'm gone and the next time I see you, I'm going to ask you some questions." He stops smiling and says, "Now Angela this is not an order, I don't want to make you do anything, but these scriptures are very important. OK?" I put my hand up to take them from him and sigh; "Ok Mr. Chapman." He pulls his hand away from me to keep me from taking the paper from him and I look dead in his eyes with puzzlement. He says, "I just told you I'm in love with you and still you call me Mr. Chapman." He breaks out in a smile and I smile back as I snatch the paper from his hand.

As I put the paper down on the table, I'm thinking, 'wow, how strong he is yet, there's something so sweet about him also.' I slowly look up into his eyes, ooh help me Lord! He can't finish his food and I never touched mine, for some strange reason I'm not the least bit hungry; neither one of us can eat. There's such a soft, gentle look in his eyes; I'm almost embarrassed to look at him. I feel so sexy now and I need to pass this test; I think I might like Mr. Chapman but I need to make sure this is not lust. I put my hand on his and say, "Malik, I really am sorry for thinking you were trying to intimidate me. I think I trust you a teeny bit now. Do you accept my apology?" He moved his hand from mine and said real softly, "Yes Angela." Man I want to kiss him! I look away from his eyes and see the paper, so I pick it up, fold it and put it in my purse then I pushed my plate to the side and he put his plate on mine and got up and threw the food in the trash. I watched him as he walked back to our booth, he looked at his watch and picked up the cups and asked me if I wanted the rest of my lemonade. I told him no thanks and stood up; I guess he has to go. He turned around and walked back to the trash and threw away the cups and walked back to the booth to get his Bible.

I felt as though he was troubled; he was moving real slow and his eyes were almost racing around the room. I could tell he was not observing his surroundings, this time he was thinking intently. When he walked up to me I put my hand on his chest to make him pause and asked him what was wrong. He stood there looking at me with that look and grabbed my hand and moved it to his side. He shook his head "no" and gently gave my hand a squeeze and led the way out of the building straight to the door of my truck and he let my hand go. He bent down almost to my ear and said, "Angela, for the first time in over 2 years I have a reason to come back from a mission. I didn't care if I lived or died before; now I want to come back to you. Baby I love you; don't forget that." He stood straight up and walked to his car door and placed both elbows on top of his car twirling his keys in his hand and say, "I'll call you as soon as I can."

As I opened the door to my truck I fought hard not to turn and run to him and kiss him; I was so scared I might not ever see him again. When my door was completely open; I turned around and looked at him, he was still standing there watching me and twirling his keys; I slightly raised my voice and said to him, "Mr. Chapman, you better make sure my Malik comes back to me. You hear me!" He breaks out with a full smile and shakes his head yes!

When I reached the end of the parking lot I looked at him in my rearview mirror and waved. I can't tell if the smile on my face made my heart feel warm or if my heart being warmed caused the smile on my face; whichever came first I'm liking this! I really like Malik and this time it's different I didn't kiss him, I passed part one of the test, I did it! Thank You Jesus! Now I remember when we were standing at my truck the first time, when I wanted to kiss him and he told me 'this is why we must meet publicly,' this is the first time a man my heart skips a beat for, has told me that he loves me; and I know he respects me. Holy Spirit You are awesome! Bring my man back to me safe and protect him from all harm. Wow what a blessing it is to walk in obedience. I thanked and praised the Lord all the way home.

I went in the garage and took inventory for Thursday and made a note to order the table cloths I need for Saturday's wedding reception. 5:45 pm the house phone rings. Hello; "Hey, I'm on my way; I'll be there in a minute, bye." It's Dora and I know it's about Parker so I go in the house and make us a garden salad and put on a pot of water for tea. I want to hear everything.

She comes in the back door and I look at her and see her smiling so big. I smile back at her and walk over to a kitchen chair and pull it out for her to sit. She blinks her eyes as if she's flirting and strolls over to the table and acts like she's going to sit down but she springs up and does her little shimmy and screams "OOHH Angie, let me tell you what happened!" We stand at the table and she starts. "I went to work this morning and he was in the employee parking lot waiting for me to pull up. I didn't notice him until I stepped out of my car and he was standing next to my bumper. I nearly jumped out of my skin and he apologized for startling me. As he walks towards me, he lifts both hands half up, as if to stop me from running from him, and says, 'Dorinda, I need you to listen to me; I really like you, I have for as long as I've known you. I'm a little nervous because you're so beautiful.

I've watched you to see if you had a boyfriend but I can't tell because so many guys call you, I want to take you to the movies and get to know you. If you don't date coworkers I'm willing to transfer to another location. Dorinda, please give me your answer.' I stepped up to him and said, "Parker, I will be honored to go to the movies with you. I apologize for the delay in my answer, but I was totally taken aback when you asked me." I tilted my head and asked, "What are you referring to when you say a lot of guys call me?" He says, "You know, Ernest, Karl and Howard. I hear you mention their names often, so I thought they were friends of yours." Angie, I was so mad at him, I poked him in the chest and severely said, "Parker do you think I'm a loose woman? Is that why you want to go to the movies with me?"

I think if he had said yeah; I would have punched him in the eye. He says, 'No! Dorinda I know you're a spirit filled woman and I'm spirit filed and I think we are very compatible; in fact we might be soul mates. I would never take advantage of you and would defend your honor. I just can't figure out why you talk to all those guys on the phone. But, I thought if you talked to them, maybe I had a chance with you.' Believing him; I back off from being in his face and after a few moments I say, "Parker, Ernest and Howard are my brothers and Karl is my cousin. We are a very close family and there are a lot of us. That's what you get for eave dropping in on my conversations." I smiled and he smiled as though he were relieved. Then he says, "Let's walk and talk we don't want to be late. What types of movies interest you?" So we're walking and talking as we get into the office, and I notice the whole office is staring at us. I'm thinking what's their trip?

Girl; later I'm in the restroom and I hear two women coming in talking and one says do you really think they spent the night together? And the other one goes well I know I would jump at the chance to sleep with Parker, he's fine and a good man too. The other one says I hear you; I'd be on that myself. Angie, after I washed my hands; I stood there to see who these hefa's were; putting me in Parker's bed, and I wanted them to see me, I was mad as fire. They opened their stall doors to come out and took one look at me and froze looking like the cat that ate the canary! I told them; "Not that it's any of your business; I don't sleep with men that are not my husband. And Parker is my man and you both had better stay from around him. You got that!" I twirled around and strolled out of the restroom.

Girl I went to my desk and sat down, I couldn't believe what I had just done. I felt so empowered, I got up and marched over to Parker's desk and told him I wanted to go to "The Hat" for a pastrami sandwich today for lunch and he said, "Ok, I'll come get you at 12:30." Angie we went to lunch and talked and laughed.

He is so nice and he's not nerdy like I thought. He was very comfortable with me and told me I was his soul mate and we were going to be married some day. He said it in a jokingly way but he checked out my reaction to what he said. I stopped laughing and looked him in his eyes and said, "Oh, you think so do you!" He nodded and said very seriously, "Yeah, me thinks so!" I told him he would have to pass my father and brother test first and Angie he smiled so big. He really likes me and.... I really like him; isn't that crazy!"

As I stand here looking into her eyes, I feel her happiness, like I'm sharing the emotion with her. I can't believe Dora is in love and the man is spirit filled! I ask, "Well did you give him your cell number so he can call you tonight?" As she shakes her head yes she says, "Yep he asked for it while he walked me to my car after work. Angie I'm so happy." She reaches out for me and I reach out for her and we lock foreheads and tears of joy are running down both our faces as I tell her that I'm so happy for her!

We sit down to eat and still I'm not hungry. I just drink my tea. She asked why I wasn't eating. I told her that I had a love story too. I had lunch at the Rib Shack with Malik, or rather I looked at my lunch at the Rib Shack; and I told her everything that happened. Dora and I both sat there with napkins crying because she knows how much it means to me to have a man I am interested in, to be first to tell me that he loves me. After we cried her cell rang and it was Parker. I kissed her on the cheek and let her out. I stood in the driveway watching her smiling as she talked looking so happy. I have never seen Dora glow as brightly as she is today.

I cleaned up the kitchen and get another phone call, this time it's Dad and we talk for hours about what his favorite foods were and mine; we did comparisons the whole time we talked. I found out so much of what I like, he does too. I also realized my temper comes from both him and Mother. She was quick to blow; short fused, but Dad takes a lot before he blows; but once he's mad it must be dealt with because he does not back down. He says he's just realizing his temper needs some taming and, he's allowing the Holy Spirit to teach him how.

Before we finished our conversation, his tone turned very serious and he began explaining to me that his sister, my Aunt Bernadine, has emphysema very bad and she wants him to take me to her house this Sunday for dinner; she wants to see me and promises to cook if I come over. I told him I would go to dinner with them but she didn't have to cook we could go out. She doesn't need to go through the trouble of cooking since she's not doing well. He said he would talk to her and see if she would agree to that and get back with me. I told him that I loved him and had learned a lot about myself through him and thanked him for having the wisdom to bring us together as father and daughter.

Later, after I read my scripture, I prayed for Malik, and before I went to bed, I put on some worship music and invited the presence of the Lord. I worshipped the Lord and thanked Him for the great and marvelous things He had done in my life thus far; and for working in me.

WEDNESDAY:

Today I still had the spirit of worship on me when I awakened and I was led to meditate on Psalms 139, the whole chapter. My heart leaped within me as I read verse 14 thru 16; **"I will praise You, for I am fearfully** and wonderfully made; Marvelous are Your Works, And that my soul knows very well."**

I thought about how God purposefully made me to look like my Dad and how He knew my looking like my Dad would be the fuel to melt the ice around my heart against him for not wanting me to be born! Wow, Holy Ghost, You really know ALL Things!! (15) **"My frame was not hidden from You, When I was made in secret, And skillfully wrought in the lowest parts of the earth."**

This verse made me think about how God knew my father would not want me to be born and how family members encouraged Mother to have me and, I was hidden from my father for 26 years yet not from the Lord because He provided the support Mother needed to raise me without a father figure in our home, how great You truly are!

And verse 16 really spoke volumes to me; **"Your eyes saw my substance, being yet unformed. And in Your book they all were written, the days fashioned for me, when as yet there were none of them."** The revelation came to me how God saw my overactive appetite for sex when He fashioned me in Mother's womb, yet His grace was sufficient enough to cover me until **I was able** to desire a handle on it; with His help. My heart felt the love God has for me, even during my weakness, and I felt so much love for the Lord; Him dying for me to set me free while I was yet a sinner! I worshipped from the very depths of my heart.... I cried and hugged my bible so tight knowing Jesus is the Word; it was like hugging Jesus and telling Him how desperately I love Him...my devotion lasted for almost 2 hours. I felt like I was floating when I came out of my bedroom, how I appreciate the Holy Spirit! After breakfast, I made my confirmation calls and baked the cakes for Saturday and put them in the freezer and then I did all my prep work for tomorrow. By 4:30 pm I was done. I talked to Aunt Flora and Dora and told them I would be able to attend Bible Study tonight. I took a long hot bath while listening to some Gospel music and changed for church. As I looked into my purse for my truck keys; I moved everything around inside my purse, trying to find my lipstick and saw the piece of paper Malik had given me at the Rib Shack and I put it on the table thinking 'when I get home from Bible Study I'll read the scriptures tonight as my devotion.'

I arrived at church ten minutes early and was surprised to see Dora standing outside talking on her cell phone; smiling and glowing. One look at her face and I knew it was Parker on the other end and she's got the 'Love Jones' bad! I smile and wave at her and keep walking because I know she doesn't want to talk with me standing out here looking in her mouth. As I step pass her she says, "Hold on; hey Angie where you goin?" I stop and turn around and point towards the church. She puts her index finger up at me and says into the phone, "OK, make a left, alright, now you should see me in a few moments standing in front of the church." I realize she's giving Parker directions and I'm glad I made it tonight. "I see you; make a left into the parking lot. Ok." She closes her cell phone and smiles at me. We hug and she says, "That was Parker. Angie I'm so nervous he's going to meet the family and if they don't like him I don't know what I'm going to do; I'm so in love with this man!" I rub her arm and tell her, "Dora everything is going to be fine; if he loves you we'll know it, quit worrying." As we stand there waiting for Parker, she has wrinkles on her forehead and is fidgeting with her cell.

Parker arrives and he has a grin from one ear to the other and; sees no one but Dora standing here; as he's walking up to her, he places his Bible under his arm and extends both his hands out for both of hers. "Dorinda, am I making you late?" She shakes her head 'no' as she places her hands in his, palms down, she smiles and does her little shimmy. She slightly pulls him towards me and introduces us; "Langston this is my cousin Angie but we are more like sisters. Angie; meet Langston Parker." She looks at him smiling, then she turns to look at me, her smile is gone and she's reading my face as I move my eyes towards him, I notice his hand is extended to me so I oblige him with a handshake and say, "It's nice to meet you, is it Langston or Parker?" He smiles as he looks directly into my eyes and says, "Parker is fine." I direct my eyes back to Dora and raise my eyebrow and smile as I nod my head yes. She breaks out in the most glowing smile as she grabs hold of his arm and directs him up the steps and into the church. I follow right behind them; I don't want to miss the reactions from the pews when Dora walks in on the arm of a man! This is waay better than pay per view!

Now the order to Wednesday Night Bible Study is as follows: promptly at 7:30 pm the choir enters into the sanctuary from the back prayer room, which is on the right side of the platform. They enter in the order of singing sections beginning with the Sopranos then Altos and last are the Tenors. The last choir member to enter is the choir director and as soon as she steps up onto the platform whichever Pastor is teaching walks up to the podium and that's the congregations cue to stand for prayer. While prayer is going forth no one is permitted to enter the sanctuary so everyone hurries to get into the sanctuary before the choir director enters.

Sister Sadie Jones who everybody calls Sister Sadie is one of our ushers and she; like all of the ushers are very friendly but, Sister Sadie smiles real big and makes sure everyone being seated gets her personal eye contact, even if 10 people are waiting to be seated; no one moves until she has everyone's eye contact, then she says, "This way please," as she turns around to escort you to your pew. Well, not tonight; Dora and Parker walks up arm in arm and Sister Sadie turns to greet the attendee with her big smile and sees its Dora with Parker and right away her smile drops as she notices their arms are locked. Her eyes bulge and began a ping pong match. She looks at Dora then Parker; Dora then Parker, back and forth. Dora says to her, "I left my purse and Bible earlier on my pew Sister Sadie; can you seat us please." Sister Sadie starts walking backwards still playing ping pong with her eyes. After a few steps Dora slips her arm away from Parker's and places each of her hands on top of Sister Sadie's shoulders and turns her around. While Dora is turning her around; her ushering skills kicked in and she broke out with her enormous usher smile.

I decide to let Dora and Parker go ahead of me; I'll sit **behind** Dora tonight; I want to observe everyone's reactions. As I stand in the door way, I scan the room and see Sister Spivey; the first Soprano, entering the platform and she does a double take; walking and watching Dora with her arm attached to Parkers' as they walk to the pew. Sister Spivey is now half way down the back row and she slows down as her jaw drops. She now turns her whole body to face the congregation. She has come to a complete stop; she is maybe 5 chairs away from her seat and has stopped choir traffic. Like dominos, each choir member steps up onto the platform and turns their head to see what Sister Spivey is hypnotized by. Now my eyes are focused on Aunt Brenda as she turns to look behind her to see what has stopped the choir. She does a double take herself as her jaw drops and she hits Uncle Odell on the leg. He turns his head slightly and when he sees Dora; he turns all the way around and commences to stare.

Now Sister Sadie has reached the pew, she extends her hand out for Dora and Parker to be seated. Her eyes are still on their ping pong game and she drops her hand and stands there and joins Uncle Odell and Aunt Brenda staring. I glance back to Aunt Brenda and Uncle Odell and notice they both are now on their knees on the pew and are holding on tightly to the top; with both their mouths wide open!

Dora bends down and shoves her Bible and purse over making room for Parker and it looks like some space for me also. Parker is following her lead as he stands there watching her so he will know what to do. Uncle Odell is so into Dora and Parker; his eyes are wide as he stares with puzzlement at Parker's face; like he wants to reach out and touch him to see if he's real. Then I notice Aunt Flora and Uncle Lester and Uncle Howard's rows, and they are all standing up and turned facing towards Dora and Parker. Just then there comes a big loud 'THUMP' and everyone turns to look towards the choir stand just as Daryl Judson, or as we call him behind his back, "Chunky DJ"; one of the lead tenors; is also looking towards Dora with his mouth open and all of the choir members in front and back of him are trying to lift his heavy behind up off the floor.

I'm still standing in the doorway waiting for Sister Sadie to come seat me and I have my hand over my mouth, hugging my Bible, almost hunched over laughing! I watch Aunt Rose Marie and Uncle Howard as they both inch their way next to Dora. Aunt Brenda and

Uncle Odell are still holding onto the top of the pew, staring at Parker as if he's an animated Mannequin. Dora pulls Parker close to her and turns to Uncle Howard and Aunt Rose Marie and introduces them. As Parker reaches his hand out to shake Uncle Howard's hand, Dora steps behind him and looks back at me and motions for me to come sit. "We seem to have a very important visitor tonight. I hope my teaching will be remembered with the same relevance." States Pastor Anderson over the microphone. This calls the congregation to order and everyone takes their places for the service. Sister Sadie passes me as I go sit next to Dora; she raises her eyebrows at me and smiles. While prayer is taking place Dora elbows me and when I look at her to see what's up; she is smiling and gives me the OK sign with her fingers and does her little shimmy again. I am so happy for her, Parker is so handsome.

He's about 6 feet tall, caramel complexion with a strong square shaped dimpled chin, slanted dark brown eyes covered with a pair of brown Kam Dhillon eye glasses and a nice grade of hair with short shinny twists and long side burns. He is built like he lifts weights and is dressed in a light and dark brown short sleeved two piece linen slack set with dark brown Sperry Top-Siders and, he's carrying a black eel skinned Bible cover.

The lesson taught tonight was from Proverbs 3: 1-8 and did Pastor Anderson break it down for us! He began with the condition of our heart and told us if we don't enter the presence of the Lord with a heart to receive; we might as well stay home and watch television because the Lord's vision for our life will never be made manifested to us. Then he taught us the importance of allowing mercy and truth to be bound around our neck becoming magnets, drawing to us favor and understanding and allowing them to flow through us; to others and God. The part that really pricked my heart was when he said we are to allow ourselves to trust in the Lord and stop leaning towards our carnal thinking.

Pastor Anderson urged us to seriously acknowledge the plans the Lord has for us before we make any decisions that will affect us; that way we will be stressed less and healthier in all areas; physically, mentally and spiritually. He took time explaining when we are faced with any dilemma; we will become strengthened and confident, knowing God will direct us in the direction He has for us.

I listened attentively to the message thinking about how I need to be more trusting when it comes to the plans God has for me; and stop thinking I'm so wise in my carnal thinking. That hit home with me! Because I realized I don't think about a future with a husband and kids and, with my sex drive; I definitely need to be married. I'm so busy keeping busy, I have never once stopped to consider the plans the Lord has for my future, not once. Geez was my eyes opened!

Before we were dismissed Pastor Anderson asked if the visitors had any remarks, and Parker stood. He spoke loud and clear, as he told us he attends Greater Grace Westside; Pastor Blevins White and First Lady Loretta White were the overseers. Pastor Anderson thanked him and made a remark about his stopping choir traffic will probably be talked about more than his bible teaching. Most the congregation chuckled, and there were a few "amens" then we were all dismissed.

As everyone huddles in around us watching Dora and Parker, a pin could be heard dropping as Dora grabs her things and Parker's hand and off they go pushing me out to the isle and on out the church doors, right into the parking lot where he walks her to her car and closes her door for her, then he walks over to his BMW X6 and in a few moments, he's pulling out of the lot, right behind Dora. The whole church was standing there watching until his car is out of sight; then we scramble to our own vehicles and head home with some good Word and juicy gossip; church don't get better than this!

Before I get out of the parking lot my phone rings, its Dora. "Well, what you think cuz?" "I think you have been found to be Parker's good thing and Dora; I am sooo happy for you; you deserve nothing but blessings!" "Oh Angie thanks so much, your opinion carries a lot of weight with me. That's my other line; oh its Mom, I love you and I'll talk to you tomorrow after I get off work, bye." Click. I am smiling so big, Dora is in love and she's being loved.

I remember once when we were 14; Marvin Hamilton followed her around everywhere she went and she acted like he was invisible, when I asked her why didn't she talk to him, she told me she was going to fall in love one time and the Lord was going to bless her for keeping her eyes on Him. Tonight I saw her words come to life and my heart is filled with happiness for her; 26 and still a virgin, she deserves all the love and favor coming her way. When I pulled up into my driveway Ernest, Dora's baby brother was parked there waiting for me.

There are 15 of us cousins and Dora, me, Kozette and Ernest are the youngest, and the rest of the cousins are older than us; they range from 46 years old, on down to Connie being 33. Then there is a seven year gap; Dora and myself, 26, Kozette, 23 then Ernest, 20.

So I feel sorry for him being the youngest of us all and the male cousin closest to him is Bernard and he's 34; Howard Jr.; his older brother is 38 and teases him about being the baby a lot. I locked my truck and walked over to his and he rolled down his window and says, "Cuz I need to talk to you, got a minute?" I reply, "Always for you come on in."

He followed me inside to the kitchen, pulled out a chair and sat in it backwards with his arms on the back of the chair and he watches me as I sit down close to him. My eyes are glued to his and he says, "Angie I need some money can you give it to me and I work for you later and pay you back?" "Ernest how much money do you need?" He replies "$200 dollars." I continue, "I work hard for my money and anyone that works for me has to be willing to work hard too." As I look at Ernest, I realize he wants me to give him the money, he didn't offer to work first, then get paid, so I say to him, "You won't be 21 until when, November, so you can't serve drinks and that's where you can make good money because all of the tips are yours. If you want to work set up and clean up you have to work with Bobby Ray; if you want to work as a waiter you have to work with Willie and let me tell you; they don't want to look bad and will only work with people that want to work. Now you think about that and call me tomorrow before 2 pm and I'll give you one of their numbers but Ernest, you have got to be serious because if you think you're family and I will cut you some slack; you are dead wrong, so you'd better think hard ok?"

"Man Angie, you sound like I have to work on a chain gang; are you a hard task master?" I softly sock him on the arm and say, "You better believe it!" Then I give him a smile. He looks serious, lowers his head and stares at the floor; so I lean in towards him and asks,

"What's going on Ernest?" Seriously he replies, "Angie if I tell you, promise you won't tell daddy." I sit up straight and look at him until he gives me eye contact and say, "I can't do that; it sounds serious, and, if I think it's something Uncle Howard should know, Ernest, I'll tell him and I'll tell him while you're still sitting here. So whatever it is, you were man enough to get to this place; and you've got to be man enough to take what comes." "Alright Angie, I'll think about what you said and call you tomorrow." I told him, "If you call after 2 pm I won't be able to get you uniformed and no uniform; no job." He gently smiles and says, "Man Angie, you so hard." "Ernest; life is hard." He gets up and pulls the chair back in the position he found it and I stand up and grab him and give him a good hug and tell him, "If we learn to consult the Lord in everything we do, we won't get into so much hot water," and I let him go. After I walk him to the door, I lock up and get ready for bed.

I have my devotion and turn off the light to get some sleep when I remembered Malik had given me some scriptures and I will be busy until Sunday so, I turned the light back on and headed to the kitchen, got the paper he gave me and went back to bed. I prayed for him; that the Lord would keep him and those with him safe and unharmed. Then I unfolded the paper and noticed he had written a note in handwriting that looked like chicken scratch. I thought, 'wonder if he's a doctor, this looks like a prescription.' After maybe 10 minutes, I was able to make out what it was; it read:

> Angela please read the following in this order; after you're done you'll know why, Malik.

So I pulled out the Amplified and read the scriptures in order. #1) Genesis 2:18 **"Now the Lord God said, it is not good (sufficient, satisfactory) that** the man should be alone; I will make him a helper meet (suitable, adapted, complementary) for him." #2) Genesis 29:10, 11, 20 "When Jacob saw Rachel daughter of Laban, his mother's brother, and the sheep of Laban his uncle, Jacob went near and rolled the stone from the well's mouth and watered the flock of his uncle Laban. Then Jacob kissed Rachel and he wept aloud. And Jacob served seven years for Rachel; and they seemed to him but a few days because of the love he had for her." #3) Genesis 34:3 "But his soul longed for and clung for Dinah Jacob's daughter, and he loved the girl and spoke comfortingly to her young heart's wishes." #4) I Corinthians 7:6-9 "But I am saying this more as a matter of permission and concession, not as a command or regulation. I wish that all men were like I myself am [in this matter of self- control]. But each has his own special gift from God, one of this kind and one of another. But to the unmarried people and to the widows, I declare that it is well (good, advantageous, expedient and wholesome) for them to remain [single] even as I do. But if they have not self-control (restraints of their passions), they should marry. For it is better to marry than to be aflame [with passion and tortured continually with ungratified desire].

When I finished reading all of the scriptures, I went over each one again; except this time I read the whole chapter of each scripture and some of the scriptures I read 4 and 5 chapters; they were so interesting. Then I laid down and thought about why Malik would ask me to read these particular scriptures. I reminisced on every conversation we had and how he looked at me every time we met. I realized he liked me from the second time we met, at his party, and I was so busy trying to run from him because of my hormones I couldn't see his heart. I thought he was like Elvin and Derek; just looking for a silly woman.

I took time to really examine my heart because I know I like Malik; I need to know I like him for the man, the person he is and not for his muscles. I must not pity him because his wife died but like him as a person. So I laid there and thought about how he talked to me and what he said and how he treated me and when I remembered how I wanted to kiss him the first time we left the Rib Shack and how he was the one to stop us I cried. This man respects me and yesterday he told me he was in love with me and I didn't believe him; thinking he hasn't known me long enough. After reading most of the book of Genesis, I understood how some men know as soon as they meet their wives, that they love them; I believe that's what Malik wanted me to see in the scriptures he gave me.

I didn't sleep most of the night; I tossed and turned sifting through my emotions. I have to know how I feel about him and I must not be influenced by his liking me; I need to know what's in my heart. Man oh man did I wrestle! At 2:30 in the morning I broke down and cried. I like Malik and know he has come into my life at this precise time so that I may forgive my father; so I can be validated as a woman. When the revelation came to me that I could not possibly admit I liked Malik had I not forgiven my father; I lost it!

CHAPTER NINE

Ernest Goes To Jail
Oops' I'm in love!

THURSDAY:

Last night I fell asleep crying and this morning I woke up with burning swollen eyes. I thought 'I'll read First Corinthians 7 as my scripture' but I couldn't move into praise and worship; I was stunned at what Paul said to me! Yeah, it was as though he was talking to me directly. The phone rang and it was Shelby County Sheriff; Ernest had been arrested for attempted robbery and called me. I called Dad and told him what happened and asked if he would go with me to see what can be done; by him working with the juvenile system he would know how to talk to who ever was in charge, he agreed to meet me there.

By the time I arrived, Dad was waiting for me inside the station. He knew someone that gave him the 411 on what actually happened. Ernest and two other friends Rubert and Spider tried to rob a liquor store in Shelby County while the owner was manning the store. The owner informed the officers it was obvious to him the boys were amateurs as he watched them amble around the store. They didn't have any weapons but Spider was wearing a fleece hoodie and with his hand in one of the pockets; pretended to have a gun and threatened the owner. Ernest and Rubert stood behind Spider and cheered, "Yeah, yeah" to intimidate the owner, but he knew they were selling wolf tickets; that's when he reached down under the counter and pulled out his magnum and made them sit on the floor with their hands up until the sheriff arrived.

Dad and I were called to the back and my Dad took care of everything, I just sat there and listened. The officer knew my Dad and had him sign some forms and told us Ernest would be released later. Dad asked for copies of the paperwork and after they were made and given to him we left. He walked me to my truck and told me Ernest was in a lot of trouble but he would help him get it off his record so it wouldn't follow him the rest of his life. I thanked and hugged him and headed home to cook for the 7pm baby shower over in Germantown.

It was 10:30 am, when I walked in the door; I changed into my nursing shoes and apron and went to the garage and started cooking. First Aunt Flora phoned, and then Aunt Shirley, both wanted my opinion on Parker. Aunt Shirley commented on how Dora acted like she was walking down the isle to her wedding with Parker on her arm; I just listened. I learned a long time ago what ever is said to Aunt Shirley gets repeated but with her flavor added to it, so I keep my mouth shut and ears open.

Just as I finished my last dish Aunt Rose Marie called. I thought it was about Ernest but she was asking if Dora had said anything to me about how serious she and Parker were. Everyone knows Dora will tell me how she feels before telling Connie, because Connie pushes Dora to get married and have kids all the time. I told her Dora has only expressed to me she really likes him and I had met him for the first time last night along with everyone else.

5pm, I was done cooking, packing up and had cleaned the kitchen, so I headed into the house to get my paperwork together, then I was going to take my shower and get dressed for tonight. After getting the file for the baby shower, the phone rang; I thought it was Bobby Ray telling me he was on his way to get the set up sheet but it was Dora. "Angie you better get over here; I'm at Mom's, Howard Junior has gone crazy on Ernest and if that wasn't bad enough; Bernard and Howard Junior is going at it something fierce, please hurry." Click. I placed the file on the desk, grabbed my purse and took my apron off while I ran out of the house. I prayed all the way over Uncle Howard's even though it's only a five minute drive; I prayed for peace all the way. We have never had anyone in our family ever go to jail and I feared Uncle Howard with his Army background was going berserk on Ernest.

When I pulled up, I had to park mostly on the sidewalk; only my bumper fit in the driveway there were so many cars parked, it looked like Sunday dinner was going on! I walked through the kitchen door and could hear the shouting. Everyone was in the back or as we called it the den. A room Aunt Rose Marie had added on when she was teaching Cosmetology and Barbering. This room is where she taught all of us cousins to do each other's, and our own hair. The room is almost the size of a two car garage. She had knee high custom storage built on the two walls without windows and they double as seating also. Uncle Howard has a 50 inch flat screen on the wall you see as soon as you walk into the den and, there are two 8 feet long, big pillowed, red leather couches facing each other, and a large round wood and glass coffee table in the middle of the couches. When I entered the room, family was sitting and standing all in the den.

My Dad was standing by the T.V. which was on, but muted and he was holding in his hand some of the papers given to him at the police station. Ernest had on a white extremely large Tee shirt with drops of blood on the front and the chest pocket was ripped and hanging off. He was holding in his hand a paper towel and used it to wipe the blood forming on his lip that was big, red and swollen. The coffee table was broken and pushed up against one of the couches. A'letha, Dora and Kozette were in front of the storage on the left of the room pacing and their lips were moving, so I knew they were praying in the spirit.

Aunt Rose Marie was standing behind the couch that was moved out of place and Aunt Brenda was standing next to her. Aunt Shirley was standing in front of the television to the right of Dad with her hands on her hips and Bernard was going off saying how Howard Junior wasn't qualified to judge anybody. Howard Jr. had a kitchen towel wrapped around his right hand and so did Bernard so I couldn't tell which one had given Ernest a big lip.

Uncle Howard was standing next to Ernest staring at him and Uncle Lester was sitting on the storage to the right of me and as Bernard's shout simmers, Uncle Lester stands up looking at Bernard. Now its obvious Bernard's done with his ranting so Uncle Lester stands next to Aunt Shirley and begins to speak, "Ok, now that everyone has spoken their minds, let's allow Ernest to explain himself; and please let him finish his say." Everyone looks at Ernest and he twiddles with the paper towel in his hand and begins.

"First I need to apologize to Mom and Daddy. Mom, Daddy I am sorry, H J is right I was raised to know better than that. I wanted to go to the One4Five concert next week and needed some money. When I asked Daddy he told me to be a man and get a job and then I asked Mom, she said real men don't ask women for money. When I asked Angie for some money she told me I had to work for it first; I just felt like I didn't have any other way to get some cash; and when Spider and

Rubert didn't have their money either we thought we would go to Germantown and hit up the liquor store and we got caught." Aunt Rose Marie says to Ernest, "Baby I hope you have learned a lesson. Ernest you had better pray you don't have a record for the rest of your life." Uncle Howard says to him, "Son, you have got to be a man and pay for your mistake. You did the crime so only you can do the time." He puts his hand on Ernest shoulder and Ernest grabs his Dad and hugs him. While his face is buried in Uncle Howard's shoulder, he says in a trembling voice, "I'm sorry daddy; I really am." Now everyone in the room heads for Ernest and lines up for a hug, Howard Jr. says, "Bro I'm sorry I had to hit you, but I meant what I said."

After I hug Ernest I walk over to Dora and she tells me what happened. My Dad called the number on the paperwork for Ernest so he could advise him as to what he should do next and the number was disconnected so, he used map quest to get the address on the paperwork. He knocked on the door and asked for Ernest. Uncle Howard recognized him and asked if he were Nichols and let him in the house. He asked Dad what brought him over and Dad told Uncle Howard what had happened with Ernest. Uncle Howard had Aunt Rose Marie get Ernest out of his room and when Ernest walked into the living room and took one look at my Dad, he went off on him saying he had no right coming to his house. He and Uncle Howard started a shouting match and Ernest was waving his arms at Uncle Howard and getting up in his face, so Aunt Rose Marie called Howard Jr. and told him to get over to the house because Ernest had been arrested and she was afraid Uncle Howard was going to hit him.

Howard Jr. told Roslyn he had to go see what was happening and Roslyn phoned Connie and Connie phoned Dora and told her Ernest had been arrested and Uncle Howard was real upset. By the time Dora arrived she said Howard Junior and Ernest were in the den; going at each other and Uncle Howard stepped in between the two of them and Ernest called Uncle Howard an old man and told him to get out of the way. That's when Howard Jr. grabbed Ernest by his shirt and punched him in the mouth. Ernest hit the table and Howard Jr. pulled him up and hit him again and told him that old man was his father and he was living in his house and he had better not ever disrespect him again.

Aunt Shirley called Aunt Rose Marie to gossip; probably about Dora; and heard all of the commotion and called everybody and told her son, Roderick to get over Uncle Howard's and stop Howard Jr. from beating up his brother but Bernard arrived before Roderick and Bernard hit Howard Jr. for hitting his brother and Uncle Howard had to get Bernard off Howard Jr. and that's when Dora called me. They all apologized to one another and we all ended up hugging each other and started leaving. Dad stayed to talk to Ernest, Uncle Howard and Aunt Rose Marie about what options there was available for Ernest. By the time I left it was 7:45 pm so I headed home changed into my uniform, grabbed the paperwork and went straight to the booking.

Everything was set up and going good. Wila was handling the table and I went into the kitchen and helped with the dishes. I had a chance to tell each one of them I had family issues and was proud of having a staff so good I wasn't missed. When Bobby Ray had a few minutes alone with me he asked if I was alright and needed any protection, he could get me something tomorrow that was not registered; meaning a gun. I told him it was not that kind of trouble and he told me if I needed anything just let him know. I thanked him and was glad to have a friend like Bobby Ray looking out. Friends and workers don't come better than him; look up the word dedication of a close friend in the dictionary and a picture of Bobby Ray is what you'll find.

We finished at 9:30 and I settled everything with the host and she gave me names and phone numbers on 3 separate sheets of paper inquiring if I were free on the dates written down and what occasion they were celebrating. I took the papers home so I can follow up on the dates tomorrow. I was so tired when I got home I laid across my bed thinking I would rest a few minutes and I ended up going straight to sleep with clothes and shoes on.

FRIDAY:

7:20 am. My phone rings and its Dora having me on speaker as she gets ready for work. She tells me that Ernest is sorry for what he did and now he's scared he has messed up the rest of his life. He realizes a concert is not the root of his trouble; it is the enemy who does not want the will of God to be made manifested in his life. Then she started about Parker and how she is in love and he is talking about them getting married. He wants to introduce her to his family Saturday. She is excited but I know Dora and can tell by her tone she is troubled about something so I ask; "Dora what's wrong?"

"Oh Angie, I think my love for Parker might be blinding me to what I should be doing; like slowing down. I love him and want to be with him all the time but then I wonder if we should wait and date for 6 months or a year. Angie I don't know if I should follow my heart or my head. What you think?" "Dora I can't tell you what to do but I can tell you I truly understand how you feel. Talk to Aunt Rose Marie maybe she has some wisdom for you." Silence.... Then Dora says, "I think she will be worried I don't want to wait because I want to have sex, I don't think she can be open minded Angie I am her baby girl." "I don't know Dora; she is pretty level headed; where you think you get it from? Tell her how you feel then ask for her opinion. Dora; do you just want to have sex with him?"

"NO! I mean... I do... but, not until we are married. I want to be with him all the time, he's all I think about; I just love him Angie; I just love the man." "Well, my advice is to talk to your mother, I sure wish mine were here, I'd be talking to her right about now, that's for sure." "Oh yeah, how is Mr. Chapman and have you been a good girl?" "You know, I can truthfully say yes I have. Dora he respects me and... I think I love him for that." "Um he respects you and you love him, sounds serious to me. Well, thanks for your ear cuz, I'm off to work now but I'll chew on what you said, love you, bye." Click.

Now she has me thinking about Malik and those scriptures he had me read, so I pull the scriptures out and began to read the whole book of Genesis and before I realize it; its 11:30 and I get showered, dressed and I'm headed to the garage to cook. I had to put Aunt Shirley and Aunt Flora on speaker when they called, but I was at the transferring to bowls stage when Aunt Brenda and Kozette called me talking about Parker and Ernest.

After I finished cooking and cleaning the kitchen I phoned Dad to get an update on Ernest and he was so happy he was able to help. He told me how much it meant to him that I would think to call him and that made him feel like a father. I could tell he was getting emotional when he said the words, "like a father." I detected a slight tremble in his voice. I was getting emotional myself feeling my heart swell with love and gratitude for him wanting me in his life. The Lord is so good to me .....Dad told me he was able to get Uncle Howard some information and refer a good attorney to represent Ernest.   Then he told me Aunt Bernadine wants us to have dinner after church Sunday and he wanted to come to church with me and we could leave from there to pick up Aunt Bernadine then head for dinner. I agreed and we told each other that we loved one another and hung up. I am so happy my father is in my life and we are having a good relationship, I think I smiled for an hour. I put all of my paperwork in the folder and was changing into my uniform when Bobby Ray and Jimmy Lee came to get the food.

Tonight is an anniversary party for Brian and Patty Landers, Brian is a salesman at the Chevy auto lot in Germantown. He and his wife are celebrating being married for 12 years and since her parents are here visiting from Florida, Brian and Patty decided to make a nice production out of their anniversary. Because it's the end of August we will be outside on the patio and they have a pool and a custom bar so this should be very nice. I gave Patty some tips for decorating with small clear lights; I don't like doing that because in the past, whenever I have given decorating advice, it was added to what was already planned and the decorations ended up being way too much. I believe simple is elegant and lights are all you need to set the atmosphere for whatever occasion. I left the house headed to Germantown thinking about Malik and the scriptures he had given me.

I arrived early and ended up helping with the light placements and it was gorgeous; they even had floating candles in the pool. The back yard was beautifully landscaped and the floor plan was laid for entertaining. The kitchen door was exclusively used by us and the sliding glass doors were left open for the guest to use. It was perfect. I manned the table and stood near it most of the time, so I had a view of the patio and the podium they had set up. I was replenishing the bowls when Brian took the microphone and gave a beautiful tribute to his wife. He started off saying how he knew as soon as he laid eyes on her, she was going to become his wife, and how he had to convince her to have lunch with him and 2 months after their first date, they were married. I realized I was standing there listening and not working.

When her father took the microphone he told his version of how he thought Brian was a hustler but watching him with Patty; he knew Brian loved his daughter and then his only worry was how he could communicate that fact to her mother. After her father spoke, 6 or 8 of their friends had a few words to say about how amazed they are to see the love they still have for each other after 12 years and 3 kids. When someone announced Brian and Patty would start the dance, I watched how tender he was with her as they danced and I found myself crying; standing there crying! While we were cleaning up Vicki stood behind me and said, "Boss it's ok to be in love, the only way to benefit from it is to yield to it." I turned around and looked at her and she smiled at me and said, "Yeah, just yield its wonderful!" And she walked away. I stood there and wondered how she knew I was in love when I had just realized it myself!

On my drive home I kept thinking about what Vicki said. I pulled up in the driveway and went straight to the garage to clean up, still thinking about Vicki's words. Then I showered and crawled into bed, tired, but I couldn't stop thinking about Malik, so I prayed for his safety and those with him and decided to read the scriptures he had given me; this time in the order he wanted me to read them and only what he wanted me to read. I felt as though a light was on every word I read; I could see Malik telling me he loved me and wants to marry me. I thought 'how cleaver he is to propose to me through scripture; his game is so bold and, is in all capital letters!'

Then I read 1 Corinthians 7:6–9 again and thought he has been battling with his flesh like I have. That's why he wants us to only meet in public places. Oh how my love for him expanded; he loves me enough to respect me even when I didn't respect myself he loves the Lord enough to put his flesh to death, wow. I began thanking the Lord for bringing Malik into my life, and then I prayed that we both keep our flesh under subjection so the blessing would rest on our marriage as a result of our obedience to the Word. I turned out my light and thought 'did I just pray for my marriage? Am I ready to marry Malik? I love him but I need to know for sure I'm not just sexually attracted to him; there can be no doubt its love.' I laid there in bed and began to pray in the spirit and before I knew it I was praising the Lord for being All Knowing and I began telling Him how much I love Him and I slid into worship and fell asleep and I'm talking some sweet sleep.

SATURDAY:
Today is a full day for me, the wedding reception is at 3 pm so we must be there at least an hour and a half early so I climbed out of bed and my move was on. 1 pm Bobby Ray called to say he would be here in 20 minutes. I finished garnishing and began to get myself ready.

The reception was at a local union hall and we had our work cut out for us setting up. We hustled and ran the whole time. This was a group of alcohol drinkers and in an hour, they were real rowdy! The men were hitting on all us women and Jimmy Lee had to calm Maynard down when he thought one of the men hit Vicki on the butt. She told him she was not touched and he calmed down but he watched her like a hawk. I made a mental note to add $50.00 to all of their pay for today. I was so tired when we pulled away from that parking lot I realized I was drained from the tension. When we pulled up in my driveway I went into the garage and started cleaning up. It was almost 11pm when I went into the house and took a shower and went straight to bed. I turned off my alarm, prayed for Malik, read the 23rd Psalms and went to sleep.

SUNDAY:

I was up by 8 am and rested; I didn't realize how tired and drained I was from yesterday until now. I haven't slept that long in a good while. I went into the kitchen to get some toast and tea and noticed there was a message on my business phone so I retrieved it. "Hey Angela I made it back and I felt your prayers, thanks. I'll see you tomorrow, love you." Click. I felt myself smiling so big; I love that man!

I arrived for Sunday School just before it started and there was Dora and Parker. As soon as I slid next to Dora, she hunched me to follow her out of the pew. We went outside and stood in front of the church. She was so excited and animated, shimming and getting on her tip toes as she tells me, "Angie I took your advice, called Mom and had her meet me at the Rib Shack Friday night. I told her that I was in love with Parker and wanted to spend every moment I was awake with him and did not want to have sex with him until we were married. Then I asked her if she thought I was moving to fast and Angie, she laughed and told me I was in love and she was happy for me and understood exactly what I was feeling. Then she told me the whole story of how she and daddy got together.

All these years Mom and Daddy have always joked with us kids on their anniversary about them having to get married, well Friday she told me why. When they met at the church cookout, daddy fell in love with her the moment she turned around to face him and he said because he had been in the war and saw so much death and lives being shattered and changed, he was not going to waste time because he appreciated life. Mom said she thought he was mental and was afraid of him at first but Aunt Shirley pleaded his cause and when Aunt Brenda told her he has always been serious and suggested Mom just go on one date to see if he was sane; she did, and fell in love with daddy.

They dated for a month and daddy said he had to marry her or he would burn and the Bible says it is better to marry than to burn." Dora and I both are laughing; she continues, "So they picked up their marriage license and went straight to a Wedding Chapel. When they say they had to get married they don't mean because of Howard Jr. even though he was born nine months later they mean they had to marry to honor the Word. Angie I feel so much better after talking to Mom, thanks because I never would have talked to her if it wasn't for you." We hug and put our foreheads together and I tell her how happy I am for her as joy tears start falling from our eyes. We go to the restroom and blow noses then return to the sanctuary.

As soon as I sit down here comes Malik sitting down next to me looking at Parker and Dora as he give them nods. He leans in and pecks me on the cheek and

I can smell his cologne and realizes I don't want to tare his clothes off and I smile to myself for passing that test. For the first time in my life I love a man and I feel secure; I don't have to do anything to make him stay with me, I know Malik's not going anywhere; he has given me scripture to prove it.

After Sunday School we move to our set in stone seats and we are packed like sardines. Malik is sitting on the end, Dora is next to me and Parker is next to her and the whole row is filled. As the choir comes out we stand and Sister Sadie escorts Dad to our row. Malik grabs my hand and steps out in the isle. He looks at Dad, nods and extends his hand towards the 6th pew. He turns his head towards me and says, "Let's make our own row." As my Dad enters the row Malik lets me know it's my turn. While we stand there waiting for Dad to get his spot, here come Aunt Flora, she reaches out and hugs me and pats Malik on the arm and motions for Dad to move down. When we were all situated I realized Malik was right; I don't have to sit with Dora's family, I have family of my own; my grandmother my Dad and my man! As the opening prayer went forth I let the tears fall as I heard the words, "Father, we thank you for all you have done for us." With my heart I told the Lord, 'I really do thank You!'

Today Pastor Jenkins is preaching and his scripture is from 1 Kings 13:11–32. His title was "KNOW God and NO Man can lead you astray!" He started off telling the story of a young man of God, who knowing the Word, allowed an older, seasoned man of God lead him astray and; it cost him his life. Having every one of us sitting in our pews holding our breath, Pastor Jenkins read verses 11 through 22, then he took us to Colossians where Paul was teaching in chapter 2, verse

4, it reads **"Now this I say lest anyone should deceive you with persuasive words."**

He told us to keep our ear towards the Word and always ask the Holy Spirit for understanding. He said that being born again believers; we are supposed to know the Word **and** expect the Word to be confirmed, if we do not get confirmation; it's simple, it's not the season for that particular Word. He took us back to 1 Kings 13, and finished verses 23–32 and wrapped up his teaching with an invitation to those who wanted to be filled and also for those who wanted prayer for more hunger and thirst for the presence of the Lord; to come to the alter. So many went forward and I heard my Dad and Malik pray in their heavenly language, so I began praying in mine, it was so awesome!

After service we stepped into the isle and Aunt Flora talked to Dad and asked if he was coming to the family dinner and he tells her he was taking me to dinner with his sister Bernadine and asked if she wanted to join us. She says, "Nichols, I just got my family back last Sunday and I need to be with them, but I want to thank you for giving me my only grandchild; Angie." He looks puzzled and Malik is standing there looking at Aunt Flora as she puts her hand on Dad's shoulder and says, "De Anne was my baby not my sister. I lied and kept that family secret too long; I'm free now and Angie is sweet enough to allow us to have a grandmother and granddaughter relationship. You all go and break bread together; we will have plenty times to have Sunday dinner as a family." She turns and looks at me while pointing her index finger towards Malik and says, "Angie bring this young man over next week so I can get to know him. Now you all have a good time and I'll see you soon." She reaches over and pulls me down towards herself and kisses me on my forehead and gently runs her finger over my cheek. I grab her and we hug one another so tight we both say at the same time, "I love you," she steps around me and leaves.

Dad looks at me and asks, "Is she alright? You know, getting dementia." I smile at him and say, "No; she was telling the truth for once in 45 years and she feels great." I turn and start walking out; quickly glancing at Malik and Dad asks, "Do you think De Anne knew Flora was her mother?" I told him I didn't think so. He shook his head and said, "That don't beat all, Angie, we have some catching up to do." He turns to Malik and says, "We're going to the steak house over on Fountain Avenue, you like their food?" Malik says, "I'm new to Memphis I'm not familiar with the steak house but you all go and have your talk." Malik touches my hand and says, "Angela I'll call you later ok." Dad says, "Man come on with us it's not that expensive." Now we have reached outside the church and he continues, "Look you follow Angela home so she can drop her truck off, and I'll pick up my sister and we'll meet you at the steak house, Angela knows where it is." Malik says, "Uh, Sir I can't follow her home, I'll take her in my car and bring her back to get her truck." Dad says, "Well ok," and he gives me a kiss on the cheek and walks to his car. I'm thinking 'Malik is wise not to know where I live so there won't be any late night creeping, Lord I love this man!'

CHAPTER TEN

Nichols verses Chapman
And the winner is...

We walk to Malik's car and he opens the door for me and I remember what he told me about his late wife, Theresa. When he gets in the car he tells me I can put my Bible in the back, I don't have to hold on to it, his driving was not that bad. He looks at me, smiles and says, "That was a joke." I smile back at him, I am nervous being alone with him in his car and he asks, "Ms. Bowen did you have time to look over those scriptures I wrote down?" I tell him to turn left and say yeah. We go a few blocks in silence then he says, "Angela I want you to understand how I feel about you and I don't want to scare you or give the impression I'm crazy or just want to sleep with you; Baby I want to marry you." He looks toward me and I slowly look at him. When our eyes lock I feel so much love for him and I know he loves me too so I tell him, "Malik I love you too and the scriptures helped me understand how a man can love a woman at first sight. And, I thought it was very creative of you to have me read scripture stating a man should get married if he can't exercise self control; that was original; I took it as a proposal. Have you used scripture before, make a left at the light, to ask someone to marry you?" He looks in his rear view mirror, put his right turn signal on and pulls the car over to the curb and puts it in park and turns off the ignition. He turns to me and says real slow, "Angela, I married Theresa before I was saved and I didn't love her as soon as I met her; we were more in lust than love so I do know the difference; between love and lust."

Now he looks at the dashboard and back to me and says, "Woman, I love you and want to marry you; you have blown my mind." Now he tenderly says, "Angela, baby I just don't want to scare you that's all. We met a week ago and I don't want you to think I only want to marry you to get you in my bed. I've been married; and yes, I like doing what married people do, so I'm not going to tell you that I'm not attracted to you sexually; because I am; but, baby I love you like I never knew I could love a woman. Am I making any sense to you?" "Yes Malik you are." I look at him and smile, he starts up the car and except for me giving him directions; we arrive at the steak house in silence.

We get there before Dad and Aunt Bernadine and decided to sit in the waiting section inside. Malik starts smiling and looking at me so I ask, "Why are you smiling?" "Angela you told me you love me; you've made me happy baby that's all." I smile but my mind is thinking about Dad and Aunt Bernadine having some questions about Aunt Granny; so I think I'd better try and fill Malik in on what's going on. "Malik my Aunt Flora told me a week ago Thursday, she was really my grandmother and Sunday she revealed the secret to the whole family. My Dad and his sister don't know about my Aunt Granny so I'm sure they will have some questions. I haven't seen my Aunt Bernadine since my high school graduation. She was the one who kept my Dad informed about me all the years I never heard from him." He says, "So you really meant it when you told me you had a lot going on right now, baby I'm sorry I didn't know." When I looked towards the door I saw Dad and Aunt Bernadine arriving.

Seeing Aunt Bernadine caused me to feel sad, she was almost bent over and was grasping at each breath she took. We both get up and walk towards them, Dad was helping her walk up the concrete walk and Malik walked to the door and held it open for them and I followed right behind him. Dad introduces Malik to Aunt Bernadine and she stands still to shake his hand and looked up and she sees me and smiles so big. I step up and hug her as I fight back tears. I had no idea she was this bad off. She starts crying and I step back and tell her not to cry before she has me crying and she raises her hand to my cheek and says, "Angie you look the same as when you graduated high school." She reaches inside her purse and pulls out a handkerchief and blows her nose then continues; "Let me look at those Bowen hips," now she's trying to turn my body around as she says, "Girl, how do you stay so youthful?" The hostess comes to inform us our table is ready and we all follow her to our table.

Dad and Aunt Bernadine sit side by side and Malik and I sit side by side; I'm facing my aunt and Malik is facing my Dad. Dad looks at me and says, "Angela what's this Flora being De Anne's mother, fill us in. I was telling Bern about it on the way here and… you telling me De Anne never suspected anything. What do you know?" I told them a short version of what Aunt Granny told me and the waiter came and took our orders. While waiting on our lunch, I told them about her accepting the Lord at Wednesday night Bible Study and the next day she told me the truth. Aunt Bernadine said, "The truth really does make one free; if only we would believe the Word of God will accomplish exactly what It is sent out to accomplish; if we will just learn to take the Lord at His Word, don't you think so Sticky." I quickly turn my head towards Dad and say, "Sticky? Is that your nickname?"

I'm laughing and looking at Dad. He has a serious expression on his face as he says, "Yeah and no body but Bern can call me that, do I make myself clear?" Aunt Bernadine says with a slight giggle, "He hates that name, mama gave it to him because she said she was always having to wash his face and hands when we were little; he was always sticky." Now both she and I have our hands over our mouths laughing and looking at him, as he rolls his eyes at us and adjusts his posture in his chair, our food comes and Dad reaches for Aunt Bernadine's hand and Malik's while I reach for Aunt Bernadine's hand and for Malik's and we stop laughing as he blesses the food. As I lift my head up, I glance over at Malik and he slowly glances at me. I feel like laying my head on his arm; I feel so safe and secure; like I'm sure he will always be here for me. I'm lovin me some Malik!

Aunt Bernadine says, "Malik tell me something about yourself." He puts his fork down and says, "I'm 30 years old, been a Marine since age 18, I was married and my wife died 2 years ago, I transferred here from DC almost 3 weeks ago and I am madly in love with your niece and your daughter sir." Now he is looking at Dad. Dad puts his fork down and says, "So you're telling me you met Angela 3 weeks ago and think you are madly in love with her, is that what you're telling me?" "No sir, I believe I met Angela the same night you did sir." Dad slightly moves his chest forward and says, "And you think you love her?" "Sir I am positive I am in love with Angela your daughter." "Malik are you sure her owning a lucrative business has nothing to do with you loving my daughter." Oh no! I know where this is going; I want to see how Malik handles himself.

"Sir I made over 90k last year, I plan on taking care of Angela, not Angela taking care of me. Sir I love your daughter like I have never loved a woman in my life and I want to marry her." I looked at Malik and he was looking directly at Dad and he was serious as a heart attack. Dad was looking just as serious at Malik; it was as if they were at the OK Coral and about to pull out guns when Dad says, "Son, I believe you do love my daughter." It was then I realized I had been holding my breath and started breathing again; relieved there would be no gun fight! Whew, that was intense!

Dad continues, "Can you guarantee me some grandchildren." Malik looks at me and says, "Sir I guarantee we will try." He smiles at me and looks back at Dad. Aunt Bernadine says, "Lord Sticky I thought you were going to run the young man off; I don't know about you but he has convinced me he loves her." Still looking Malik in the eyes, Dad says, "Bern, he's convinced me too." He extends his hand to Malik and says, "I had to find out man, she's all I have." Malik says, "She's all I have too sir." Then we all ate our food while Dad tells Aunt Bernadine about how Malik kept me off him. The way he told it, was a lot funnier than I remembered.

The bill came and Malik said, "Mr. Nichols I got this, you save your money after all your daughter's getting married." Dad looks at me and asks, "When and where; and who in the world can cater your wedding?" He and Malik chuckles; I was feeling like I was in the 3rd grade again I didn't know what to say. I looked at Aunt Bernadine and she was waiting for me to say something. Malik says, "We'll let you know, I'm working on a plan that will save you some money." Aunt Bernadine goes, "Ahh, you know what to say to Sticky don't you." "There you go Bern, just because you are the oldest doesn't mean I'm not a man." She takes both her hands and squeezes his jaws together and puckers her lips and makes kissing sounds at him and he rolls his eyes at her and pushes her hands away and says,

"Come on Bern we're in public I'm not your little baby brother." He looks at her out of the corner of his eye, sighs and leans in towards her and lets her kiss him. While she kisses him he rolls his eyes around then he hugs her, begins shaking his head while looking at Malik saying; "Man; women!"

Aunt Bernadine looks at me and says, "Come on; let me go to the ladies room before we go." I help her walk to the restroom and she's talking to me the whole while we walk, "Now Angie what's going on with you and Malik; most women can't shut up talking about getting married, you on the other hand act like you don't know you're even getting married, spit it out, come on." We get to the rest room and sit on the bench and I tell her, "He just proposed to me in the car on the way over here and I wasn't expecting him to even come to dinner with us so I'm just stunned that's all." "Do you love him Angie?" I smile, shake my head yes and say, "I really do Aunt Bernadine; I love Malik I just don't want to have sex with him before we get married and that's a challenge for me right now." She pats me on my hand and says, "De Anne used to talk to me like this when she was courting Sticky; some times she gave me too much information but she loved my brother. Baby, listen; why don't you just go and get married; it's not like you're 18 or 19 years old! He says he's 30 and you'll be what 27. You two know you love each other, well that's just my opinion Angie, do what you want, you're grown. Now help me in there so I can get Sticky home before dark." She leans in towards me and almost whispers, "You know he was afraid of the dark when we were little," and she breaks out laughing. I can't imagine my father afraid of anything; but I humor her and smile.

After walking Dad and Aunt Bernadine to the car,

we all hugged and Dad whispered in my ear "I like Malik for you." Then he shook Malik's hand and said, "Malik; you have my blessing; make sure you keep my only baby happy alright." Malik looking directly at him says, "Thank you sir, Yes sir I'll do my best." As Malik and I turned to walk to his car, he put his hand in my back directing me. I feel so safe with him and I so desperately want to pass this test so I start thinking on what I'll say to him during the drive back to pick up my truck. He opens the door for me and I glance at him and he's grinning so big like the day we were at the Rib Shack. He gets into the car and turns to me and starts, "Angela Bowen will you marry me?" His smile is so big I look into his eyes and cup my hand on his cheek and shake my head yes as I say, "Yes Malik Chapman; I'll marry you!" He reaches for my hand and turns it palm down and kisses the top and holds it with both his hands and tells me, "Angela, you won't regret becoming Mrs. Chapman; baby I love you, you truly are my good thing. I can't kiss you, but don't take it personal Angela I respect you and want our marriage blessed; so let's be obedient ok?" "I agree." Was my response. He kissed my hand again and tells me, "Angela, you won't regret becoming Mrs. Chapman; baby I love you." And gently put my hand down and turned to start the car and I say, "Malik, I love you." He looks at me and breaks out in that big smile again.

After driving a few blocks he says, "I have a sister living in Baltimore, my father died of a heart attack when I was 17 and my mother died of a blood clot to the heart 4 years ago." I asked "Are you close to your sister?" He answers, "Not really, do you ever wish you had siblings?" I tell him, "When I was little and had to go to bed alone I remember wishing I had a sister to talk to; but Dora and I are so close, I feel as though she's my sister." "Angela the only thing I can tell you about my job is I do a lot of training. Is there anything you want to ask me?" "How old is your sister?" "We are nine months apart; I'm the oldest." He gives me a glance and a smile and says, "People thought we were twins; by the time we were 7 we stopped trying to explain, what can you say?" I blurted, "That it was a miracle there were only two of you!" We look at each other and laugh so hard.

He asked me about my mother and I talked about her all the way to the church. I was surprised when we pulled up into the parking lot; I didn't have to tell him once when to turn, he had memorized the way.

He put the car in park and I told him; "Malik I agree with you about being obedient to the Word of God and not giving place to fornication." "Angela, I'll call you later, you know if I had your home phone number I wouldn't have to call you on your business phone." "Oh I'm glad you thought about that; here let me give it to you." I went into my purse and pulled out a business card and wrote my home and cell number on the back. I handed him the card and said, "Malik I love you." I opened the door and got out of his car and went straight to my truck. I got in, started it and looked over at him; he had such a sad look on his face. I reached into my purse and held up my cell and mouthed CALL ME and turned it on. He nodded and pulled out his cell phone and called me. As I backed out of the parking lot I answered, "What's with the sad face?" He responds; "Angela I want to be with you all the time. All I think about is you and, hey, what if we go to the mall and talk, you have anything you have to do?" "Well no, not really... follow me." "OK baby, bye."

We went to the mall and sat on a bench and talked. He told me that he didn't want to rush me and wanted me to be sure I wanted to be married to him and asked if I had any questions for him. I explained to him the scriptures helped me understand how someone could fall in love at first sight; I was wrestling with the possibility of wanting to marry because of not being able to exercise self control. You know; what if we get married and after a roll in the hay we have regrets. I looked him in the eyes looking for a response and never flinching, he says, "I never knew I could love like I love you and if you need more time to be absolutely sure you love me; I'll wait. Angela love is unconditional and because we all have faults, love covers them. I love you; if I wanted sex I wouldn't be asking you to spend the rest of our lives together. Baby, what is it exactly you doubt?" He looked into my eyes and I felt as if he was looking at my heart. I tell this man exactly what I feel and I have never done this to any other man; what is it about him? I don't even blink; it's as if I'm under his truth spell I say, "Malik, I have never been able to separate love from sex. I meet a man and bam, I'm in his bed." He interrupts me never changing his expression; still looking into my eyes "So you're saying you just walk up to a guy and say hi let's have sex." "NO! Well, maybe I've come close to that, but, that's not what I'm saying.... See; I knew you would think I'm easy." I look away from him thinking how close he hit the nail, almost right dab on the head; now I can feel tears forming. "So, you're saying, you have sex and afterwards you realize it wasn't love; I don't think you're easy I think you made a mistake and haven't forgiven yourself.

Angela the enemy; our adversary, is the only one that doesn't want you to forgive yourself. Baby listen, my wife died from a drug overdose and I thought it was my fault. I was on a self destruct mission; I didn't care if I lived or died because I didn't think I deserved to live because I thought Theresa and my son died because of me. I moved here to Memphis and was here less than 2 weeks and I meet you. If Theresa had never died, I wouldn't even be here and we would not have met. Baby we're yoked up." I look into his eyes and feel as though it's just the two of us here. Ooh I love this man! Geez!

A few minutes later he says, "Let's walk the mall." I said Ok and stood up; when he stood he grabbed my hand and off to the directory we go. He looked over the directory and put his finger on a jewelry store and turned toward me and said, "Angela trust me ok." I nodded yes and as he's guiding me to the store he says, "I know you have good taste in clothes; you wear nice suits to church but I don't know your taste in jewelry so pick out something you like." I felt my heart racing; the thought of him wanting to marry me is beginning to sink in. As we walked a little further I found myself thinking 'am I ready for marriage, not just the bedroom part but the cleaning, encouraging, sharing, building up, supporting; all of the interactions I've seen my aunts do for my uncles, geez Angela, you ready for the responsibility?'

When we arrive at the store I looked at the sets in the window where we stood and then I crossed to the other side and asked him if he was afraid I would spend all of his money or go over his credit limit and I watched his reaction; he laughed and walked up to me and said, "I don't believe in credit cards; it's strictly cash and carry with me. Do you have a lot of credit cards?" "No, it's cash and carry with me also." He smiles big again and says almost in my ear "We just might be soul mates."

I step back and glance at him and he shakes his head yes and winks at me; out comes this enormous smile on my face, 'I love this man; we really are soul mates and he's right; I need to forgive myself of my past and start living the abundant life The Lord has in store for me; for us.' I continue looking in the window and say, "Malik! I think I found it; that one right there." "You know your size?" "Yep, 6." "Thanks Angela for trusting me; I know that wasn't easy for you but you're catching on baby, you're catching on." He stands there smiling and before I realize it, I reach out and hug him and say, "Thanks Malik for believing in me."

He looks at his watch and asks me if I want to go to lunch tomorrow with him; he has a surprise for me and I shake my head 'yes' to agree. "How is 11:30 am for you?" "That's good as long as I'm back in time to get my laundry done." He gets serious and says, "Angela I love you baby." I respond just as serious and tell him that I love him too. He takes his index finger and runs it softly down my check as we stare into one another's eyes and he smiles and says, "I do believe we passed the test! Do you hear that song playing?" I listen and it's 'We're in this love together; by Al Jarreau' I shake my head yes and he says, "I think we have our song." I'm thinking, 'how romantic; most men could care less about a song but my man picked ours; Thank you Lord I finally did something right!' When the song ends the announcement of the mall closing in 15 minutes airs.

Sadness covers both our faces and he says, "One good thing about this ending; we can look forward to tomorrow." But there's no enthusiasm at all in his voice; and I feel the same as he does, I don't want to go home. He grabs my hand and we head for the parking lot walking as slowly as we can. When I open the door to my truck, I turn and tell him, "Malik thank you for helping me deal with my past; I appreciate you for that." "Angela the sooner we get over the past; the sooner we can move forward. Can I call you later?" I say to him, "Give me your number; I'll call you." I reach into my purse and get my phone and enter it as he dictates it to me. He looks at me with puppy eyes and says, "Bye baby talk to you later." And he turns around and walks away. I honestly do not want to leave him I want to be with Malik; not for sex but for his company; I am in love!

I rush home and change my clothes and go into the kitchen to call Malik when I noticed there was a message on my business phone so I hit the button. "Angela I guess you're not home yet; I just wanted to tell you that I like Malik. He is a man and he definitely loves him some Angela; you call me when you get a chance, love you baby, bye." It was my dad, calling to give me his blessing; he approves of Malik. I can't believe the day I met my father is the same day I meet my husband to be. That blows my mind; maybe I'm moving too fast, I don't really know him but I'm in love with who I know so far. He says we are soul mates and I'm beginning to think he's right. In fact he's been right on everything he's told me. Today he mentioned I need to forgive myself; something I never thought about. I feel so cheap when I remember the past men in my life, so I keep myself busy and try not to think about it. When I do remember; I don't feel worthy of a future with anyone because I fear I'll end up in some man's bed and left alone afterwards, geez I never realized the power harboring secrets carry!

My home phone rings and I jump and lift the receiver up and can hear Malik, "You made it home ok? Are you alright?" I reply, "Yeah I was going to call you but my dad left me a message and I couldn't wait to hear the verdict on you; Aunt Bernadine thinks I should marry you tomorrow and my dad says he likes you. Malik do you think we're moving too fast after all we haven't known one another for two weeks yet and here we are talking about marriage." He says, "When you look at less than two weeks; it seems like a short while, but Angela we are not teenagers, we both love each other. What reason do we have to wait? Can you think of anything we need to wait to do that we can't do together as a married couple?" I think for a second then say, "Well, the only thing I can think of is we don't know one another." Quickly he replies, "Well, I've heard a lot of married couples say you really, really don't know the other person until you live with them, so, I want to spend the rest of my life getting to know you baby just cross that one off your list.

Angela I know we're meant to be together so whatever comes our way; with the Lord on our side it's already worked out." I tell him, "Malik I love you and I'm scared; this is happening so fast and that's what scares me." "I know baby; the unknown scares us all." Then he begins to tell me about when he and his sister, Makeba were scared of the dark; we talked until almost midnight taking turns sharing about our childhoods.

When I turned my light off to go to sleep I remembered what Malik told me about forgiving myself and I couldn't go to sleep. After 20 minutes of tossing, I got up and went to the back of my Bible and looked up the words 'forgive, forgiven and forgiveness,' I thought it was interesting how the word forgotten was right after forgiveness; mmm.... Because there were so many scriptures I wrote them down and read every one of them. The scripture that ministered the most to me was in Psalms 32:5 the Amplified states; **"I acknowledged my sin to You, and my iniquity I did not hide. I said, I will confess my transgressions to the Lord [continually unfolding the past till all is told]—then You [instantly] forgave me the guilt and**

iniquity of my sin. Selah [pause, and calmly think of that]!"

I cried when I read this scripture; the Lord has forgiven me, now I need to forgive me. After all these years I had never forgiven myself. I knew I was forgiven but my attention had been on running from men and by me never forgiving myself; my past behavior resurfacing itself, was what I was running from..... thank you Jesus! I prayed, cried and ended in praise. I got out of bed and danced myself happy I know I'm forgiven and now; I've forgiven myself; talk about liberty! I crawled into bed thanking and praising the Lord for His Word as I fell asleep.

MONDAY:

7:20 Dora called and had me on speaker again. She was so excited; she met Parker's family after he had Sunday dinner with our family. Aunt Shirley has the largest house of all of us. Her living room and formal dinning room is combined and when we set up for dinner, her formal dinning room has 2 extra fold up tables in it and there's 1 fold up table in the living room close to the other two tables. The formal dinning table and chairs seats all of the aunts and uncles and we call it the big table, the other tables seats the rest of us; we sit 8 per table. All of the grand children eat in the big den Uncle Henry had added on. Aunt Shirley had the floor tiled, so the clean up after the little ones would be easy. Eunice has a 9 year old daughter, Stephanie, and Wanda Faye has an 8 year old daughter, Rene' and the two of them keep the rest of the little ones in line.

Dora tells me when she walked in the house with Parker; there was a place setting added for the two of them at the big table and Aunt Shirley put them between Uncle Howard and Aunt Rose Marie. She says

Uncle Howard asked Parker where his family was from, and how many were there, he wanted to know what each one of them did and asked Parker had he attended college and where. She said Parker did real well, after the second question he relaxed and gave colorful answers. When she went into the kitchen to clean up Uncle Howard told Parker he was the first young man I had brought to dinner and I must like him so, what were his intensions for his baby daughter and Parker told him he wanted to marry me after a respectable courtship of course. Uncle Howard asked Aunt Rose Marie if Parker had passed her test and she said yes.

"Angie; I'm so glad the family likes Parker, what do you think about him?" "Well Dora, all I can say is; he is handsome, works and seems to be in love with you; I give him a pass also. Besides I think you two make an attractive couple and will probably have some beautiful kids." "Oh cuz thanks; you know your opinion means the world to me, thanks Angie. I gotta go but, call me tonight and fill me in on Malik; I kinda owe him, he broke the ice for me with Parker last Sunday. Every time I think about Aunt Brenda passing you that note I can't help but smile. Love you cuz, bye."

I got up at 8:15 and made a cup of tea and I have my devotion in the kitchen and began to thank and praise the Lord, and I entered into worship and when my Bible fell open again, the letters looked as though they were 30 inch font; they leaped out at me and I read Psalms 92: 4 & 5; **"For You, LORD, have made me glad through Your work; I will triumph in the works of your hands. 5) O Lord, how great are Your works! Your thoughts are very deep."** I sat there and thought about how the Lord has brought Malik into my life at this particular time. How he said his late wife died and that brought him here, to Memphis. I thought about how the Lord knew to time my meeting my dad; and how Malik happened to look up at the precise moment. When I thought of how Malik has helped me see myself and, get an understanding through scripture; I meditated on how great the works of the Lord is and pictured the depth of His thoughts, and I had tears form in my eyes; my eyes of understanding the great works of God! Wow, the Lord is so good!

10 a.m., my home phone rings it's Malik "Good morning." He says, "Good morning to you" I reply. He asks, "Baby do you know of a nice place we can get lunch?" "Yes; what do you want soups, sandwiches, steak, what's your choice?" "I'm a meat eater, steak sounds good or Seafood." "Ok, let's meet; which is closer for you, the Rib Shack or the church?" He says, "The church." I reply, "Ok I'll meet you there in what; 30 minutes?" "Angela, I need to ask you something, do you always carry your driver's license and social security identifications with you at all times?" I answer, "Well, yeah, why?" "That's part of my surprise, I'll meet you at the church; love you baby." As I hang up, I realize how excited I am about seeing Malik and it feels good to have peace about us being in love so soon after we met.

When I pull up into the parking lot, he's already there. I get out of my truck and walk to his car. He gets out and opens the car door for me. When he gets back into the car he asks what time do I have to get back home and I tell him in time to do my laundry. He smiles real big and starts the car.

We arrive at a real nice diner I know that has good rib eye steak sandwiches and different meats are added in the salads. We eat and talk asking each other questions like what kinds of foods we like, are you a morning or late night person, things like that. When we finish eating he picks up the check and leans in towards me and says, "Angela trust me ok; I won't trick or hurt you baby I love you, and want to surprise you ok?" I feel real comfortable with him and strange as it seems to me, I do trust him so I tell him ok.

He never told me where we were going and I watched how he drove as if he knew exactly where he was going, so I was very relaxed. When he ended up downtown on Washington Avenue I thought he was lost but when he pulled into the parking lot of the County Clerk; I felt my heart beat so fast; 'I know he doesn't want to get married today!' I turned to look at him and he says, "No baby, I'm not forcing you." He parked and turned to me and says, "Angela will you marry me?" "Malik this is too fast." "I know baby I thought we would get our license out of the way." I looked at his face; reading it actually, looking for his expression to reveal his intentions for coming here. He asks, "Baby, are you ready to commit to a license?" He puts his hand into his pocket and comes out with a ring box and presents it to me with a big smile and raises his eyebrow as he opens the box and says, "Are you?"

I look at the ring and recognize it's the ring from the mall. I look at him and tears began to fill my eyes; tears of joy. He really wants me to be happy. I look deeply into his eyes and shake my head yes as he takes the ring out of the box. He gently lifts my hand up and while slipping the engagement ring on my finger he says, "Angela, say yes and make me the happiest man in Memphis." Now the tears are flowing, I say, "Yes Malik, yes." After he slips on the ring, I lean towards him and we hug. He gets out and comes to open my car door. I'm looking at the ring on my finger and can't believe I'm engaged; and to a man that loves me and wants me to be happy!

He takes my hand and we go inside and straight to the information desk. He asks the security officer sitting behind the booth, "Where is your water fountain?" The man stands and gives direction and before we walk away Malik asks what floor we can get a marriage license. Again the guy gives us instruction and we're off to the water fountain and he's still holding onto my hand.

We stand at the fountain and he says, "Angela I want you to hold the spigot down for me. Baby I'm going to put my hands under the water and completely cover and wash them; when I'm done, I'll hold it down for you to do the same. I know the water is cold, but this will be symbolic of us washing our past deeds away ok?" "Ok," I watch him as he washed his past deeds away and when he held the spigot down for me, I began crying because I visualized the symbolism; my past was actually swirling down that drain. He let go of the spigot, stepped towards me and took both my hands and tenderly rubbed them and said, "Angela I love you baby and I promise, you will never regret today." He takes me into his arms and hugs me and kisses me tenderly on my forehead. I feel so safe in his arms and feel my past has been erased. All I could do was cry as he held me.

It's difficult to describe the emotion I felt. I felt weight lift off me and I became light as a feather; as if I could fly away. If Malik wasn't holding me, I could have floated away. I actually felt as though Malik was the only man in my life. I was anew, just for him. After I absorbed the freshness; I went into my purse and took out a tissue and blew my nose, then I told him, "I'm ready now."

Twenty minutes later, we walked out of the County Clerks office holding hands and I had a marriage license folded up in my purse that was valid for 30 days.

During the drive back to the church I asked Malik how he knew where the County Clerks office was. He told me he used the yellow pages and glanced over at me and smiled. "No, I used map quest last night and made a trial run." When he pulled up into the church parking lot I realized I did not want to leave him. He turned off the ignition and slowly turned to me looking at me with that pitiful look he had yesterday. I said, "I know Malik I don't want to go either. I love you and want to be with you; I mean not sexually but just be with you. Malik I love you." He smiles and says, "And I you baby. Do you have to go home now; I really want to spend some time with you." "No, I have time; I know a park close by." "Just tell me how to get there." He starts up the car and we go to the park and sit on a bench.

I ask him why he wants to get married so soon." He looks real serious and answers, "Angela my job is life threatening and I don't take life for granted; tomorrow is not promised to any of us." "Sooo, you're telling me, when you leave on the next mission as you call it; there's a chance we may not see each other again." "That's right." "So when we get married I'll have to worry about you not coming home?" "Yes baby, but I put in for fewer missions last Tuesday. I want to be home more with you, when the paperwork clears; I will only go on quarterly missions." "Malik, that's 4 times a year I'll have to worry about you; I don't know if I can do that." We look at each other in silence for a few minutes and he says, "Baby don't worry, pray for me while I'm gone." He takes my hand and kisses the back of it and tells me he loves me and as we look into each other's eyes, I know I love this man and I agree; we do tend to take life for granted. I say, "Let's get married in

3 weeks." After a pause he smiles at me and softly asks, "You sure baby?" I shake my head and say, "Yes I am." The grin that he sported; was so wide!

We began to talk about what we think makes a healthy relationship; we were there until after 3pm. We went to dinner and as soon as we were home; we talked on the phone until after 1 am. When I went to bed I thanked and praised the Lord for the marvelous works He had done in me and for making me ready to love and be loved; I sighed a long deep sigh; while thinking 'no more secrets for me; the truth truly does make you free!'

Epilogue

The next morning I phoned Aunt Flora and told her I was engaged to Malik and she told me to bring him by her house for lunch today; she was not taking no for an answer. When I told Malik, he agreed to spend some time with my grandmother. By the time we arrived at her house all my aunts and uncles were there. Aunt Flora had phoned Aunt Shirley and she called everyone else. When I told them I preferred a small wedding at the courthouse, nothing fancy; my aunts all told Malik and I how they had already talked and decided I was well past grown and whatever we decided; it was ok with them. They would give us our wedding gifts at one of our family Sunday dinners.

Uncle Lester volunteered to counsel us on premarital counseling so we could save on our marriage license. He told us the counseling also helps us to get to know each other's views on some important issues that were sure to come up in our future. Some things we really need to be on the same page about; like raising children, in-law boundaries and spiritual views. Malik told him we already had our license but we will consider the counseling to help us in the other matters. We shared with them how we met and Malik told them about himself and of course they asked a lot of questions.

Malik went back to work Wednesday and we talked on the phone every evening. We only saw each other at Wednesday night Bible study, but we stayed on the phone until the wee hours sharing our devotion time, and we discussed what was important to us and what things were absolutely not acceptable in our marriage.

The following Sunday at dinner I introduced Malik to the family and Dora and Parker announced their engagement. Their wedding is set for June 8 of next year. Dora wants a big wedding, she and Parker both have savings and Parker said he would take her anywhere she wanted for their honeymoon.

A couple days later, Malik took Ernest to the Marine base and later told me that he was a good kid who happened to have made a mistake and he deserved a second chance. Ernest had a court hearing and both Aunt Rose Marie and Uncle Howard took him to court. When they arrived, Dad and Malik were there. Dad spoke on Ernest behalf as a witness to his character and Malik helped in presenting to the judge a plan having Ernest work off his sentence and take the entrance exam for the Marines. The judge agreed and told Ernest he had made a mistake in judgment of character when choosing his friends. He sternly stressed to Ernest that he must keep his nose clean or the agreement will be revoked. Well, he cut his friends loose and is working hard at proving he is repentant of what he did and is responsible. I had a long talk with him and he apologized for trying to hustle me and thanked me for not giving him the money up front.

My dad brags to everyone who listens that his daughter is getting married and will make him a grandfather, hopefully real soon! He keeps telling me my clock is ticking and I should not waste time and for me to hurry and get started on his grandsons and oh yeah; he'll take one granddaughter or two at the most. Then he says he'll take whatever so long as they're healthy and have our gaps.

Due to Malik's mission schedule, we will marry next week on Monday. The following Tuesday after we're married will be his last mission before going on quarterly. My schedule has me working Thursday so we will have a short honeymoon for now but we plan on going somewhere possibly a cruise later this year. Surprisingly I'm not at all nervous I really am looking forward to becoming Mrs. Chapman and starting a life with Malik. The way he looks at me and listens to my every word; I can't describe in words, but I know he loves me. My heart feels the love he has for me and that makes me want to love him right back, I am so glad I can trust him; the Lord surely does work in mysterious ways. When we talk about God's timing; I am at awe of His wonderful works; no one can compare to his majesty! Absolutely no one!

Summary

In this story, the woman who was lied too now has to confront "truth." Truth is what is accurate and what is real. Her life was built on secrets and lies. Meaning, her character was built upon hidden, concealed false statements. This is the definition of secrets. Secrets 'weaken' and; reduces the value of relationships not only as we see in this story between the family members but also in our relationship with God. Secrets also cause separation in friendships.

Statements made with deliberate intent to deceive; this is the definition of lies. Lies hinder our ability to walk upright; being fearful of exposure. The root word for lie is "to fail; disappoint" and because a lie is deliberate; it destroys.....**Truth must be confronted**.

What has occurred is the foundation of De Anne and Angela's lives were built on secrets and lies. Secrets and lies were the blueprints used to define their life. Even unaware of the secrets and lies, their lives were nonetheless influenced by them. Everything has its time and season and now that revelation has come to Angela, correction and forgiveness must now exist for her to have a healthy, fruitful rest of her life.

Think of a house being demolished while someone is still living in it. Not a pretty site is it! That's what it feels like when you find out the life as you know is a lie! Only the Holy Spirit can do a work that absolute without destroying everything in the house and; can only destroy the parts of the foundation that needs to be destroyed! Trust Him to do a great job, He does all things well. His blueprint of you is customized just for you! Allow the Holy Spirit to direct you and supervise the new construction [understanding and healing] room by room, or issue by issue; until every area is stable and sturdy.

Because there is so much to deal with emotionally; the root **must** be dealt with, or the root of bitterness will spring forth. Bitterness breeds resentment and resentment distorts how you view things and once our eyesight, or view is distorted, contamination sets in the heart and every opinion you have now is tainted. Truth is not seen even when it is staring you in the face, all because of bitterness! Ephesians 4:31 tells us, **"Let all bitterness, and wrath, anger, and clamor, and evil speaking, be put away from you, with all malice:** Also Hebrews 12:15 says, **"Looking carefully lest anyone fall short of the grace of God; lest any root of bitterness springing up cause trouble, and by this many be defiled:"**

Let the Holy Spirit tell you why the secret and lie was conjured up, He will tell you the truth. That opens the door to understanding. Make sure you give Him permission just as Jesus did in Matthew 26:39; **"He went a little farther and fell on His face, and prayed, saying, "O My Father, if it is possible, let this cup pass from Me; nevertheless, not as I will, but as You will."** Jesus was giving the Holy Spirit permission to do what was best for Him. The truth pill is real hard to swallow and we feel better off not knowing it; however if it's time to deal with this, deal with it or it can cause detrimental repercussions.

While new construction is being performed, you must allow your new interior decorator [the Holy Spirit] to instruct you on what will be tasteful in portraying the new found you. The word of God <u>must</u> become your manual now. Remember lies are deliberate and learning how to react to what was done to you the healthy way, is better for you. Because, if you render evil for evil; you will reap evil right back. Let Holy Spirit teach you how to reply in an orderly way; you can be deeply emotionally injured and yet reply without the police having to come to the house! Let Him teach you how.

Seek after and know your purpose. Just think for a moment; what in you, is so valuable, that the devil was intimidated by your life? ...... Concentrate on your calling; why you are here and what changes should you make in your life that can better it and the people you will come in contact with. Concentrate less on your mishap and more on what is so valuable in you; so powerful, your enemy wanted it destroyed! Forgive those who were trusted with your future and were purposefully unproductive, they are sure to reap what they sowed. After all it was not their sole purpose to destroy you; it was the enemy that used them!

Let's take a look at 2 Samuel 4:4. See the beginning of Mephibosheth, son of Jonathan who was the son of Saul. Mephibosheth was dropped by his nurse at the age of five and became crippled in both feet for the rest of his life. By the actions of one person, his life was full of disadvantage. He was forced to live in Lodebar. A place of no pastures where there was no provision at all. David summoned Mephibosheth out of the place of no provision, and into a place setting at the table in David's house, a place made just for Mephibosheth to sit for the remainder of his life. Mephibosheth lived a life of favor, honor, privilege and great acceptance for the rest of his life! A life intended for a Kings grandson. You should see the similarities in your life. A life that began in disadvantages and now, by the grace and love of God; you are summoned out of that life and into the victorious life designed just for you! If you thought you had a good life before the truth was revealed; watch how much better it will become, you can't imagine!

John 8: 31 & 32 instructs us who believe in Jesus and walk in his teaching, to know the truth and become free by it. Holy Spirit wants us to always consider the truth (referred this way because He is a Person). We tend to be afraid of what we are not familiar with. We find fault or a reason not to confront the unknown, because deep inside of us we know facing the truth will cause us to make some changes in our life when the truth is exposed. That's why we are so hesitant to face the truth and why some of us actually run from it. When you have been exposed to the truth, it is the Holy Spirit that gives you understanding of that truth; to liberate us. Our enemy, the devil, does not want truth to prevail in our lives; he is the father of lies and a master of deception. Once we learn the Holy Spirit can be trusted, we will no longer be a consumer of the devil; buy the lies he sells. The devil wants to keep havoc in your life and once you find out the truth, your life will be enhanced and you will continue to seek after truth.

When you find yourself getting fearful, remember the opposite of fear is love. You are only afraid because you can see yourself disappointed, hurt, or embarrassed if you believe on what the Word says. Pull those imaginations down and meditate on II Timothy 1:7. It clearly states **"For God has not given us the spirit of fear, but of power and of love and of a sound mind."** Meditate on scriptures like Psalms 25:2 **"O my God, I trust in You: let me not be ashamed..."** And verse 3; **"Indeed, let no one who waits on You be ashamed"**...Or Psalms 31:1 **"In You O Lord, I put my trust; let me never be ashamed..."** These scriptures and many others will give support to building your faith and your spirit man.

Remember, God loves you and would never put you in a place you are not capable of maintaining. His love for you will enable you to grasp onto the truth and will not shatter you, as you embrace understanding and healing. Allow yourself time to heal from all of the demolition that has been done inside of you. With healing comes an understanding and with understanding comes forgiveness. Embrace them all, and experience **THE MAGNIFICENT, NEW AND IMPROVED, YOU!**